ALTERNATIVE LOVES

IRISH LESBIAN AND GAY STORIES

EDITED BY DAVID MARCUS

FOREWORD BY AILBHE SMYTH

DAVID MARCUS was born in Cork, studied Law at UCC and was called to the Bar in 1945. From 1968 to 1986 he was Literary Editor of the *Irish Press*, for which he established and edited 'New Irish Writing', a weekly page of short stories and poetry which became a national institution. He has edited many anthologies of short stories, most recently *Irish Love Stories*.

AILBHE SMYTH is a feminist critic and scholar, founder and director of the Women's Education Research and Resource Centre at University College, Dublin.

First published in 1994 by
Martello Books
An imprint of Mercier Press
16 Hume Street Dublin 2

Trade enquiries to Mercier Press
PO Box 5, 5 French Church Street, Cork

A Martello Original

Foreword © Ailbhe Smyth 1994
The acknowledgements page is an
extension of this copyright notice

ISBN 1 86023 001 6

10 9 8 7 6 5 4 3 2 1

A CIP record for this title is available
from the British Library

Cover illustration and design by Brian
Finnegan
Set by Richard Parfrey in Avant Garde
and Garamond Narrow (120% wide)
10/14
Printed in Ireland by ColourBooks,
Baldoyle Industrial Estate, Dublin 13

CONTENTS

ACKNOWLEDGEMENTS

For permission to reprint the stories specified, we are indebted to:

Patrick Boyle: 'Shaybo' from *All Looks Yellow to the Jaundiced Eye* (MacGibbon and Kee). Reprinted by permission of the estate of Patrick Boyle.

Ita Daly: 'Such Good Friends' from *The Lady with the Red Shoes*, © Ita Daly 1975. Reprinted by permission of the author.

Emma Donoghue: 'Going Back', ©*Emma Donoghue* 1993. Reprinted by permission of the author.

Mary Dorcey: 'Introducing Nessa' from *A Noise from the Woodshed* (Onlywomen Press), © Mary Dorcey 1989. Reprinted by permission of the author.

Desmond Hogan: 'A Poet and an Englishman' from *The Diamonds at the Bottom of the Sea* (Hamish Hamilton). © Desmond Hogan 1979. Reprinted by permission of Rogers, Coleridge and White Ltd.

John Jordan: 'He Lay Down on Me' from *Collected Stories* (Poolbeg Press). Reprinted by permission of the estate of John Jordan.

Rita Kelly: 'Opening Night', from *The Whispering Arch* (Arlen House), © Rita Kelly 1986. Reprinted by permission of the author.

Ray Lynott: 'April' from *A Year in the Country* (The Irish Writers' Co-operative), © Ray Lynott 1978. Reprinted by permission of the author.

Colum McCann: 'Breakfast for Enrique' from *Fishing the Sloe-Black River* (Pheonix House), © Colum McCann 1994. Reprinted by permission of Shiel Land Associates Ltd.

Val Mulkerns: 'Memory and Desire' from *An Idle Woman* (Poolbeg Press), © Val Mulkerns 1980. Reprinted by permission of the author.

Edna O'Brien: 'The Mouth of the Cave' from *The Love Object* (Jonathan Cape), © Edna O'Brien 1968. Reprinted by permission of the author.

Julia O'Faolain: 'The Widow's Boy', © Julia O'Faolain 1994. Reprinted by permission of Rogers, Coleridge and White Ltd.

Sean O'Faolain: 'How to Write a Short Story' from *Foreign Affairs* (Constable). Reprinted by permission of Rogers, Coleridge and White Ltd.

Terry Prone: 'Blood Brothers, Soul Sisters' from *Blood Brothers, Soul Sisters* (Poolbeg Press), ©Terry Prone 1994. Reprinted by permission of the author.

Frank Ronan: 'Ringsend', © Frank Ronan 1994. Reprinted by permission of Rogers, Coleridge and White Ltd.

Padraig Rooney: 'Tabernacles' © Padraig Rooney 1981. Reprinted by permission of the author.

William Trevor: 'Torridge' from *Lovers of Their Time* (Constable), © William Trevor 1978. Reprinted by permission of the author.

FOREWORD

AILBHE SMYTH

'The embrace of love': Kate O'Brien's wondrously simple phrase
cuts through the tangled mass of 'oversights and 'mono-sights',
stereotypes and prejudice which have dismissed, disguised or
deliberately misrepresented lesbian and gay experiences in our
culture. *The Land of Spices* was banned in the 1940s because of
the homosexual relationship that phrase so strikingly if fleetingly
described, and Kate O'Brien paid a heavy price in terms of her
literary reputation for daring to so much as suggest a different
way of loving. I think of Kate O'Brien's work as an island —
sometimes appearing almost as a mirage, a trick of the light and
of history — surrounded by a monochromatic sea of sexless hetero-
reality. For sex was not allowed to be much written about at all of
course, as Edna O'Brien's fate in the 1950s should remind us.
The intolerable constraints and enforced concealments of that
long long time must surely have destroyed or seriously distorted
the lives of more lesbians and gay men than I can bear to
contemplate. The narrator in Edna O'Brien's story 'The Mouth of
the Cave', is desolate, and powerless to name the source of her
ill-being in any but the most obliquely imaged terms: 'Yet, I always
find myself taking the sea road even though I most desperately
desire to go the other way.'

How much has shifted and opened up in Ireland since then,
and in what seems a remarkably short time-span when you com-
pare the growing openness of the present with that narrowly
repressive and not so distant past. Just a dozen years ago, David
Norris took his decriminalisation case to Europe — and won, setting
Ireland on course for legal reform and equal citizenship for all,

regardless of sexuality. It was vital to hope, although difficult to really believe in 1982, that barely a decade later lesbians and gay men would march through the streets of Irish cities and towns in proud celebration of our sexuality. That huge sea-heave of social change was brought about in very large measure by the determination and intelligence of a small number of dedicated people. They hoped, believed and worked for a society in which diversity would become the basis of everyday experience, not something to be erased, resisted or held at arm's length, on the margins of social, political and cultural life.

At about the same time as the Norris case, Mary Dorcey's poetry collection, *Kindling*, was published by a British feminist press. She was the first Irish writer I ever knew to be openly lesbian, and her work seemed to me back in the early 1980s to be extraordinarily brave and immensely enriching and inspiring – as it is still. She wrote from an experience, a reality, a truth which had of necessity to confront the 'barbarous law and comfortable prejudice' of a deeply homophobic society which did not want to know, to hear, to see, far less to embrace, the legitimacy of other ways of living and loving, of creating and imagining. It would be hard to overestimate either the difficulty or the importance of Mary Dorcey's writing against the heterosexual grain when, for all practical purposes during the 1980s, she was a lone voice: 'It was not in the light we lived, but in the spaces between – in the darkness.' Illuminating the darkness means that there is now a space which Irish lesbian and gay writers can inhabit with some dignity, if not yet absolute ease. For the difficulties do indeed persist, as the 'emigrant' setting of many of the stories here makes clear: 'Missing it's easy after the first time,' Cyn says of Ireland in Emma Donoghue's story 'Going Back'. For the 'Wild Colonial Boy', the ironically named narrator of Colm McCann's fine and poignant story about AIDS, 'Breakfast for Enrique', going back is not even a question.

There are many reasons why I don't subscribe to the notion that literature and politics do or ought to occcupy impermeably separate domains. One of the most compelling reasons is my strong sense that tangible social and political change is never achieved without the ability to imagine the world otherwise, to find the language which can give shape and substance to our unnameable, and thus unnamed, longings. I believe that the willingness to explore what has been sealed tight by stifling layers of convention and fear, the capacity to imaginatively reorder history and reality and to conjure alternative visions have been crucial in creating the new possibilities we see beginning to emerge in Ireland now, although by no means always smoothly and unopposed, to be sure.

The stories in *Alternative Loves* deal with many themes, for love – of whatever kind – is never singular, always complicated, always risky. Many of the writers here are not gay or lesbian and some were a surprise to me. So much for my preconceptions, now under revision. But one of the many strengths of the collection is the expansive range and variety of the voices it invites us to listen to, for there is no such thing as the 'definitive' lesbian or gay experience – or story. Why should there be? It is only a homogenous heterosexual culture which imposes spurious and controlling unity. In this collection, different generations, perspectives, politics and styles jostle one another intimately, pre-cariously, contradictorily, non-judgementally, passionately. As in the strongest kind of loving.

HOW TO WRITE A SHORT STORY

SEAN O'FAOLAIN

One wet January night, some six months after they had met, young Morgan Myles, our county librarian, was seated in the doctor's pet armchair, on one side of the doctor's fire, digesting the pleasant memory of a lavish dinner, while leafing the pages of a heavy photographic album and savouring a warm brandy. From across the hearth the doctor was looking admiringly at his long, ballooning Gaelic head when, suddenly, Morgan let out a cry of delight.

'Good Lord, Frank! There's a beautiful boy! One of Raphael's little angels.' He held up the open book for Frank to see. 'Who was he?'

The doctor looked across at it and smiled.

'Me. Aged twelve. At school in Mount Saint Bernard.'

'That's in England. I didn't know you went to school in England.'

'Alas!'

Morgan glanced down at twelve, and up at sixty.

'It's not possible, Frank!'

The doctor raised one palm six inches from the arm of his chair and let if fall again.

'It so happened that I was a ridiculously beautiful child.'

'Your mother must have been gone about you. And,' with a smile, 'the girls too.'

'I had no interest in girls. Nor in boys either, though by your smile you seem to say so. But there was one boy who took a considerable interest in me.'

Morgan at once lifted his nose like a pointer. At this period of his life he had rested from writing poetry and was trying to write short stories. For weeks he had read nothing but Maupassant. He was going to out-Maupassant Maupassant. He was going to write stories that would make poor old Maupassant turn as green as the grass on his grave.

'Tell me about it,' he ordered. 'Tell me every single detail.'

'There is nothing to it. Or at any rate, as I now know, nothing abnormal. But, at that age!' − pointing with his pipe stem. 'I was as innocent as . . . Well, as innocent as a child of twelve! Funny that you should say that about Raphael's angels. At my preparatory school here − it was a French order − Sister Angélique used to call me her *petit ange*, because, she said, I had "*une tête d'ange et une voix d'ange.*" She used to make me sing solo for them at Benediction, dressed in a red soutane, a white lacy surplice and a purple bow tie.

'After that heavenly place Mount Saint Bernard was ghastly. Mobs of howling boys. Having to play games; rain, hail or snow. I was a funk at games. When I'd see a fellow charging me at rugger I'd at once pass the ball or kick for touch. I remember the coach cursing me. "Breen, you're a bloody little coward, there are boys half your weight on this field who wouldn't do a thing like that." And the constant discipline. The constant priestly distrust. Watching us like jail warders.'

'Can you give me an example of that?' Morgan begged. 'Mind you, you could have had that, too, in Ireland. Think of Clongowes. It turns up in Joyce. And he admired the Jesuits!'

'Yes, I can give you an example. It will show you how innocent I was. A month after I entered Mount Saint Bernard I was so miserable that I decided to write to my mother to take me away. I knew that every letter had to pass under the eyes of the Prefect of Discipline, so I wrote instead to Sister Angélique asking her to pass on the word to my mother. The next day old Father George Lee − he's long since dead − summoned me to his study. "Breen!" he said darkly, holding up my unfortunate letter, "you have tried to do a very underhand thing, something for which I could punish you severely. Why did you write this letter *in French*?"' The doctor sighed. 'I was a very truthful little boy. My mother had brought me up to be truthful simply by never punishing me for anything I honestly owned up to. I said, "I wrote it in French, sir, because I hoped you wouldn't be able to understand it." He turned his face away from me but I could tell from his shoulders that he was laughing. He did not cane me, he just tore up the letter, told me never to try to deceive him again, and sent me packing with my tail between my legs.'

'The old bastard!' Morgan said sympathetically, thinking of the lonely little boy.

'No, no! He was a nice old man. And a good classical scholar, I later discovered. But that day as I walked down the long corridor, with all its photographs of old boys who had made good, I felt the chill of the prison walls!'

'But this other boy?' Morgan insinuated. 'Didn't his friendship help at all?'

The doctor rose and stood with his back to the fire staring fixedly in front of him.

(He rises, Morgan thought, his noble eyes shadowed. No! God damn it, no! Not noble. Shadowed? Literary word. Pensive? Blast it, that's worse. 'Pensive eye!' Romantic fudge. His eyes are dark as a rabbit's droppings. That's got it! In his soul . . . Oh, Jase!)

'Since I was so lonely I suppose he *must* have helped. But he was away beyond me. Miles above me. He was a senior. He was the captain of the school.'

'His name,' Morgan suggested, 'was, perhaps, Cyril?'

'We called him Bruiser. I would rather not tell you his real name.'

'Because he is still alive,' Morgan explained, 'and remembers you vividly to this day.'

'He was killed at the age of twenty.'

3

'In the war! In the heat of battle.'

'By a truck in Oxford. Two years after he went up there from Mount Saint Bernard. I wish I knew what happened to him in those two years. I can only hope that before he died he found a girl.'

'A girl? I don't follow. Oh yes! Of course, yes, I take your point.'

(He remembers with tenderness? No. With loving kindness! No! With benevolence? Dammit, no! With his wonted chivalry to women? But he remembered irritably that the old man sitting opposite to him was a bachelor. And a virgin?)

'What happened between the pair of ye? "Brothers and companions in tribulation on the isle that is called Patmos"?'

The doctor snorted.

'Brothers? I have told you I was twelve. Bruiser was eighteen. The captain of the school. Captain of the rugby team. Captain of the tennis team. First in every exam. Tops. Almost a man. I looked up to him as a shining hero. I never understood what he saw in me. I have often thought since that he may have been amused by my innocence. Like the day he said to me, "I suppose, Rosy," that was my nickname, I had such rosy cheeks, "suppose you think you are the best-looking fellow in the school?" I said, "No, I don't, Bruiser. I think there's one fellow better-looking than me, Jimmy Simcox."'

'Which he, of course, loyally refused to believe!'

The old doctor laughed heartily.

'He laughed heartily.'

'A queer sense of humour!'

'I must confess I did not at the time see the joke. Another day he said, "Would you like, Rosy, to sleep with me?"'

Morgan's eyes opened wide. Now they were getting down to it.

'I said, "Oh, Bruiser, I don't think you would like that at all. I'm an awful chatterbox in bed. Whenever I sleep with my Uncle

Tom he's always saying to me, "Will you, for God's sake, stop your bloody gabble and let me sleep." He laughed for five minutes at that.'

'I don't see much to laugh at. He should have sighed. I will make him sigh. Your way makes him sound a queer hawk. And nothing else happened between ye but this sort of innocent gabble? Or are you keeping something back? Hang it, Frank, there's no story at all in this!'

'Oh, he used sometimes take me on his lap. Stroke my bare knee. Ruffle my hair. Kiss me.'

'How did you like that?'

'I made nothing of it. I was used to being kissed by my elders – my mother, my bachelor uncles, Sister Angélique, heaps of people.' The doctor laughed. 'I laugh at it now. But his first kiss! A few days before, a fellow named Calvert said to me, "Hello, pretty boy, would you give me a smuck?" I didn't know what a smuck was. I said, "I'm sorry, Calvert, but I haven't got one." The story must have gone around the whole school. The next time I was alone with Bruiser he taunted me. I can hear his angry, top-loftical English voice. "You are an innocent mug, Rosy! A smuck is a kiss. Would you let *me* kiss you?" I said, "Why not?" He put his arm around my neck in a vice and squashed his mouth to my mouth, hard, sticky. I thought I'd choke. "O Lord," I thought, "this is what he gets from playing rugger. This is a rugger kiss." And, I was thinking, "His poor mother! Having to put up with this from him every morning and every night." When he let me go, he said, "Did you like that?" Not wanting to hurt his feelings, I said, imitating his English voice, "It was all right, Bruiser! A bit like ruggah, isn't it?" He laughed again and said, "All right? Well, never mind. I shan't rush you."'

Morgan waved impatiently.

'Look here, Frank! I want to get the background to all this. The telling detail, you know. "The little actual facts" as Stendhal called them. You said the priests watched you all like hawks. The constant discipline, you said. The constant priestly distrust. How did ye ever manage to meet alone?'

'It was very simple. He was the captain of the school. The apple of their eye. He could fool them. He knew the ropes. After all, he had been there for five years. I remember old Father Lee saying to me once, "You are a very lucky boy, Breen, it's not every junior that the captain of the school would take an interest in. You ought to feel very proud of his friendship." We used to have a secret sign about our meetings. Every Wednesday morning when he would be walking out of chapel, leading the procession, if that day was all right for us he used to put his right hand in his pocket. If for any reason it was not all right he would put his left hand in his pocket. I was always on the aisle of the very last row. Less than the dust. Watching for the sign like a hawk. We had a double check. I'd then find a note in my overcoat in the cloakroom. All it ever said was, "The same place." He was very careful. He only took calculated risks. If he had lived he would have made a marvellous politician, soldier or diplomat.'

'And where would ye meet? I know! By the river. Or in the woods? "Enter these enchanted woods ye who dare!"'

'No river. No woods. There was a sort of dirty old trunk room upstairs, under the roof, never used. A rather dark place with only one dormer window. It had double doors. He used to lock the outside one. There was a big cupboard there – for cricket bats or something. "If anyone comes," he told me, "you will have time to pop in there." He had it all worked out. Cautious man! I had to be even more cautious, stealing up there alone. One thing that made it easier for us was that I was so much of a junior and he was so very much of a senior, because, you see, those innocent guardians of ours had the idea that the real danger lay between the seniors and the middles, or the middles and the juniors, but never between the seniors and the juniors. They kept the seniors and the middles separated by iron bars and stone walls. Any doctor could have told them that in cold climates like ours the really dangerous years are not from fifteen up but from eighteen to anything, up or down. It simply never occurred to them that any senior could possibly be interested in any way in a junior. I, of course, had no idea of what he was up to. I had not even reached the age of puberty. In fact I honestly don't believe he quite knew himself what he was up to.'

'But, dammit, you must have had some idea! The secrecy, the kissing, alone, up there in that dim, dusty box-room, not a sound but the wind in the slates.'

'Straight from the nuns? *Un petit ange*? I thought it was all just pally fun.'

Morgan clapped his hands.

'I've got it! An idyll! Looking out dreamily over the fields from that dusty dormer window? That's it, that's the ticket. Did you ever read that wonderful story by Maupassant – it's called *An Idyll* – about two young peasants meeting in a train, a poor, hungry young fellow who has just left home, and a girl with her first baby. He looked so famished that she took pity on him like a mother, opened her blouse and gave him her breast. When he finished he said, "That was my first meal in three days." Frank! You are telling me the most beautiful story I ever heard in my whole life.'

'You think so?' the doctor said morosely. 'I think he was going through hell all that year. At eighteen? On the threshold of manhood? In love with a child of twelve? That is, if you will allow that a youth of eighteen may suffer as much from love as a man twenty years older. To me the astonishing thing is that he did so well all that year at his studies and at sports. Killing the pain of it, I suppose? Or trying to? But the in between? What went on in the poor devil in between?'

Morgan sank back dejectedly.

'I'm afraid this view of the course doesn't appeal to me at all. All I can see is the idyll idea. After all, I mean, nothing happened!'

Chafing, he watched his friend return to his armchair, take another pipe from the rack, fill it slowly and ceremoniously from a black tobacco jar and light it with care. Peering through the nascent smoke, Morgan leaned slowly forward.

'Or did something happen?'

'Yes,' the doctor resumed quietly. 'Every year, at the end of the last term, the departing captain was given a farewell dinner. I felt sad that morning because we had not met for a whole week. And now, in a couple of days we would be scattered and I would never see him again.'

'Ha, ha! You see, you too were in love!'

'Of course I was, I was hooked,' the doctor said with more than a flicker of impatience. 'However . . . That Wednesday as he passed me in the chapel aisle he put his right hand in his pocket. I belted off at once to my coat hanging in the cloakroom and found his note. It said, "At five behind the senior tennis court." I used always to chew up his *billet doux* immediately I read it. He had ordered me to. When I read this one my mouth went so dry with fear that I could hardly swallow it. He had put me in an awful fix. To meet alone in the box-room was risky enough, but for anybody to climb over the wall into the seniors' grounds was unheard of. If I was caught I would certainly be flogged. I might very well be expelled. And what would my mother and father think of me then? On top of all I was in duty bound to be with all the other juniors at prep at five o'clock, and to be absent from studies without permission was another crime of the first order. After lunch I went to the Prefect of Studies and asked him to excuse me from prep because I had an awful headache. He wasn't taken in one bit. He just ordered me to be at my place in prep as usual. The law! Orders! Tyranny! There was only one thing for it, to dodge prep, knowing well that whatever else happened later I would pay dearly for it.'

'And what about him? He knew all this. And he knew that if *he* was caught they couldn't do anything to him. The captain of the school? Leaving in a few days? It was very unmanly of him to put you to such a risk. His character begins to emerge, and not very pleasantly. Go on!'

The doctor did not need the encouragement. He looked like a small boy sucking a man's pipe.

'I waited until the whole school was at study and then I crept out into the empty grounds. At that hour the school, the grounds, everywhere, was as silent as the grave. Games over. The priests at their afternoon tea. Their charges safely under control. I don't know how I managed to get over that high wall, but when I fell scrambling down on the other side, there he was. "You're bloody late," he said crossly. "How did you get out of prep? What excuse did you give?" When I told him he flew into a rage. "You little fool!" he growled. "You've balloxed it all up. They'll know you dodged. They'll give you at least ten on the backside for this." He was carrying a cane. Seniors at Saint Bernard's did carry walking-sticks. I'd risked so much for him, and now he was so angry with me that I burst into tears. He put his arms around me — I thought, to comfort me — but after that all I remember from that side of the wall was him pulling down my short pants, holding me tight, I felt something hard, like his cane, and the next thing I knew I was wet. I thought I was bleeding. I thought he was gone mad. When I smelled whiskey I thought, "He is trying to kill me." "Now run," he ordered me, "and get back to prep as fast as you can."'

Morgan covered his eyes with his hand.

'He shoved me up to the top of the wall. As I peered around I heard his footsteps running away. I fell down into the shrubs on the other side and I immediately began to vomit and vomit. There was a path beside the shrubs. As I lay there puking I saw a black-soutaned priest approaching slowly along the path. He was an

9

old, old priest named Constable. I did not stir. Now, I felt, I'm for it. This is the end. I am certain he saw me but he passed by as if he had not seen me. I got back to the study hall, walked up to the Prefect's desk and told him I was late because I had been sick. I must have looked it because he at once sent me to the matron in the infirmary. She took my temperature and put me to bed. It was summer. I was the only inmate of the ward. One of those evenings of prolonged daylight.'

'You poor little bugger!' Morgan groaned in sympathy.

'A detail comes back to me. It was the privilege of seniors attending the captain's dinner to send down gifts to the juniors' table – sweets, fruit, a cake, for a younger brother or some special protégé. Bruiser ordered a whole white blancmange with a rose cherry on top of it to be sent to me. He did not know I was not in the dining hall so the blancmange was brought up to me in the infirmary. I vomited again when I saw it. The matron, with my more than ready permission, took some of it for herself and sent the rest back to the juniors' table, "with Master Breen's compliments." I am sure it was gobbled greedily. In the morning the doctor saw me and had me sent home to Ireland immediately.'

'Passing the buck,' said Morgan sourly, and they both looked at a coal that tinkled from the fire into the fender.

The doctor peered quizzically at the hissing coal.

'Well?' he slurred around his pipe stem. 'There is your lovely idyll.'

Morgan did not lift his eyes from the fire. Under a down-draught from the chimney a few specks of grey ashes moved clockwise on the worn hearth. He heard a car hissing past the house on the wet macadam. His eyebrows had gone up over his spectacles in two Gothic arches.

'I'm afraid,' he said at last, 'it is no go. Not even a Maupassant could have made a story out of it. And Chekhov wouldn't have wanted to try. Unless the two boys lived on, and on, and met years afterwards in Moscow or Yalta or somewhere, each with a wife and a squad of kids, and talked of everything except their schooldays. You are sure you never did hear of him, or from him, again?'

'Never! Apart from the letter he sent with the blancmange and the cherry.'

Morgan at once leaped alive.

'A letter? Now we are on to something! What did he say to you in it? Recite every word of it to me! Every syllable. I'm sure you have not forgotten one word of it. No!' he cried excitedly. 'You have kept it. Hidden away somewhere all these years. Friendship surviving everything. Fond memories of . . .'

The doctor sniffed.

'I tore it into bits unread and flushed it down the WC.'

'Oh, God blast you, Frank!' Morgan roared. 'That was the climax of the whole thing. The last testament. The final revelation. The summing up. The *document humain*. And you "just tore it up!" Let's reconstruct it. "Dearest Rosy, As long as I live I will never forget your innocence, your sweetness, your . . ."'

'My dear boy!' the doctor protested mildly. 'I am sure he wrote nothing of the sort. He was much too cautious, and even the captain was not immune from censorship. Besides, sitting in public glory at the head of the table? It was probably a place-card with something on the lines of, "All my sympathy, sorry, better luck next term." A few words, discreet, that I could translate any way I liked.'

Morgan raised two despairing arms.

'If that was all the damned fellow could say to you after that appalling experience, he was a character of no human significance whatever, a shallow creature, a mere agent, a catalyst, a cad. The story becomes your story.'

'I must admit I have always looked on it in that way. After all it did happen to me . . . Especially in view of the sequel.'

'Sequel? What sequel? I can't have sequels. In a story you always have to observe unity of time, place and action. Everything happening at the one time, in the same place, between the same people. *The Necklace. Boule de Suif. The Maison Tellier*. The examples are endless. What was this bloody sequel?'

The doctor puffed thoughtfully.

'In fact there were two sequels. Even three sequels. And all of them equally important.'

'In what way were they important?'

'It was rather important to me that after I was sent home I was in the hospital for four months. I could not sleep. I had constant nightmares, always the same one – me running through a wood and him running after me with his cane. I could not keep down my food. Sweating hot. Shivering cold. The vomiting was recurrent. I lost weight. My mother was beside herself with worry. She brought doctor after doctor to me, and only one of them spotted it, an old, blind man from Dublin named Whiteside. He said, "That boy has had some kind of shock," and in private he asked me if some boy, or man, had interfered with me. Of course, I denied it hotly.'

'I wish I was a doctor,' Morgan grumbled. 'So many writers were doctors. Chekhov. William Carlos Williams. Somerset Maugham. A. J. Cronin.'

The doctor ignored the interruption.

'The second sequel was that when I at last went back to Mount Saint Bernard my whole nature changed. Before that I had been dreamy and idle. During my last four years at school I became their top student. I suppose psychologists would say nowadays that I compensated by becoming extroverted. I became a crack cricket player. In my final year I was the college champion at billiards. I never became much good at rugger but I no longer minded playing it and I wasn't all that bad. If I'd been really tops at it, or at boxing, or swimming, I might very well have ended up as captain of the school. Like him.'

He paused for so long that Morgan became alerted again.

'And the third sequel?' he prompted.

'I really don't know why I am telling you all this. I have never told a soul about it before. Even still I find it embarrassing to think about, let alone to talk about. When I left Mount Saint Bernard and had taken my final at the College of Surgeons I went on to Austria to continue my medical studies. In Vienna I fell in with a young woman. The typical blonde fräulein, handsome, full of life, outgoing, wonderful physique, what you might call an outdoor girl, free as the wind, frank as the daylight. She taught me skiing. We used to go mountain climbing together. I don't believe she knew the meaning of the word fear. She was great fun and the best of company. Her name was Brigitte. At twenty-six she was already a woman of the world. I was twenty-four, and as innocent of women as . . . as . . .'

To put him at his ease Morgan conceded his own embarrassing confession.

'As I am, at twenty-four.'

'You might think that what I am going to mention could not happen to a doctor, however young but, on our first night in bed, immediately she touched my body I vomited. I pretended to her that I had eaten something that upset me. You can imagine how nervous I felt all through the next day wondering what was going to happen that night. Exactly the same thing happened that night. I was left with no option. I told her the whole miserable story of myself and Bruiser twelve years before. As I started to tell her I had no idea how she was going to take it. Would she leave me in disgust? Be coldly sympathetic? Make a mock of me? Instead, she became wild with what I can only call gleeful curiosity. "Tell me more, *mein Schätzerl*," she begged. "Tell me everything! What exactly did he do to you? I want to know it all. This is *wunderbar*. Tell me! Oh do tell me!" I did tell her, and on the spot everything became perfect between us. We made love like Trojans. That girl saved my sanity.'

In a silence Morgan gazed at him. Then coldly:

'Well, of course, this is another story altogether. I mean I don't see how I can possibly blend these two themes together. I mean no writer worth his salt can say things like, "Twelve long years passed over his head. Now read on." I'd have to leave her out of it. She is obviously irrelevant to the main theme. Whatever the hell the main theme is.' Checked by an ironical glance he poured the balm. 'Poor Frank! I foresee it all. You adored her. You wanted madly to marry her. Her parents objected. You were star-crossed lovers. You had to part.'

'I never thought of marrying the bitch. She had the devil's temper. We had terrible rows. Once we threw plates at one another. We would have parted anyway. She was a lovely girl but quite impossible. Anyway, towards the end of that year my father fell seriously ill. Then my mother fell ill. Chamberlain was in Munich that year. Everybody knew the war was coming. I came back to Ireland that autumn. For keeps.'

'But you tried again and again to find out what happened to her. And failed. She was swallowed up in the fire and smoke of war. I don't care what you say, Frank, you *must* have been heart-broken.'

The doctor lifted a disinterested shoulder.

'A student's love affair? Of thirty and more years ago?'

No! He had never inquired. Anyway if she was alive now what would she be but a fat, blowsy old baggage of sixty-three? Morgan, though shocked, guffawed dutifully. There was the real Maupassant touch. In his next story a touch like that! The clock on the mantelpiece whirred and began to tinkle the hour. Morgan opened the album for a last look at the beautiful child. Dejectedly he slammed it shut, and rose.

'There is too much in it,' he declared. 'Too many strands. Your innocence. His ignorance. Her worldliness. Your forgetting her. Remembering him. Confusion and bewilderment. The ache of loss? Loss? *Lost Innocence*? Would that be a theme? But nothing rounds itself off. You are absolutely certain you never heard of him again after that day behind the tennis courts?'

They were both standing now. The rain brightly spotted the midnight window.

'In my first year in Surgeons, about three years after Bruiser was killed, I lunched one day with his mother and my mother at the Shelbourne Hotel in Dublin. By chance they had been educated at the same convent in England. They talked about him. My mother said, "Frank here knew him in Mount Saint Bernard." His mother smiled condescendingly at me. "No, Frank. You were too young to have met him." "Well," I said, "I did actually speak to him a couple of times, and he was always very kind to me." She said sadly, "He was kind to everybody. Even to perfect strangers."'

Morgan thrust out an arm and a wildly wagging finger.

'Now, *there* is a possible shape! Strangers to begin. Strangers to end! What a title! *Perfect Strangers*.' He blew out a long, impatient breath and shook his head. 'But that is a fourth sequel! I'll think about it,' as if he was bestowing a great favour. 'But it isn't a story as it stands. I would have to fake it up a lot. Leave out things. Simplify. Mind you, I could still see it as an idyll. Or I could if only you hadn't torn up his last, farewell letter, which I still don't believe at all said what you said it said. If only we had that letter I bet you any money we could haul in the line and land our fish.'

The doctor knocked out the dottle of his pipe against the fireguard, and throating a yawn looked at the fading fire.

'I am afraid I have been boring you with my reminiscences.'

'Not at all, Frank! By no means! I was most interested in your story. And I do honestly mean what I said. I really will think about it. I promise. Who was it,' he asked in the hall as he shuffled into his overcoat and his muffler and moved out to the wet porch, the tail of his raincoat rattling in the wind, 'said that the two barbs of childhood are its innocence and its ignorance?' He failed to remember. He threw up his hand. 'Ach, to hell with it for a story! It's all too bloody convoluted for me. And to hell with Maupassant, too! That vulgarian over-simplified everything. And he's full of melodrama. A besotted Romantic at heart! Like all the bloody French.'

The doctor peeped out at him through three inches of door. Morgan, standing with his back to the arrowy night, suddenly lit up as if a spotlight had shone on his face.

'I know what I'll do with it!' he cried. 'I'll turn it into a poem about a seashell!'

'About a seashell?'

'Don't you remember?' In his splendid voice Morgan chanted above the rain and wind — '"*A curious child holding to his ear / The convolutions of a smoothlipped seashell / To which, in silence hushed* . . . " How the hell does it go? " . . . *his very soul listened to the murmurings of his native sea.*" It's as clear as daylight, man! You! Me! Everyone! Always wanting to launch a boat in search of some far-off golden sands. And something or somebody always holding us back. "The Curious Child." *There's* a title!'

'Ah, well!' the doctor said, peering at him blankly. 'There it is! As your friend Maupassant might have said, "*C'est la vie!*"'

'*La vie!*' Morgan roared, now on the gravel beyond the porch, indifferent to the rain pelting on his bare head. 'That trollop? She's the one who always bitches up everything. No, Frank! For me there is only one fountain of truth, one beauty, one perfection. Art, Frank! Art! And bugger *la vie!*'

At the untimely verb the doctor's drooping eyelids shot wide open.

'It is a view,' he said courteously and let his hand be shaken fervently a dozen times.

'I can never repay you, Frank. A splendid dinner. A wonderful story. Marvellous inspiration. I must fly. I'll be writing it all night!' – and vanished head down through the lamplit rain, one arm uplifted triumphantly behind him.

The doctor slowly closed his door, carefully locked it, bolted it, tested it, and prudently put its chain in place. He returned to his sitting-room, picked up the cinder that had fallen into the hearth and tossed it back into the remains of his fire, then stood, hand on mantelpiece, looking down at it. What a marvellous young fellow! He would be tumbling and tossing all night over that story. Then he would be around in the morning apologising, and sympathising, saying, 'Of course, Frank, I do realise that it was a terribly sad experience for both of you.'

Gazing at the ashes his whole being filled with memory after memory like that empty vase in his garden being slowly filled by drops of rain.

A POET AND AN ENGLISHMAN

DESMOND HOGAN

'We'll shortly see the broad beaches of Kerry,' he said, smiling, the van ricketing from side to side and Limerick's fields passing, pastures of golden, or near golden, dandelions.

His hair swung flamingly over his face, a wild red gust of hair, and his tinker's face narrowed like a gawky hen's.

'Peader.' She swept her hand across his forehead and he laughed.

'Behold the Golden Vale.'

They got out and looked. Sandra's legs were white after winter, white as goat-skin. A sort of vulnerable white Peader thought.

Her body was tucked into a copper dress and her hair, red like his, performed little waves upon her shoulders. She looked so handsome. After a winter in Belfast that was strange. One would have thought a winter in Belfast would have changed one, broken-down factories and hills, arching with graves.

Yet in their little house off Springfield Road, they'd hid out, guns going off occasionally, televisions roaring, an odd woman calling.

Peader was working as a tradesman-carpenter-cum-electrician. A strange trade for a tinker one might have thought. Peader had picked these skills up in London when he ran away from Michael Gillespie, his tutor, in the west of Ireland.

He was seventeen and his hair was more gold than red and he'd run away from the harbour village where he'd been brought up and partly adopted by an English Greek teacher who'd retired to Ireland on the strength of a volume of poems, a hard-bitten picturesque face in *The Times* colour supplement and an award from the British Arts Council.

There in the west he stayed, making baskets, sometimes taking to the sea in a small boat, writing more poems, winning more awards, giving lectures in Greek to students at Irish colleges.

Peader thought of Michael now, thought of him because somehow the words framed in his head were the sort of words Michael would use.

'A sort of vulnerable white.' Yes, that was the state of Sandra's legs; they were pale and cold. Ready for summer.

'Let's make love,' Peader thought in his head and he didn't need to say it to Sandra. There were bushes and leaving their van there on the open road above the Golden Vale, they hid behind bushes where Sandra could have sworn there was honeysuckle just about to appear and made love, Peader coming off in her, rising like a child caught in an evil but totally satisfying act.

'Banna Strand.' Peader murmured the name of the beach. Roger Casement had appeared on that beach in a German submarine in 1916 and was arrested and hanged.

'Our first sight of the sea,' Sandra said.

'It's lovely.'

It stretched, naked, cold.

'I'd love a swim,' Sandra thought, thinking of last summer and tossing waves off the Kerry coast.

Peader didn't really notice how pale and beautiful the beach was. He was observing the road, his head full of Michael Gillespie's mythology. 'Roger Casement, a homosexual, arrived on Banna Strand, 1916, was arrested and hanged.' Items of Michael's history lessons returned.

When Peader was twelve, he was adopted by Michael, brought to his house near the pier and was given a room, alien to him, told by Michael to be calm and often, a little harassed, made his way back to his father's caravan where his father beat his brother Johnny.

The first time Michael referred to Roger Casement as being a homosexual Peader didn't know what the word meant. He must have been twelve or thirteen when Michael spoke about Casement and it was probably spring as spring was a penetrating season in the west of Ireland, lobster pots reeking of tensed trapped lobster.

When he was seventeen and running away, Peader still knew little about the word, more about a love affair with Michael.

A donkey stood out before them. 'I'll tell him to go away,' Sandra said.

She got out, hugging the donkey's brown skin, kissing his nose, and Peader watched, silenced.

Why was he thinking of Michael now? Why the silence between him and Sandra?

Perhaps because he felt he'd soon see Michael again.

They were going to a festival in Kerry; Peader had given up his job in Belfast and Sandra and he had bought antiques cheap and with a van full of them were going to sell them at the festival which included plays, dancing, lectures, music, drinking and most of all the picking of a festival queen.

Kerry had many festivals, at all times of the year and since Peader's family originally came from Kerry he'd make his way back there at odd times, like the time in London he threw up his job on a site and went to Dingle for the summer, sleeping in a half-built house, a house abandoned by a Dublin politician who had thoughts of living there when it was fashionable and when it ceased being fashionable with his mates, he abandoned the place in time for summer and Peader's stay there.

'We'll have a good time,' Sandra thought. 'We'll have a good time.' She was smoking a cigarette she'd picked up in a café in Limerick, her head slouched so that her hair fell across her face.

'How long is it?'

'Ten miles.'

Her mouth pouted. Her resistance was low; there was a

strangeness about Peader. This she knew. Her silence deepened. Cigarette-smoking was a token activity.

Maybe it was because of his return to roots Peader was silent. Perhaps he felt sad on coming back to Kerry and the towns of big houses and the verandas of hotels which held rare flowers because it was warm nearly all the year round in Kerry, a Gulf Stream climate.

'There's a rhododendron,' she shouted.

The first she'd seen that year but Peader wasn't interested and she said to herself, 'Maybe there's things I don't know.'

She wasn't really a tinker; she'd grown up in Ballyfermot in Dublin. Her father sold junk, broken furniture, broken chairs, broken clocks and her cousin played a tin-whistle and was married to a Mayo tinker, playing in Germany for a living.

He was famous now, having gone to Berlin, barely knowing how to sing but by some fluke ending up in a nightspot in a West Berlin bar. Now he had two records and his wife often sang with him, a wild woman with black hair who gave Sandra's family an association with tinker stock.

Sandra had met Peader at a Sinn Féin hop. Neither Sandra nor Peader had any interest in politics but both had cousins and uncles who supported Sinn Féin and God knows what else, maybe guns and bombing and the blowing up in the North.

Sandra had a Belfast side to her family, her mother's side, and though her mother was silent about Belfast grief, Sandra knew of cousins in the North who wore black berets and dark glasses and accompanied funeral victims, often men who'd died in action. Sandra's main association with the North was tomato ketchup spilling the day she heard her cousin John was dead, a little boy run down by an ambulance which had been screaming away from the debris of a bombing.

She'd seen Peader at the Sinn Féin hop, a boy sitting down, eyes on the ground. A woman with dyed hair sang 'I Left My Heart in San Francisco' and a girl with biting Derry accent sang 'Roddy McCordy', a Fenian ballad.

Peader asked her to dance – they'd hardly spoken, his hands left an imprint on her back and on ladies' choice she asked him up; his fingers tightened a little awkwardly about her. The girl from Derry sang 'Four Green Fields' as the lights dimmed; a song about Mother Ireland's grief at the loss of her fourth field, Ulster.

People clapped and there was a collection for internees in Long Kesh but Sandra and Peader slipped away; he slept in her house, on the sofa in the sitting-room.

He told her he was just back from England, his first time in four years. He seemed upset, gnome-like as he was drinking coffee in her home.

She sensed a sorrow but sorrow was never mentioned between them, not even when they were going to films at the Adelphi or when they eventually married, the wedding taking place at the church in Stephen's Green, her family outside, black-haired; his, the remnants from Connemara and Kerry, his brother dressed like Elvis Presley and his cousins and second cousins in a mad array of suits, hair wild on women in prim suits bought at Listowel or Galway for the occasion.

Come winter they went to Belfast, Sandra's uncle Martin providing Peader with work. Springfield Road where they lived ran through a Catholic area, then a Protestant area, again a Catholic area.

Its colour was dark and bloody. Like its history. Catholic boys walked by in blue. Protestant boys walked by in blue. One wouldn't know the difference. Yet they killed one another, violence ran up and down the road and on in the hills at the top of the road a boy was found crucified one day, a child of ten gagged to a cross by other children of ten, his hands twisted with rope and he half-dead and sobbing.

'We'll leave Belfast,' Sandra said one day, crying over the

newspaper. A little girl had been killed down the road by a bomb planted in a transistor set.

'Where do we go?' Peader brooded on the question.

He came up with an answer, drove back in their van one day loaded with antiques from a bombed out shop. Together they procured more; 'My father used to buy and sell things at the Ballinasloe fair,' Peader said, 'I can take a hint.'

His father and his father's father sold things like grandfather clocks in North Kerry. His father moved to Connemara on marrying Brigid Ward, his mother, and she dying on a wild Connemara night, after he, beating her, left her two children, John, Peader. Peader was the one taken by the poet; Peader now with what Sandra observed as ancestral intelligence returned to the feel of country things — clocks, paintings of women in white writhing as though in pain — to the purchasing and reselling of these items.

A man waved. Women wandered through the streets, country women, all loaded with bags and with the air of those who'd come from fresh land and flowered gardens. They'd arrived.

'Let's park the van,' said Peader. Sandra had long since forgotten her troubles but on seeing a young man, a Romany maybe, with black falling hair, a cravat of red and white and an earring pierced in his right ear, gold, she wondered at their purpose in coming here and felt what she could only decide was fright.

Through the day women with plants walked past their stall, geraniums dancing in pots and women laughing. Business went well.

Craftily Peader sold his wares, producing more, the mementoes of Country Antrim unionists disappearing here in the Kerry market town.

Relatives of Peader appeared from nowhere, his father's people. Mickey-Joe, Joseph-James, Eoghan-Liam. Men from Kenmare and Killarney.

They'd been to Kerry for their honeymoon, Sandra and Peader, but for the most part Kerry was unknown to Sandra apart from Peader's accounts of childhood visits there from Connemara, to Dingle and Kenmare, to the wild desolate Ballinskelligs peninsula full of ghost villages, graves, to Dun Caoin and the impending view of the Blaskets and Skellig Mhicel and the Sleeping Monk, an island which looked like a monk in repose.

'Sandra, my wife.' People shook her hand; grievously some did it, men were hurt by lack of sex. He took her hand. They were in a crowded pub and Peader stroked first Sandra's thumb, then took her whole hand and rubbed it.

'You've had too much,' said Sandra, but already he was slipping away. She was far from him.

In his mind, Peader saw Michael Gillespie making his way through the crowd that day. Michael hadn't seen him but Peader remained strangely frightened, fearful of an encounter.

All the poets and playwrights of Ireland seemed to be here for it was a festival of writers too, writers reading from their work, writers lecturing.

In the pub now Michael entered. He stood, shocked. His black hair smitten on his forehead. There was no sense of effeteness about him as there used to be. He was all there, brooding, brilliant in middle-age, ageless almost.

'Hello.'

Peader shook his head – tremulously. So tremulously that he thought of shaking rose bushes in Michael's garden in Connemara when Peader was fourteen or fifteen, frightened by rain, by shaking things.

'Michael, this is my wife, Sandra.'

Michael looked towards her and smiled. He had on a many-coloured T-shirt. 'Your wife.'

Five years since they'd met; it all cascaded now. Peader asked Michael if he wanted a drink but Michael insisted on buying drinks for both of them, Guinness heavily topped with cream.

'To your beautiful wife,' Michael toasted Sandra.

He was here to read his poems he explained, he had a new book out.

"Did you win any more prizes?' Peader asked.

'Not recently,' Michael replied. But he'd opened a crafts shop in Connemara and anyway he lectured widely now, streaming off to universities in Chicago or in Texas. He had a world-wide following.

'Good to be famous,' Peader said.

'Alone?' Michael questioned.

Sandra was now talking to a boy with a Dublin accent; he had on a cravat and they chatted gaily, obviously having found some acquaintance in common.

'Your wife is lovely.' Remarks loaded, laden with other comment.

Eventually Michael said — sportingly almost.

'How was it?'

'What?'

'London.'

'All right.'

'Big?'

'At my age, yes.'

'You managed.'

'I was careful.'

Michael looked at him. 'You look OK.'

Peader remembered the times he was thirteen, Michael minding him, giving him honey in the mornings, eggs fresh, little banquets of eggs with yellow flowing tops.

He remembered the time he was fourteen, by which time Michael had seduced him. He remembered the white pillow and in summer the grey morning that would merge into the big room and afterwards the excitement of sailing a boat or running on the sand.

'Your daddy wouldn't like it!' Michael said one day and Peader thought back to winter and the roadside caravan and his hairy father frying mutton chops that smelt like rabbits dead and rotting.

'You're more handsome than ever.'

'Am I?'

'Tough!'

'Married.'

'Your wife is lovely.'

'You said.'

'I can't say it too much. She's got a gorgeous smile.'

'What have you been doing?'

'Working, writing, lecturing. For two years I lived with an American student from Carolina, a Spanish-American girl.'

'Black haired?'

'Yes.'

'I thought you preferred them blonde.'

'Who?'

'People.'

'Peader, you've become harsh.'

Harsh. The winters were often harsh in Connemara; when Peader was fifteen it snowed and he and Michael freed a fox from a trap near a farm-yard. Peader's hair was quite blond then and rode his head like a heavy shield against the elements.

'This won't last forever,' Michael said one day, weeping.

Peader had emptied a bowl of chestnuts into the gutter at Hallowe'en. In a temper, often Peader could be brazen and perhaps it was his brazenness which drove him to run away.

It was after he'd had an affair with a girl from Clifden, cut through her thighs in a barn near the sea, in a corduroy suit with his trousers down found woman nearer to satisfaction than man.

He ran away to London, a city of many women, and found no one there interested in him.

No one beyond the odd foreman on a building site and a man

from Kerry who gave him rudimentary training in carpentry and in skills of trademanship.

'Are you going to see the festival queen crowned?' Michael asked.

'Yes,' Peader nudged Sandra. 'Will we go and see the festival queen crowned?'

Sandra turned to him. 'Yes. Here's John from Dublin.'

The Dublin boy shook hands with them. They made a party, trailing off.

'Is that the man that brought you up?' Sandra nudged Peader.

'Yes.' His reply was drowned by the crowd, noise, mingling, bunting shaking in the bustling avenues, old women crying raucously and the young holding one another.

They made their way to a square where the queen was just being crowned, a woman who looked like Marilyn Monroe, her smile big and awkward. Cheers rose about them and fights broke out.

Peader felt himself stirring with an old passion; how many times in bed with Sandra had he longed again to be fondled by male hands, and the points of adolescence, his knees, his genitals, to be fondled in the old way.

Instead of having a mother, he'd had Michael. Instead of adolescent tears and rashness, there'd been an even flow, card games, winkle-picking, mountain climbs, a spiral of strange fulfilment.

As the crowd jostled Peader felt Michael's nervous hand on his shoulder. 'Is your wife having a child?'

'Not yet.'

'Some day?'

'Seed is a strange thing,' Michael said; his words nearly drowned. 'The seed that seems lost but is devoured by an artist's vision, an artist's uncertainty, the uncertainty of reaching to people, the feeling of trying and failing and trying again and loving someone — anyone.'

'Me?'

'Yes — you were the one.'

A balloon went into the air. It slipped into the air, red, against a rather retiring-looking moon. The fireworks went off, splattered against the sky.

'Like a monstrance at mass,' Peader thought, remembering childhood and the times his father would take him to mass in Clifden, the priest turning with a golden, sun-like object to his congregation and the people bowing like slaves.

Peader virtually hadn't been to mass since he was seven — except the odd ceremony — like his wedding.

'Let's go somewhere,' Michael said. 'Peader, I've missed you, I've missed your arms and your body. I've waited for you. You can see poems I've written about you and read at Oxford and Cambridge.'

'Sandra,' Peader was going to call out to her but she was lost among the crowd with the boy from Dublin.

At three o'clock that morning Sandra made her way back to the tent she and Peader had erected earlier that day. How would she tell Peader? It had been so strange meeting John, a boy from Ballyfermot she'd dated at fifteen. He'd turned into a buxom motor bike hippie; his pink shirt had drooped open that evening revealing a strongly tanned chest.

'We're all gypsies,' John had said, 'we people from Ballyfermot.'

Ballyfermot, a working-class suburb of Dublin.

She'd lost Peader and the man he was talking to in a crowd, rather strange enigmatic Englishman, and found herself adrift with John.

They'd found their way to a pub which was situated beside a tin caravan where fish and chips were being served, and there in the pub had hot whiskeys, and recalled going to James Bond films in the Savoy together before John's motorbike vocation and Sandra's wedding. John had found money in his travels; he'd lived with an old rich Italian lady near Trieste.

'Festivals bring strange people together,' Sandra had said, getting drunker and drunker, leaning on John's leather jacket.

The tent was forgotten and Peader and the rather strange Englishman who had his arms about Peader, the man Peader had often referred to in rather sharp clipped sentences. She'd ended up lying on John's stomach.

'Let's go to the mountains,' John had said.

'No, to the sea.' Her order was relieved by her mounting the bike and making to the sea. Waves surged in and she ran beside them and John recounted more and more of his experiences in Europe, a night in Nice with a millionaire's daughter, striding by the Mediterranean on the sea-walk below the city with a bottle of champagne.

'Let's make love,' John hugged her.

She relapsed into his arms and lay with him on the sand but didn't stir to embrace him further, knowing that her faithfulness wasn't to John and the affairs of adolescence but to Peader and his toughness.

Making her way back to the tent, she thought of Peader and the difference between her and him, a difference she hadn't realised until that night, meeting John again; she'd realised and wondered at the fields of her childhood, fields on the outskirts of Dublin where tinker caravans were often encamped and which snow brushed in winter, fields grabbed by Dublin's ever-expanding suburbs. Peader had come from a different world, a world of nature continued, ever-present, ever-flowing.

He came from the sea and the west, a world of fury.

There'd been different laws there, different accidents, a savagery of robins dying in winter snow and scarecrows looking like the faces of the people, faces starved for want of love.

Coming towards the tent she heard voices within, male voices. A thought struck her that Peader was inside with the Englishman whom he'd been talking to earlier in the evening. It had been a strange, packed way they'd been talking; Peader's clipped sentences returned to Sandra. 'The day Michael and I walked to the sea,' 'the day Michael and I went sailing,' 'the day Michael and I collected blackberries.'

Sandra stopped and listened outside the tent. There was a low moan of pain and Sandra began shaking.

It wasn't cold but she was sure now of Peader's past; she knew him to be a traitor. He came from a world of lies.

'Peader,' she pulled back the drape of the tent and inside she saw Peader, arm in arm with a young boy she'd never seen before.

She began running but there was a sudden clench, Peader stopped her.

He was naked and wet. He took her forehead and he took her face.

He kissed her throat and her neck and his tongue dabbed in her mouth. And she fell before him into the cold, dirt-laden path.

His big and eager face loomed before her. 'It's all right, Sandra,' he said.

'I had to do it and I couldn't hide it from you. There's things to be done and said in life; you must go back, sometimes.'

She'd never know how Michael Gillespie had tried to seduce Peader that night, she'd never know how Peader had repulsed him and walked away, drunk, through the crowd.

She'd never know how Peader had picked up a young boy from Cahirciveen who'd been drunkenly urinating and made love to him in the tent, kissed his white naked pimples as Michael Gillespie had kissed his years before.

She'd never know but when she woke in the morning between Peader and a young boy she knew more about life's passion than she'd ever known before. She rose and put on a long skirt and looked at the morning, fresh, blue-laden, as she'd never seen it before.

SUCH GOOD FRIENDS

ITA DALY

Although it all happened over two years ago, I still cannot think about Edith without pain. My husband tells me I am being silly and that I should have got over it long ago. He says my attitude is one of self-indulgence and dramatisation and that it is typical of me to over-react in this way. I have told no one but Anthony, and I think that this is a measure of the hurt I suffered, not to be able even to mention it to anyone else. I don't think I am over-reacting – though I admit that I have a tendency to get very excited when I discover a new friend or a potential friend. This may sound as if I am wallowing in permanent adolescence, but even if this were so, the knowledge still wouldn't stop me being overcome with joy if I should meet someone whom I felt to be truly sympathetic.

It may be that I feel like this because I have had so few real friends in my life. I do not say this with any suggestion of self-pity; I am aware that such affinity of spirit is a very rare commodity and so, when there is a possibility of finding it, why, there is every reason to be excited. And it is something I have only ever found with members of my own sex.

Not that I have ever had any shortage of men friends. I have a certain bold physical appeal which seems to attract them, and before I was married, I always had four or five men hovering around, waiting to take me out. I don't deny that this gave me a satisfaction – it was sexually stimulating and very good for one's ego – but I have never felt the possibility of a really close relationship with any of these men. Even Anthony, to whom I have been married for five years, and of whom I am genuinely fond, even he spends half the time not knowing what I am talking about, and indeed, I am the same with him. Men on the whole are unsubtle creatures. You feed them, bed them, and bolster their egos, and they are quite content. They demand nothing more from a relationship, and for them physical intimacy is the only kind that matters. They don't seem to feel a need for this inner communion, they are happy to jog along as long as their bodies are at ease. I do not bare my soul to men. I tried to once with Anthony in the early days of our marriage, and, poor dear, he became upset and was convinced that I must be pregnant. Pregnant women are known to suffer from all sorts of strange whims.

You may by now think that I do not like men, but you would be quite wrong. I do like them and I am sure that living with one must be so much easier than living with a member of one's own sex. They are easy to please, and easy to deceive, and it is on the whole therapeutic to spend one's days and nights with someone who sees life as an uncomplicated game of golf, with the odd rough moments in the bunker. All I point out are their limitations, and I do so knowing that these views may be nothing more than an eccentricity on my part.

However, to return to Edith. I first met her during a bomb scare when that spate of bomb scares was going on, a little over two years ago. Before my marriage I had been studying law. I passed my first two exams and then I left to get married. About a year later I decided I would try to get a job as a solicitor's clerk, for I found I was bored doing nothing all day long and I thought it might be a good idea to keep my hand in, so to speak. It would make it easier if I ever decided to go back to College and attempt to qualify.

The firm where I got my job had its offices on the top floor of an old house in Westmoreland Street. The offices had a Dickensian air of shabbiness and dust, although I knew the firm to be a thriving one. It consisted of Mr Kelly Senior, Mr Kelly Junior, and Mr Brown. Along with five typists and myself of course. Mr Brown was a downtrodden man of the people, who was particularly grateful to Mr Kelly Senior for having lifted him from the lowly status of clerk to the heights of a fully fledged solicitor. He spent his days trotting round after the boss, wringing his hands and looking worried, and, as far as I could see, making a general nuisance of himself. Mr Kelly *père et fils* were tall dour Knights of Columbanus. They had crafty grey eyes in emaciated grey faces and they always dressed in clerical grey three piece suits. One day, Mr Kelly *fils* caused quite a sensation when he ventured in wearing a yellow striped shirt, but this break with tradition must not have met with approval, for next day, and thereafter, he was back to the regulation policeman's blue.

The typists in the office were nice girls. I had little to do with them, as I had my own room, and only saw one of them when I had any work to give to her. In the beginning, as I was the only other female in the office, I did try joining them for morning coffee. However, it was not a success. They were not at their ease, and neither was I. I didn't know what to say to them, and they were obviously waiting for me to leave until they could resume their chatter of boyfriends and dances and pop music. There was only about six years difference in our ages, yet I felt like another generation. It was because of this lack of contact that I hardly noticed Edith's existence, although she had been in the office nearly six weeks. That was, until the day of the bomb scare.

We were cursed with bomb scares that winter and particularly irritated by this one, the third in the same week. We filed out of the building, silently, as people were doing on either side of us. The novelty had worn off and these regular sorties into the winter afternoons were beginning to get under people's skin. It was bitterly cold, and I thought I might as well go and have a drink. It seemed more sensible than standing around in the raw air, making small talk. I crossed over the bridge and turned down towards a little pub that I had discovered on such a previous occasion. I sat sipping a hot whiskey, enjoying the muggy warmth, when I happened to glance across at the girl sitting opposite me. She looked familiar in some vague way, and just as I was wondering if she was from the office, she caught my glance and smiled back at me. Yes, now I remembered, she was one of the typists all right, and now that she had seen me I felt obliged to go over and join her. I hadn't wanted to − I had been looking forward to a nice quiet drink without the effort of conversation. But I couldn't be so obviously rude.

'You're with Kelly and Brown,' I began, sitting down beside her.

Her smile was diffident, almost frightened.

'Yes, that's right. And you're Mrs Herbert. I know because the other girls told me − I haven't been long there myself. My name is Edith Duggan,' she added and held out her hand, rather formally I thought. We sat side by side, both of us ill-at-ease. I was wondering what I could talk about, and then I saw, lying open in front of her, a copy of *The Great Gatsby*. Good − at least this could be a common theme.

'Please call me Helen,' I said. 'Any friend of Gatsby's is a friend of mine. Do you like Scott Fitzgerald?'

'Oh I love him, I think he's great. He's marvellous.'

Her whole face lit up, and it was then I realised what a good-looking girl she was. As I have mentioned before, I have a certain showy attractiveness myself. I know I am not basically good-looking, and I depend heavily for effect on my skilful use of paints. But I have red hair and green eyes, and with a bold make-up I am very much the sort of woman that men stop to look at in the street. I could see now that Helen was not at all like this. She was small and slight, with a tiny face half hidden under a heavy weight of dark brown hair. You would pass her by and not look at her, but if you did stop to take a second look you would realise that her features, though small, were exquisitely proportioned, that her skin had a translucent sheen and that her eyes – her eyes were deep and soft and tranquil. I was the one getting all the barman's looks, but I could see at a glance that Edith was much the finer of us. She was such a charming girl too, shy and low spoken, yet with none of the gaucherie and bluster that so often accompany shyness.

But though I was pleased by her good looks and her charm, it was not these that excited me. What excited me was a realisation that here was someone to whom I could speak. Right from the beginning, from my remark about Fitzgerald, I think we both were aware that we were instantly communicating. We talked that day, long into the afternoon, and the more we talked the more we found we wanted to say. It was not only that we shared values and views and interests, but there was a recognition, on both our parts I thought, of an inner identification, a oneness. I knew that I would never have to pretend to Edith, that she would always understand what I was trying to say. I knew that a bond and a sympathy had been established between us and that I could look forward with joy to the times that we would talk and laugh and cry together. I had found a friend.

Do women love their husbands, I sometimes wonder? Do I love Anthony? I know that I like him, that I am grateful to him, that I feel the constant desire to protect him. But love? How can you love somebody you are so apart from? We live together comfortably, but so distinctly. Anthony wants it so, although if I told him this he would be incredulous. I have come to realise as I lie in bed at night, or at the first light of dawn, with his supple body, wracked by pleasure, lying in my arms, that Anthony is undergoing his most profound experience. His body shudders, and his isolation is complete. Sometimes I am amazed by the exclusivity of his passion, although I know well that this sort of pleasure is something that you cannot share. I know, for I am no stranger to pleasure myself; I have felt a tingling in the loins, a heat in the bowels. But I have always kept a weather eye out and asked — is there nothing more? Anthony's capitulation to his body is so complete, and his gratitude to me afterwards so overwhelming, that I know that, for him, this is where we touch, this is where he reaches me. And I am left in the cold outside.

But not once I had met Edith. Anthony should have been grateful to Edith, for with her coming I stopped harassing him. He didn't have to watch me in the evenings, sitting bleakly in our elegant drawing-room, upsetting his innocent enjoyment of the evening papers. I didn't suddenly snap at him for no reason, or complain of being bored, or depressed or lonely. Edith became my source of pleasure. Soon we were having lunch together every day, and I would drive her home in the evenings after work. She soon confessed to me that she had been unhappy in the office before she met me, for the other girls were as unwilling to accept her as they had been me, although in both instances, to be fair, I think it was a sensible recognition on the typists' part of our essential difference. We just had nothing to share with them.

For a start, she was older than they were. She had been a third year philosophy student at the University, she told me. A most successful student, apparently, who had hoped to pursue an academic career. She had been working away quite happily, looking forward to her finals, when one day her mother, who had gone quite innocently in search of matches, had found a packet of contraceptive pills in Edith's handbag. It was not, Edith told me, the implication that she was sleeping with a man or men that had so shocked her parents. It was the deliberateness of the act. Young girls did from time to time fall from grace, and it was wrong and they should be punished accordingly. But that anyone, particularly a daughter whom they had reared so carefully, could arm herself with these pills before-hand — that sort of calculation denoted a wickedness and evil of a far more serious order. She was thrown out of the house that very evening and told never to darken the door again.

'The thing I regret most,' Edith said, 'was hurting them. You cannot expect them to understand, the way they were brought up themselves. It's natural that they'd react like that. But I do love them, and I really didn't want to cause them pain. They'll come round, I'm sure. I'll just have to give them a few months, and then everything will be all right I hope. I'll just have to be a lot more careful. But I do miss them, you know — particularly Mammy.'

I had known Edith about six weeks when she introduced me to Declan. She had mentioned him several times, and I gathered that they intended to get married as soon as Declan qualified. He was an engineering student. What a surprise I got the first time I saw him. I couldn't understand, and never did understand afterwards, how someone of Edith's delicacy and intelligence could fall in love with such a slob. And he *was* a slob, a lumbering six-foot-two, with a red face and a slack mouth and a good-humoured, apparently unlimited amount of self-confidence. The night I met him, he had come round after work to collect Edith, and she asked me to stay and have a drink with them. He took us to a rather draughty and gloomy pub, and having bought our drinks, sat opposite me and fixed me with a disapproving eye.

'What,' he asked, 'do you think of the situation in South Africa?'

I later discovered that being a swimming champion all through his school days and most of his college days, Declan had come late to the world of ideas. But not at all abashed by his late start, he was now determined, it appeared, to make up for lost time. I found his zeal rather wearying, I must admit, and I resented the off-hand way he dismissed Edith's comments. I wondered what would happen when he discovered Women's Lib. With a bit of luck he might offer to liberate Edith by refusing to marry her.

In the meantime I realised that Edith would not take kindly to any criticism I might voice and that I had better be careful to simulate some sort of enthusiasm. So next day when she asked me what I thought, I told her I found him very interesting, and that I'd like them both to come to dinner soon and meet Anthony. We decided on the next night, and I said I'd come and collect them as Declan didn't have a car. I planned my dinner carefully and told Anthony to provide an exceptional claret – it was a special occasion. At these times, I'm pleased to be married to a wine merchant, for Anthony can produce the most miraculous bottles, guaranteed to revive any social disaster. I did want Edith to be happy, to like my home and my dinner and my husband. I didn't want to impress her – I knew anyway that the trappings of wealth would leave her unmoved – but I wanted to offer her something, to share whatever I had with her. I was afraid she might be bored.

But I needn't have worried. The evening was a tremendous success and Anthony and Declan seemed to take to one another straight away. Anthony is a most tolerant man, and cannot understand my own violent reactions towards people. I don't think he notices them very much. Once he has had a good meal and with a decent cigar in his hand, he is prepared to listen to all kinds of nonsense all night long. I was amused that evening at the interest he seemed to be showing in Declan's lengthy monologues, nodding his head intelligently and throwing in a 'Really – how interesting' every now and again. Afterwards he told me he thought Declan a 'rather solemn but quite decent chap.'

I blessed his tolerance that night, for I thought it might provide a solution to a problem I saw looming. I had no interest in being lectured to by Declan, and on the other hand, if I saw as much of Edith as I wanted to, if I could take her to films, concerts, even perhaps on holiday, then I knew Declan would begin to resent me and feel perhaps that I was monopolising Edith. But if I could manage to arrange these foursomes, then Anthony would keep Declan happy, and I would have Edith to myself.

And how happy I was at this prospect. The more I saw of Edith, the more I admired and loved her. She had a quietness and repose about her which I found particularly attractive – I am such a strident person myself. I always look for the limelight and though I have tried to cure myself of this fault, I know I am as bad as ever. But Edith actually preferred to listen. And when she listened, you knew that she was actually considering what you were saying, and not simply waiting for an opportunity to get in herself. I talked a lot to Edith, more, I think, than I had ever talked to anyone in my life. The pleasure I got from our conversation was enormous. The world suddenly seemed to be full of things and people and ideas to discuss. I asked for no other stimulant than the excitement generated by our talk, and I looked forward to our meetings with a sense of exhilaration. I loved to buy things for her too. I have always liked giving people gifts, but through being married to Anthony my sense of pleasure had become dulled. Mind you, I don't think it was Anthony, most men would be the same. You can buy a man only a certain number of shirts, and after that – what is there? But with Edith the possibilities were endless. She dressed quite badly – I don't think she ever thought about the way she looked. But I, who saw all the possibilities of her beauty, felt like a creator when I thought of dressing her. A scarf to bring out the purity of her skin, a chiffon blouse to emphasise that fragile line of her neck – the changes I could make in her appearance! Of course I had to be careful not to offend her, as I knew that one so sensitive might be made to feel uncomfortable by all these gifts. So sometimes I would pretend that I had bought something for myself and it didn't fit and she would be doing me a favour by taking it. Or I would accept a pound for a leather bag which had cost me fifteen, saying that I had picked it up cheaply but that the colour wasn't right.

Creating this new Edith re-awoke all my interest in clothes and make-up. I seemed to have been dressing myself and putting on my face for so long that I felt I could do it in my sleep, and I had some time ago grown bored with myself. Besides, presenting my rather obvious persona to the world was a straightforward task, and the subtleties which I used in dressing Edith would have been lost on me. And as Edith saw her new self emerging, she grew interested too. I wondered how this would affect her attitude towards Declan. As she began to realise what a beautiful girl she was, might she not also realise what a slob Declan was, and get rid of him? Not that I thought very much about Declan any more. He was by now busy preparing for his final examinations and when he did have time to go out with Edith he seemed quite happy for them to come and have dinner with us, or at Anthony's club. Anthony had even interested him in wine, and as they sat sniffing their glasses and delicately tasting, we sat giggling over ours, having quaffed too much of the stuff in a most unconnoisseur-like fashion. Edith and I both agreed that we knew little about wine, but knew what we liked. Sometimes, when Declan was studying, I'd go round to Edith's flat for supper, and we'd get through a bottle of plonk enjoying it just as much as any rare Burgundy. This formed a bond between us and gave us a nice comfortable sense of vulgarity, of which Delcan would have disapproved for intellectual reasons and Anthony for social.

I was happy. It is a state you have to be in to recognise. Before I met Edith, it had never occurred to me that I was unhappy. I knew that I was bored a lot of the time and often lonely. I felt that something was missing from my life and various well-meaning girlfriends had told me from time to time that what I wanted was a baby. Instinctively I knew however that this was not so. I have always rebelled at the idea of becoming a mother; I could never see myself, baby at breast, looking out placidly at the world. Now I knew that my reservations had been right: I would probably have made a very bad mother, and I would not have fulfilled myself. All I needed all that time was a friend. A real friend.

But it seems to be a rule of life that, having achieved a measure of happiness, clouds begin to float across one's Eden. I don't know when things started going wrong with Edith and myself, for my state of happiness had begun to blur my perceptions, and I wasn't as conscious as I should have been of all Edith's reactions. Then little by little I noticed changes in her. She started to make excuses about not coming out to the house with me. When I'd ask her to go to a concert or lecture she'd say no thank you, she was doing something else. She grew irritable too, and would cut me off short when I'd begin to talk about something. Then she took to avoiding me in the office or so it seemed to me, and she started bringing sandwiches in at lunch time, saying that she had no time to go out to lunch as she was doing extra work for Mr Kelly.

When I was certain that I had not been imagining Edith's attitude, when I could no longer fool myself that everything was as it had been, I grew very upset. What upset me most, I think, was that I could not offer an explanation for her behaviour. I knew I was not the most tactful person in the world, but I had felt that Edith and I were so close that there was no need for pretence; and anyway I couldn't remember having said anything so awful that she would stop wanting to see me because of it.

One afternoon I became so worried that I burst into tears in the office. Mr Kelly junior was with me at the time, and I think I frightened the poor man out of his wits, for he told me that I looked tired and to go home at once and not to bother coming in the next day, which was Friday. That weekend I did a lot of thinking. Away from the office I grew calm, and I began to think that things would sort themselves out if I could remain calm. Maybe I had been seeing too much of Edith, and if I left her alone for a while she would probably recover her equilibrium and everything would be all right again.

When I returned to the office, I stuck to my resolution. I

remained perfectly friendly towards Edith, but I stopped asking her to come places with me, and I began to have my lunch half-an-hour earlier than the rest of the office. It was so difficult, this calm indifference, but I knew it was the only way. Then one morning as I was taking my coat off, one of the typists rushed into my room.

'Isn't it awful, have you heard?' she said.

'No, what is it, what's happened?'

'Edith Duggan's mother was killed last night. Run over by a bus as she was crossing the road. She died instantly. Edith, the poor thing, went to bits, I believe. They couldn't get her to stop crying.'

God, how awful. I felt quite sick. What must Edith be feeling? I knew she had loved her mother . . . and that she should have been killed before they could be reconciled . . . The guilt she must be feeling, added to the pain. I must go to her, I knew. I put my coat back on and got her home address from one of the girls, and left without even telling Mr Kelly where I was going.

The house was a shabby semi-detached with a few sad flowers struggling for life in the patch of green outside. A man I took to be Edith's father answered the door. He showed me in to the little front room and there I saw Edith, sitting white-faced and stiff, staring at nothing. She looked up and gave me a wintry smile.

'Edith, what can I say —' I began, but she interrupted me with a shake of her head.

'I know. It's all right really. I understand. It was good of you to come.'

The words sounded so small and distant in that front parlour.

'Oh. Edith, my poor, poor Edith.' I ran towards her and put my arms around her, kissing her, kissing her to comfort her. Suddenly she tore at my arms and flung herself from me. She ran behind the sofa and stood there, trembling.

'Get out of here,' she shouted. 'Leave me alone. Go away you

— you monster.'

I tried to say something, but she began to scream some incoherent phrases about the girls in the office and how stupid she'd been and how could I have come there then. I could still hear the screams as I made my way down the path.

She didn't come back to the office. Anthony suggested that she had probably been reconciled with her father and was now staying at home to mind the family. I worried about her, for it seemed to me that the shock of her mother's death must have unhinged her mind. How else could I explain the dreadful things she shouted that day in her front room?

Then about a month later, as I was walking down Grafton Street one afternoon, I saw her coming towards me. She saw me too, and as we drew level I put out my hand. She looked at me, directly into my eyes, with a cold hostility.

'Hello Helen,' she said, and she sounded quite calm. 'I'm glad I've met you like this. You see, I want you to realise that I meant what I said that day. I wasn't hysterical or anything like that. I do not wish to see you ever again.' Then she stepped aside and walked on down towards O'Connell Street.

I felt my stomach heave as she walked away. I felt I could never get home, that I would have to stand there, in Grafton Street, rooted to the spot in horror. I twisted and turned, like an animal in a cage, not wanting to face the fact that Edith's shouted obscenities were the result of no temporary derangement. When I did get home and told Anthony, he refused to discuss it. He said that the only thing to do was to put the whole business out of my mind, forget about it completely. But how could I forget? How can I shrug off the pain and the pleasure, as if it had never happened? I can find no way of doing that, no way of wiping out the profound sense of loss I am left with. You see, we were such good friends, Edith and I. Such good friends.

APRIL

RAY LYNOTT

He asked himself if he had any sense of humour left. There was irony in accepting the notion of male monthlies, phases of the moon. He threw the magazine down and paced the room to the calendar behind the door. Four, five days or was it a week or more, his mind full of acrid rubbish. From the calendar page a little round moon stared at him like an eye and now he did laugh, as one might smirk in a mirror, half-bravely.

He turned. The window framed a primrose light hovering on the world outside. Easterday in twenty-four hours. It was always a cold holiday despite the full moon, new light.

'Infinity of space . . . the constancy of death . . . ' Phrases from the text he had left on the desk. But the other rubbish burned on. The image of the old priest with the grey long lady's hands — saint's hands, a silly classmate called them; the face of the boatman, strong-skinned, sun-brown, laughing. Both images singeing every part of his being as scrap ends of hair are singed.

He crossed the room to sit in the armchair where he had thrown the magazine and he began to page through it again.

'Immaculate, tasteful small cottage, terraced, shuttered, in Chelsea area, near Chelsea Gardens. Viewing by appointment. Godfrey Street SW3.'

Other houses were in Knightsbridge, Pimlico; there was a mews in Victoria, a stone gate-lodge in Cornwall. Full pages of women posed in wide-skirted print dresses, face after made-up face with its confidence and daredevilry. He turned the pages more slowly. Men challenging. Young moustached men in white open shirts. Older men suave in yachting blazers, beside boats, all sleek. All speak-easy, all brave, all out of no world he was part of. He didn't find it easy to accept now that he had walked from any shop that morning clutching *Harper's and Queen*.

He had been tired for weeks. The winter was longer than people had patience for. And random sun-teasing days out of the gloom, like treacherous pools in a bog, only emphasised the encircling hold winter still had. Maybe one could enjoy the odd sunny day if one had the strength, built up the strength as one was supposed to build up faith.

'The theologian's pyramid, based in Reason, apex in Faith'. It was the old priest's sharp voice . . . 'apex in Faith'. A joke.

He threw the magazine on the floor behind him as he got up to cross the chill room to his desk. The homily lay half-finished. He had set himself to speak only by implication of the risen Christ – eyes to see, let them have ears to hear. There were notes to the side of the page – 'Infinity of space . . . the constancy of death'. Underlined 'Let us think of the body being driven every minute to shred itself down to a last particle that will be nothing but the earth again. Let us think of our minds like light capable of travelling . . . '

There was nothing of a sermon in it. Yet there was the truth he could tell them. I went into Sligo today, an ordinary April day. My spirit had deserted me. I sat in the lounge of the Great Southern Hotel and I drank three large whiskies before eleven o'clock. Then I went boldly to the newsagent's and I bought *Harper's and Queen*. For the photography, I told the girl.

He laid both hands over the scribbled papers on the desk, sat, put his head down on his hands and waited for the soft drowsing to come as it always did since ever he was a child in need of soothing.

Outside there was the faint purring of cars, then the angelus bell. They made the distance comfortable. In the room there was some sharper whizzing in the fireplace, soot falling, a click at the window where the sun was stretching the wavin eave-runs, even the wood of the desk underneath him full of breathing.

With his eyes shut, he felt all movements one after another, distinct, painless. And then streets astride the greenish river, children, dusty cars from the hills and people shouting something he found it hard to hear. He didn't have the language and thoughts of these people who wanted to barter their half-joys and their boredom in any market, thinking it would make them less forlorn. All he should do was remind this mountain people that they had a name and a pride. Remind himself.

He raised his head suddenly. The thought had been strong — a name and a pride. What was he dredging now, he asked himself. He was bewildered.

Sparrows were playing outside in the sunshine of the gravel path, two wild creatures angry with each other, wings flippittering. Then they were gone. He looked over at the magazine on the floor in the middle of the room, splayed like any model within its pages. Godfrey Street SW3. What blame to the people? What was a priest worth except as a saint, with or without saint's hands. Play on their football teams, organise their Bingo and concerts, teach their children, amuse their old parents, bind and swaddle, comfort with doctrine and discipline. Otherwise — out.

There was a tightening at the back of his head. Five years before, in the seminary, he was the one who believed in people. 'You should have been an actor,' the grey old Spiritual Director had told him. 'Start a new pantheism with everybody and everything becoming God.' A grey bitter old man in a room that smelled of floor polish and chest ointment. His death made them all say he was a saint, so who was the actor? All the white surplices billowing out as they lifted the yellow coffin into the cemetery through the Roman archway. '*Justorum animae in manu Dei sunt*.' Green trees, birds and first flowers of spring were all out that day. Now, outside, another spring.

He thought he heard a knock at the door and went across the room. In the hallway the sun was shining from the front porch down past him to the kitchen door and the stairs beside it. The hall was empty. It might have been Mary Monaghan in the kitchen, he told himself. Empty sunlight on the ordination class photograph hanging opposite, and on the line of dusty geranium pots at the skirting. Then, he wasn't sure. There, down in the shadow at the stairwell, coming forward smiling, out of the empty place, sun-brown . . .

He banged the door shut and stood behind it. The boatman. Enough to think of the priest, and the other came. Brown-skinned, the knitted cap the same as had been on the lad's head that day. 'Boat, boats out.'

The others also touting. 'Boats to the pool – boats to the islands.' But the lad stood out from the rest. 'To any of the islands, sir. A boat out. Anything you want.' The face, the dark eyes looking straight at him. 'Anything you want, sir.' For God's sake, it was what the young boatman had said to draw him that day. Face with weather in it, the eyes not fine, but steady except for split seconds of speed and depth. His own age.

'Where do you go?'

'Out on the pool, if you like, sir. Or the main island and the garden or any of the islands, or just around.' A pause, and then again, 'Anything – you like, sir.'

With the knitted cap, he was wearing a ridiculous version of a navy-blue blazer and slacks, blazer and slacks creased and stained beyond any semblance of fashion.

A few moments studying each other. There had been no motion of will, no wavering or turning except to look down the length of the red boat against which the lad rested.

Even five years distant the image burned as strongly. His first holiday as a priest, alone for the day, he had dressed himself in jeans and a T-shirt. Now it could be recalled detail by detail, more minutely than – ordination itself, more real.

He turned quickly where he stood in the room. The April sun was over the house, leaving short shadows on the gravel path. The sparrows had come back.

He was thinking of the grey priest in the wintry room.

'The eyes, guard the eyes, *custos oculorum*. You deny Christ when you refuse discipline.'

In open sunshine the courtesy of the boatman had been natural and easy.

'Would you like to put the book and things behind the bucket at the back where they'll be dry, sir.'

Together they pushed the red boat while the other boatmen touted on the slipway towards people coming down. There was urgency, not talk of money.

'Don't you need some others to make up a party?'

'The way business is, sir, I'm glad to get yourself and I'll only be charging you your seat. To tell the truth, I'm not pushed about a boatload, we'd be waiting for a fair while and I'm as pleased to get her out and get a bit of exercise, sitting waiting does a body no good.'

Offshore before he realised, allowed himself to think. Passing other boats. In some there were only couples who had hired the boats themselves, laughing women leaning back with their faces up to the sun, men open-shirted rowing. But in one boat it was a long-haired girl with a smiling face who was rowing steadily, taking the boat out past the others and talking intently to a young man sitting opposite her with his elbows on his knees, hands supporting his chin, lost in admiration. The sound of their voices carried over the water. The girl would never tire, infinite resources of a sea-woman out of legend.

It was the way his stupid escaping mind wanted to fool itself that day.

The priest remembered now how he had leaned back against the side of the boat feeling the steady one-two of the boatman's strong even rowing. He watched the water dripping from the rising oar and then he closed his eyes and let himself be carried forward, conscious only of the rhythm.

'You deny Christ when you refuse discipline.'

The grey priest always challenged. And there was never any courage with which to counteract.

In the boat the other, now in shirtsleeves without the blazer, hummed for a while quietly. The priest remembered that they had been looking at each other quite unselfconsciously before the boatman asked him if he was from Dublin.

'No, I work near Sligo.'

'I passed it once when I went to the brother's wedding. He's an electrician in Donegal. I remember Sligo, coal ships in at the harbour.'

'That's right, you can see the harbour from the Donegal road.'

'Are you married yourself?'

'No.'

'Nor meself either. The brother has four children now. I think children is as good a reason for getting married as any other. Would you like children yourself?'

'If, eh, I'd get married first, think about it then.'

'Aye, we were nine of us in the family, maybe that's why I'd like a few kids. Used to the noise like.' His laugh went out from the boat on the shining water.

They had gone beyond the bay almost to open sea. There was an island, rhododendron bushes holding a few purple blossoms and masses of dark green. But they were going past it, the boatman in complete control, no longer calling him 'sir', talking about winters on English building sites earning the money that had bought him the boat. Another island that had been hidden behind the first, hardly more than massive boulders out in the sea with a cluster of trees and a green strip down towards an apron of shingle. No jetty nor any sign that boats put in there. The boatman was laughing again. It was the kind of laugh that could be remembered because it went with the rowing, effortless and strong as it brought them closer to the deserted sunlit place.

'This island hasn't much except the ground you see, but it's better for swimming.' Together they were pulling the boat up on the shingle. 'It's as safe as a wash tub. The odd basking shark comes farther out, but no fear of them and no currents or weed either because of the stones.'

'I didn't bring anything.'

'Any what?'

'Togs.'

'What togs d'ye need, aren't we as God made us.'

It was impossible to remember exact shades of those first moments on the rough shingle island. He had never intended. He had left the hotel that afternoon, his mother reading in the lounge, he was going for a walk around the golf course. Why? What tempering had there been?

The answer never came. Each year questions multiplied. And now on an April day watching sparrows and sun through glass he knew there was no movement of his spirit towards quietness and peace.

Two of them lying back in the teeming sunshine. The chaos beginning. The other standing, taking off shirt, pants. Naked, expecting companionship into the sea.

'Come on, you can swim, can't you?'

'No, you go. I'll — I'm not a good swimmer.'

Nothing fine or innocent. Near to the spirit of the grey priest — 'Choice of either Christ or the very material of your own body, turmoil.'

The brown-skinned boatman looked like a native of the sea finding his second nature out on the shining water.

Turmoil was a favourite word of the old priest — 'If you cannot put order on your thoughts and desires, then the sum total of your life will be turmoil.' As if salvation was saving coppers in a jar.

The sun had been a glory in the sky that day. Sun on land, sun on sea and the liquid body propelling itself outward, no boats anywhere. The girl with oars in her hand, where had she gone?

Where were girls in his thoughts? In prayer he used to try to encompass it, he had no name for it, turmoil. Even now when prayer withered there were almost tears at the confusion. Let me pray, let me – 'I will go to the altar – God who gives joy to my youth –'

That day when the boatman came back from the sea the water was glistening on him, naked.

'I never feel as mightily as out in that water. There's often a day or two I'd come out and dive off of the boat and just swim on and on and then back to it.'

'Would you not be afraid of losing it?'

'Not if the sea's like this, how could you?'

'I could. Takes courage.'

'Sure what courage is in it?'

The sound of the sea below, beating out moments of time. The sun had moved and the afternoon seemed to be resting between them. The boatman, half-dressed now, was lying back nearby. Should one be alone in anything one did, he had asked himself. Instead of an answer he heard the other's voice.

'I wish you were a woman.'

'What?'

Fingers had come over at his shoulder. 'I wish you were a woman.' Squeezing through the cotton T-shirt, digging slightly below his shoulder blade. The voice was quiet. Heads back, faces turned on the shingle. He could feel the other's breath. He moved quickly, standing.

'Do you want to go?'

'What?'

'To be going, do you want to go?'

'Oh no. Well, I suppose. It'll be late otherwise.'

'Plenty of sun, but whatever you say.'

Neither of them stirred. What had happened in that moment, that day? He remembered falling back on his hunkers in case he had seemed rude. The boatman leaning on an elbow.

'You like it here?'

'Yes.'

'I said to myself you would, soon as I saw you.'

'What do you mean?'

'When you were coming along down from the hotel, at the corner. I don't know. There's an English lad comes every year, army lad. I take him out. He likes it here, too. And every Christmas the parcel of clothes comes and a tenner.'

He had stared at the boatman. Englishman, the same journey, money. The small undistinguished face, lying against the shingle, old as the place itself. What was the man thinking?

Then for whatever reason he had found himself letting out a convulsive laugh. The boatman smiled, asked if it was the clothes that made him laugh because they were so odd. He said no, something else altogether, hearing the coldness in his own voice.

Even after five years it was a bitter feeling when he remembered that oblique moment, the irony, need to get away, outrage and a thousand other shades all in that nervous rumpled laughter.

Sometimes now he would stand wishing that time might catch up with the fury of those thoughts and that there might be one simple purpose, the strength in one moment. That moment would become the next and then the next and –

He moved again to the armchair.

Grey priest and boatman, shadow on shadow, often the faces merged. Copper pence in a jar. Tenner.

He could see through the window to a field beyond the house where a pair of jackdaws were hopping clumsily. He glanced over at the magazine, women fighting back at him, magazine men mocking.

He laid his head against the chair, closed his eyes.

When he woke it was late evening. Mary Monaghan knocking at the door was calling him to supper. There were no faces, no feelings. It was a calm space for the first time in weeks.

He could even approach decision now, he knew, if that was what he wanted.

SHAYBO

PATRICK BOYLE

Y ou'd be right in thinking that an underground jakes is a poor place for a smoke and a chat. The more so when the sun is knocking sparks off the glass roof and stirring up a stink that would bloody near talk to you. But when you haven't the price of a packet of fags and when Shaybo Gallagher, the Corporation attendant, is a countyman of your own, a bit of hardship is neither here nor there.

'Hey!' he calls out, when he sees you stowing away. '*You're* a stranger. Come over here and tell us the news.'

Shaybo's cubby-hole is so small that there's only room for the one chair, but give the little whitterit credit, up he gets.

'Take the weight off your feet, old stock,' says he. 'It's tiring work walking the streets on a day like this.'

And on top of that, he produces the packet. A twenty Players, not long opened. Good for an hour or two of Shaybo's blethering.

'The city's choked up with yobs from the country,' he says. 'Up for the match. Oh, a shower of ignorant gulpins. They've made a hames of the joint already.'

He aims a kick at a terrier dog about to lift a leg against the door jamb.

'Hump off!'

It's a poor class of a man takes his spleen out on a brute beast. But there you are. What more can you expect from a shithouse warden?

'It'll have to be cleaned down from stem to stern,' says he. 'It is far from public conveniences these gentlemen were reared. Coming up from the Kerry mountains or the bogs of Cavan with but one thought in the heads – to rid themselves of the load of dirty black porter they've incurred in their travels. Clambering up on the seat and squatting down on their hunkers as if they were in their own haggards.'

He goes ranting on with this class of chat as though he wasn't born and bred, like many a better man, in the wilds of Donegal. Sight nor sound of a flush lavatory did he see till he came to work in the city thirty-odd years back. Damn the bit he knew what the chain was even for. Or where the used paper should go. To listen to him now, you would think he is gentry.

'Mean scuts they are too. They would stand outside an occupied cubicle for twenty minutes at a time, waiting for the customer inside to finish his business. Ducking in past him as soon as the door is opened. You can be full sure the ratepayers won't fatten on what they get by way of contributions from the crowd of country hallions heading for Croke Park.'

As he is giving out the pay, you can hear in the background the clatter of the crowd coming and going. The mutter of voices. The shuffle and stamp of impatient feet on the tiled floor. The swish of water from the pipes. And, from the closets, the odd cough or grunt or maybe even a rumbling fart as some poor bugger strives to relieve himself. A pleasant class of a commotion, one you could listen to for hours, if you've the smokes to go with it.

Shaybo is now holding forth about the way people look down on a lavatory attendant. And, God knows, you could hardly blame him. You'd see folk cringing away from him in disgust who'd find nothing bothersome in the company of a cow doctor – a man very apt at any time of the day or night to ram his arm, shoulder deep, up the backside of a brute beast.

'The truth is, it's a job like any other,' he says. 'The pay is good. The hours not too long. The work light. Granted it's not the best place to be in the real hot weather. Or when the crowds flock into the city for an All Ireland final.'

You could say that again. There's a hum rising, thick as a cloud of midges, that only cigarette smoke would disperse. Shaybo takes the hint and when the fags are lit, he says:

'You'd be surprised at the folk come in here. All classes of people. Even the clergy. Priests, Christian Brothers and the like.'

They'd be the queer asset in any public lavatory! It would be very liable to put a man off his devotions if he found a parish priest mounting the pulpit beside him and proceeding to let his dog off the chain.

The traffic had slackened a lot.

'It's the same every Sunday at this time,' says Shaybo. 'Everyone's at Croke Park, Dalymount Park, the Phoenix Park. They could be devouring pints somewhere or other. Or maybe be at the pictures. Wherever they get to, they don't come down here. A different class of a character altogether you'd find using a public convenience during a slack period. Queer-hawks of one sort or another. Slipping in here looking for company. The Guards are death on them. There's polismen smelling around this place at every hour of the day or morning. In full canonicals or in civvies. Out to plague and pester these poor angashores. And you'd wonder why. For they're a decent harmless enough lot. They may have their little weaknesses, I'll grant you that. But sure none of us is perfect. And few as quiet and civil and well-mannered as these lads.'

To hear the little pigmy giving off, you would think it is a meeting of the Sacred Heart Confraternity he is talking about instead of a gathering of blackguardly rascals intent on every manner of villainy and rascality. Take care but maybe Mister bloody Shaybo himself isn't properly battened down and shipshape. Why else would he be taking up the cudgels on behalf of a crowd of bloody half-in-halfs? Oh, he could be a dark horse, all right. Isn't he forever running to the altar rails and to evening devotions. Sure these craw-thumpers are all the same, the world over. Master hands at deception.

He gives me a nudge.

'Psst! Here's one of the regulars now. Out and in here a dozen times a day. Blondie, I call him.'

Well, the Lord knows, you couldn't mistake him. Strutting along, his hips clashing like a pair of cymbals. A tall fellow with fair wavy hair, a nose you would love to flatten and a double-breasted suit with padded shoulders and french letter fitting. A shockproof, fully automatic, twenty-two-carat bum-boy.

'Watch the antics of him,' says Shaybo.

Blondie minces down to the far end of the urinal. Stops at the hand basins. Takes out a pocket comb and starts preening himself up. Cocking his head this way and that to see what he looks like. The kind of carry on that would give you the sick.

'Hush!' says Shaybo. 'He's watching everything in the mirror. You don't want to let him know he's taped.'

Sure enough, when you study closer, it is sticking out a mile that what Blondie is really doing at the hand basins is lamping the establishment. He stands there combing his hair, all the time grinning and grimacing into the mirror, until the last customer has emptied his bladder and gone his way rejoicing. Then he strolls across to the stall at the very end of the line, mounts the ledge and lounges there. Waiting.

'Isn't he the last word?' whispers Shaybo. 'He's the daddy of them all, I tell you.'

You would think he is talking about a prize fighter. Or a politician. Instead of a scrubby, smirking pansy.

'Someone's coming,' Shaybo mutters. 'With any sort of luck, we should have a right bit of gallery.' He leans out to look up the stairs. Ducks back immediately. 'Be cripes, it's a plain-clothes man. I'd know by the cut of his jib.'

Indeed, like Blondie, you would know him at once. Close-cropped bullet head, wattles of flesh creasing the collar of his jacket, splay feet treading cautiously: a rozzer if ever there was one. At the foot of the stairs slowing down, like you would do going into a place of worship. Sizing up the available space. Then, believe it or not, he heads straight for the only occupied stall in the tool house. A thing no decent law-abiding citizen would dream of doing. For a man is entitled to a bit of privacy on a job of this kind. Unless the jakes is packed out.

'There'll be trouble come of this,' Shaybo says, watching the rozzer take up pumping stations beside Blondie.

Flutes in their fists, they stand side by side, paying no attention – or so you'd think – to each other. But you are sorely mistaken if you think they are making proper use of the facilities provided by the Corporation. You would be fully assured of this when you see Blondie reach his free hand across in the general direction of the rozzer's fly.

'That's torn the coupon,' says Shaybo, starting off down the jakes at a run. He has rubber-soled shoes and the pair of bucks know nothing till he is upon them.

'Hey you!' he shouts, giving the rozzer a push in the small of the back. 'Enough of that.'

The rozzer lurches forward against the slippery porcelain. Claws wildly at it with both hands, seeking purchase to push himself upright. He fails. The feet go from under him, skidding off the ledge to the floor, sending him sliding down to crash on his mouth and nose into the trough. You can say without a word of a lie that he swallows back a mouthful of porter piss that would soften the cough of a chief superintendent. To crown the poor bugger's misfortunes, doesn't the bloody spray take it into its head to start working, drenching the sleeves and shoulders of his nice new suit. You'd have broken your arse laughing at the cut of him, lying there wriggling and gasping like a freshly caught conger.

Shaybo leans over him.

'What are you supposed to be doing down there?' he shouts, above the roar of the spray. 'This is no place to be doing your barrack square exercises.'

The rozzer struggles up to his hands and knees, clear of the spray.

'What's wrong?' he asks the tiled floor. 'What's going on here?'

He shakes his head violently, scattering water all round, in an effort to clear his head. With the clatter he got, he must be just about half-conscious.

'You should be ashamed of yourself,' says Shaybo. 'Nosing your way into Corporation property on your filthy errands. Those that sent you here must have the queer dirty minds.'

The rozzer turns his head up sideways. There is a dazed expression on his face.

'Someone gave me a belt of a fist,' he says. 'When my back was turned. Gave me a bloody judas.'

Shaybo leans closer, hissing into the astonished face.

'No one hit you. Though if someone did, I wouldn't raise a hand to stop him. What right have you to come in here starting trouble. I keep a decent law-abiding establishment, I'll have you know.'

You would find it in your heart to be proud of the little banty cock. Not since the force was started could there have been a rozzer talked to in this fashion. Though it's to be admitted that a copper is not at his best kneeling on the floor of a piss house with his flute hanging out and him wringing wet from wallowing in the lavatory trough.

He gets to his feet and stands there swaying, gaping in bewilderment at the little circle of curious customers that's after gathering. It is worth noting that there is no sign of Blondie. Wisely enough, he has skipped it. After starting off the whole bucking rumpus.

Shaybo hasn't finished with him yet.

'Put away that truncheon of yours,' he says. 'And button up your spare. Don't you know full well, if you're conversant with your manual of instructions, that exposing your person in public is a criminal offence?'

He pauses to let that shaft penetrate.

'Whether in uniform or in plain clothes,' he finishes.

While the rozzer, red faced and all thumbs, is tucking away his paraphernalia, the crowd of earwigging gulpins mutters:

'What's the row about?'

'Didn't you hear what the man said?'

'Exposing his person, no less.'

'A drunken polisman, they say.'

'Disgraceful!'

'What's happening anyway?'

Shaybo, with flapping hands, shoos them off.

'It's all right, gentlemen,' he says. 'Everything's under control.'

For sheer brass neck and general effrontery, you must hand it to the little weasel. Making an unprovoked attack on a law enforcement officer, accusing him of unspeakable practices, humiliating him before a gathering of scandalised citizens and then calming the enraged populace with a few words of soft sawder. Though to be strictly accurate, you have only to take a look at the rozzer with his arms hanging the one length, the water dripping out of his sleeves and running down his cheeks, his face twisted with suppressed rage, to know that there is one member of the company far from calm and reassured.

'Look!' he says, displaying his sodden jacket with the sleeves already riding up the wrists. 'Look at the state of my clothes.'

God knows, if he weren't a plain-clothes cop – the type of creeping Jesus nobody likes – you would feel sorry for him.

'Sure it's a thing of nothing,' says Shaybo. 'The cleaners will put it right for you in jig time.'

He takes the rozzer by the arm and leads him past the scattering of customers now absorbed in their devotions.

At the foot of the stairs he halts.

'You'd be as well though,' says he, 'to get out of those wet duds before you do another short arm inspection.'

He pauses.

'Elsewhere,' he adds. And there's a growl in his voice that would do credit to a mastiff.

The rozzer shambles up the stairs without another word out of him and Shaybo comes strutting back to his cubby-hole.

'It'll be the queer while,' says he, 'before that fellow comes down here again on his filthy pursuits. This place would get a bad name if that kind of carry-on were to continue.'

In the name of God, what class of a joint does the little pintle think he is running? A convent or a crap house? He is getting too big for his boots, Mister bloody Shaybo. He wants taking down a peg. But if you're smoking a man's cigarettes, your hands are tied.

He is still holding forth like an outraged abbess when there's the sound of footsteps on the stairs. Standing at the door, he has a clear view of all comers and you can see by the look on his face that a stumer is on its way.

'And what brings *you* back?' he demands, as the tow headed pansy puts his head round the door.

'He's gone, I see,' says Blondie, in a sour tone of voice.

'If it's your playmate you mean, I ran him out of here.'

'It's a pity you couldn't mind you own business instead of interfering in what doesn't concern you.'

'What's that?' Shaybo yelps.

You can see he is shook. But the silly slob should know that a queer the like of Blondie specialises in biting the hand that feeds him.

'I had him on the hook. You made a bags of the whole thing by butting in.'

'Do-you-do-you-do you mean . . . that you should have been allowed . . . without let or hindrance . . . to . . . to — '

'Sure, I do. I know how to handle these customers.'

'You know . . . how to handle . . . these – ?'

'Yeah. It's my job.'

Shaybo takes a deep breath. Lets it out slowly through his nose.

'Well, you made a poor fist of the job here today, if I may say so. Did you not tape the class of a gentleman you were propositioning?'

'Of course I did. Isn't he a notorious character? Known in every public lavatory in the city.'

'Why did you tackle him so? You could have landed yourself in the Bridewell.'

Blondie switches a pair of lamps on Shaybo that would shrivel your soul.

'Didn't I tell you it's my job? How do you think vice in this city can be stamped out without the work of the Special Branch?'

It would make the day for you, if you were to see the cut of Shaybo. The legs must be going from under him for he is propped up against the door jamb like a sagging bolster. His face is twisted up and his eyes squeezed tight. The fingers of his locked hands are squirming furiously. There are sounds coming from his open mouth that could very well come from someone after getting a woeful kick in the fork. At length the words come.

'Special Branch?' he squeaks.

'Yes.'

'You mean . . . that all the times you came in here . . . day and daily for weeks past . . . you were on duty?'

'That's right. It was suspected at Headquarters that these premises were becoming a centre of homosexual activities.'

Shaybo's eyes were scampering around in their sockets like hunted sheep, trying to evade the expressionless face of his tormentor. He runs his tongue round his lips. Whispers hoarsely:

'Suspected . . . homosexual . . . activity?'

'Yes. That's what I was on the track of today.'

'But . . . but . . . but I don't understand. Wasn't that bullet-headed fellow a plain clothes man? How could there be . . .'

Shaybo dries up. And no wonder. The thought of two rozzers tricking with each other's tools in a public lavatory would be enough to put you wondering what capers they would be at in the privacy of the barracks day room.

Blondie snorts.

'Plain-clothes man, how are you! Is it trying to insult the Force you are?'

'You mean –' Shaybo moistens his trembling lips. 'You mean . . . he's not . . . a policeman?'

'Of course not. He's a wretched little homo. And but for your intervention, I'd have him up on a charge of indecent behaviour.'

This is too much for Shaybo. He burst out:

'Indecent behaviour, is it? Sure no man's accoutrements would be safe with you around. Didn't I see you with my own two eyes interfering with that poor fellow who had no other errand in here but to make his water? And then you talk of bringing a charge against him. It's little short of felon setting, that's what it is. Felon setting.'

Blondie gives him the kind of look you'd give to a turning worm.

'My man,' says he, in a voice these gentlemen use when they are very liable to take out the notebook, 'any more trouble from you and I'll book you for obstructing an officer in the execution of his duty.'

Shaybo's eyebrows are up in his hair and his jaw is dangling by its own weight. There is no fight left in him. All that is wanted now is a blow of the chopper to finish him off.

Blondie squares his shoulders. Clears his throat. Swings up the blade.

'In the course of my investigations here,' says he, and you could almost hear the icicles tinkling in his voice, 'it has become evident that you have been turning a blind eye on what is happening under your nose.'

He breaks off to turn to the little group of gougers, their heads stuck out trying to catch what's being said above the swish of the pipes.

'Move along there,' he says. 'Be off about your business.'

When they are gone, he turns back to Shaybo.

'Furthermore,' says he, bringing down the chopper, 'your behaviour would lead to the belief that you are in sympathy with the activities of these immoral characters.'

Well, that's a real slaughter-house blow and no mistake. Who would ever think that this little maggot, a notorious candidate for beatification, is all the time running a class of a knocking shop instead of a gent's lavatory? The novenas will have to come thick and fast to atone for this transgression.

As Blondie turns away and moves off towards the stairs, you'd be inclined to think that the entertainment is over. But no! Shaybo starts clearing his throat, rasping and raking and hawking till he drags up a bloody great ball of phlegm that must have had roots growing down to his navel. With the force of a sling shot, he sends it cracking off the tiled floor at Blondie's heels.

'Jesus curse you!' he murmurs fervently.

Blondie stops in his tracks. Wheels round slowly. Comes back a pace.

'What was that you said?' he demands.

'My Jesus, mercy!' Shaybo spits out the words as though he is pronouncing a malediction.

'What kind of a war-cry is that?'

'It's a pious ejaculation. Entitles you to three hundred days' indulgence.'

'And what's the idea of this?' Blondie points to the green gobbet, still quaking like a jelly.

'I'm a bit caught in the throat. It'll maybe clear up if I keep spitting.'

They stay eyeing each other while you would count ten, neither moving a muscle.

'If you take my advice,' says Blondie, at length, 'you'll mind your step in future. Or you'll be in trouble.'

His gaze swivels slowly round the empty stalls.

'Big trouble.'

He turns on his heel and starts off up the stairs again.

Not till the footsteps have died away does Shaybo's face uncoil. He opens and closes his lips, searching for spittle. Sucks up a noisy breath through his nose. Hawks deep in his throat. Spits dry.

Straightening up, he moves across to the back of the cubby-hole. Rummages around on the shelf. Picking things up and putting them down again. His legs are shaky enough, so is his voice when he says:

'Very few around for the day of a match.'

He stands there, staring into space, with not a word out of him that you'd throw to a dog, until a group of schoolboys comes trampling down, shouting and jack-acting. Then he rouses himself. Rubs his hands together briskly.

'The sun splitting the trees and not a potato washed,' he says.

He picks up a long-handled mop. Goes to the door.

'The crowd'll be along any minute now,' he says.

Leaning on the mop handle, he gazes down the length of the jakes. There is only one customer left. An old buff with a dark suit and a bowler hat. A bank director or the like. Rushing off to a board meeting, you'd say, for he keeps glowering impatiently down at the unceasing dribble. You would cripple yourself laughing at the contortions of him when he starts stowing away. Hard put to it you'd be to say whether it is the crown jewels or a dangerous reptile that he is stuffing down the leg of his trousers, jiggling and jerking with one knee bent to make full sure the pants are slung on the usual side and the last drop shaken from Fagan. In spite of all his precautions, he moves off stiff-legged, letting the cat out of the bag, so to speak.

Shaybo is muttering to himself.

'Tck! Tck! Tck!' He shakes his head sadly. 'Blondie — of all people. You'd lose faith in human nature after the likes of that.'

THE MOUTH OF THE CAVE

EDNA O'BRIEN

There were two routes to the village. I chose the rougher one to be beside the mountain rather than the sea. It is a dusty ill-defined stretch of road littered with rocks. The rocks that have fallen from the cliff are a menacing shade of red once they have split open. On the surface the cliff appears to be grey. Here and there on its grey-and-red face there are small clumps of trees. Parched in summer, tormented by winds in winter they nevertheless survive, getting no larger or no smaller.

In one such clump of green, just underneath the cliff, I saw a girl stand up. She began to tie her suspenders slowly. She had bad balance because when drawing her knickers on she lost her footing more than once. She put her skirt on by bringing it over her head and lastly her cardigan which appeared to have several buttons. As I came closer she walked away. A young girl in a maroon cardigan and a black skirt. She was twenty or thereabouts. Suddenly and without anticipating it I turned towards home so as to give the impression that I'd simply been having a stroll. The ridiculousness of this hit me soon after and I turned round again and walked towards the scene of her secret. I was trembling, but these journeys have got to be accomplished.

What a shock to find that nothing lurked there, no man, no animal. The bushes had not risen from the weight of her body. I reckoned that she must have been lying for quite a time. Then I saw that she, too, was returning. Had she forgotten something? Did she want to ask me a favour? Why was she hurrying? I could not see her face, her head was down. I turned and this time I ran towards the private road that led to my rented house. I thought, Why am I running, why am I trembling, why am I afraid? Because she is a woman and so am I. Because, because? I did not know.

When I got to the courtyard I asked the servant who had been fanning herself to unchain the dog. Then I sat out of doors and waited. The flowering tree looked particularly dramatic, its petals richly pink, its scent oppressively sweet. The only tree in flower. My servant had warned me about those particular flowers; she had even taken the trouble to get the dictionary to impress the word upon me — *Venodno*, poison, poison petals. Nevertheless I had the table moved in order to be nearer that tree and we steadied it by putting folded cigarette cartons under two of its legs. I told the servant to lay a place for two. I also decided what we would eat, though normally I don't, in order to give the days some element of surprise. I asked that both wines be put on table, and also those long, sugar-coated biscuits that can be dipped in white wine and sucked until the sweetness is drained from them and re-dipped and re-sucked, indefinitely.

She would like the house. It had simplicity despite its grandeur. A white house with green shutters and a fanlight of stone over each of the three downstairs entrances. A sundial, a well, a little chapel. The walls and the ceilings were a milky-blue and this, combined with the sea and sky, had a strange hallucinatory effect as if sea and sky moved indoors. There were maps instead of pictures. Around the light bulbs pink shells that over the years had got a bit chipped, but this only added to the informality of the place.

We would take a long time over supper. Petals would drop from the tree, some might lodge on the stone table, festooning it. The figs, exquisitely chilled, would be served on a wide platter. We would test them with our fingers. We would know which ones when bitten into would prove to be satisfactory. She, being native, might be more expert at it than I. One or other of us might bite too avidly and find that the seeds, wet and messy and runny and beautiful, spurted over our chins. I would wipe my chin with my hand. I would do everything to put her at ease. Get drunk if necessary. At first I would talk but later show hesitation in order to give her a chance.

I changed into an orange robe and put on a long necklace made of a variety of shells. The dog was still loose in order to warn me. At the first bark I would have him brought in and tied up at the back of the house where even his whimpering would be unheard.

I sat on the terrace. The sun was going down. I moved to another chair in order to get the benefit of it. The crickets had commenced their incessant near-mechanical din and the lizards began to appear from behind the maps. Something about their deft, stealth-like movements reminded me of her, but everything reminded me of her just then. There was such silence that the seconds appeared to record their own passing. There were only the crickets and, in the distance, the sound of sheep-bells, more dreamlike than a bleat. In the distance too, the lighthouse, faithfully signalling. A pair of shorts hanging on a hook began to flutter in the first breeze and how I welcomed it, knowing that it heralded night. She was waiting for dark, the embracing dark, the sinner's dear accomplice.

My servant waited out of view. I could not see her but I was conscious of her the way one sometimes is of a prompter in the wings. It irritated me. I could hear her picking up or laying down a plate and I knew it was being done simply to engage my attention. I had also to battle with the smell of lentil soup. The smell though gratifying seemed nothing more than a bribe to hurry the proceedings and that was impossible. Because, according to my conjecture, once I began to eat the possibility of her coming was ruled out. I had to wait.

The hour that followed had an edgy, predictable and awful pattern – I walked, sat on various seats, lit cigarettes that I quickly discarded, kept adding to my drink. At moments I disremembered the cause of my agitation, but then recalling her in dark clothes and downcast eyes I thrilled again at the pleasure of receiving her. Across the bay the various settlements of lights came on, outlining towns or villages that are invisible in daylight. The perfection of the stars was loathsome.

Finally the dog's food was brought forth and he ate as he always does, at my feet. When the empty plate skated over the smooth cobbles — due to my clumsiness — and the full moon so near, so red, so oddly hospitable, appeared above the pines, I decided to begin, taking the napkin out of its ring and spreading it slowly and ceremoniously on my lap. I confess that in those few seconds my faith was overwhelming and my hope stronger than it had ever been.

The food was destroyed. I drank a lot.

Next day I set out for the village but took the sea road. I have not gone the cliff way ever since. I have often wanted to, especially after work when I know what my itinerary is going to be: I will collect the letters, have one Pernod in the bar where retired colonels play cards, sit and talk to them about nothing. We have long ago accepted our uselessness for each other. New people hardly ever come.

There was an Australian painter whom I invited to supper having decided that he was moderately attractive. He became offensive after a few drinks and kept telling me how misrepresented his countrymen were. It was sad rather than unpleasant and the servant and I had to link him home.

On Sundays and feast days girls of about twenty go by, arms round each other, bodies lost inside dark commodious garments. Not one of them looks at me although by now I am known. She must know me. Yet she never gives me a sign as to which she is. I expect she is too frightened. In my more optimistic moments I like to think that she waits there expecting me to come and search her out. Yet, I always find myself taking the sea road even though I most desperately desire to go the other way.

BREAKFAST FOR ENRIQUE

COLUM McCANN

T he only older men I know are the ones who rise early to
work. They fish the ocean for sea trout and haddock, flaring
out their boats from the wharf before the sun, coming back by
mid-morning with huge white plastic barrels full of fish, ready for
us to gut. They pull hard on untipped cigarettes and have big
hands that run through mottled beards. Even the younger ones
look old, the hair thinning, the eyes seaward. You can see them
lurch, slow and gull-like, back to their boats when their catch has
been weighed, stomping around in a mess of nets and ropes.
They don't talk to the fish-gutters. They hand us a sort of guilt, a
quiet disregard, I believe, for the thinness of our forearms.

I think of them always in the mornings, when the light comes
in through my curtains. The light is like an old fisherman in a
rain-slicked coat, come to look at Enrique and me, wrapped in
our bed sheets.

It's a strange light that comes this morning, older, thicker-
wristed, pushing its way through the gap and lying, with its motes
of dust, on the headboard. *Goddamn it, aren't you two just the
salt of the earth?* Enrique is curled into himself, the curve of his
back full against the spindle of his legs. His hair is all about his
face. Stubbled hairs in a riot on his chin. His eyes have collected
black bags and his white T-shirt still has smatterings of spaghetti
sauce from yesterday's lunch. I move to brush my lips against his
cheek. Enrique stirs a little and I notice a little necklace of blood
spots on the pillow where he has been coughing. *Get up out of
bed you lazy shits.* I smooth his brow where, even in sleep, the
sweat has gathered.

I climb naked out of bed, swinging my feet down into my

slippers. The floor is cold and I step carefully. Last night I smashed the blackberry jamjar that used to hold our money. The glass splayed in bright splinters all around the room. I move over to the window and Enrique murmurs into the pillow. The curtains make the sound of crackling ice. The ghosts of old fishermen can tumble here in droves now, if they want, spit their epithets all around the room. *What the hell sort of mess is this? You're late for work, Paddy-boy. No foghorns going off this morning. You gut the fish along the side, asshole.*

Our window looks out to a steep hill of parked cars. This morning they are bumper to bumper. Drivers have turned their steering wheels sideways so their vehicles won't roll down the hill and fling themselves towards the sea. Two weeks ago Enrique and I sold our car for $2,700 to a man with lemon-coloured hair, and already all the money is gone. Bags full of medicine and a little bit of cocaine. I put our last line on his belly last night but he was sweating so hard that it was almost impossible to snort.

I look up the road towards the deli. The light in the street has a huge whiteness about it, slouching on the buildings, falling against the ironwork railings. What I like most about the street is that people put flower pots in their windows, a colourful daub of Mediterranean greens and reds. Doors are painted in a medley of colours. Curtains get thrown open early in the mornings. There's a cat on the third floor across the street, jet black, with a dappled blue bandanna. It is forever cocking its head sideways and yawning in the window. Sometimes I bring home some sea trout and leave it on the doorstep of the house for the owner.

I cover myself with my hand and step out through the French doors. A chill wind is coming up from the waterfront, carrying the smell of saltwater and fresh sourdough. Already some of the fishermen will have unloaded their catch and Paulie's fingers will be frantic in his hair. *Where's O'Meara this morning?* they'll say to him, *has he found himself a ferret?* The three other fishgutters will be cursing over slabs of fillets, while the minute hand of the clock on the warehouse wall circles. The plastic gloves will be covered in blood. Strings of fishgut will have fallen on their boots. *That bastard's always late anyway.*

I should pull on my old jeans and whistle for a taxi, or hop on the trolley, or ride the old bicycle through the hills, down to the warehouse, but the light this morning is curiously heavy, indolent, slow, and I feel like staying.

Enrique is coughing in the bedroom behind me, spitting into the pillow. It sounds like the rasp of the seals along the coastline cliffs further up the California shore. His skin is sallow and tight around his jaw. The way he thrashes around in the bed reminds me of a baby corncrake I once took home after an oil slick in my hometown near Bantry Bay, continually battering its blackened wings against the cage to get out.

He should wake soon and perhaps today he'll feel well enough to sit up, read a novel or a magazine. I bend down and pick up the large pieces of shattered glass from the floor. There's a long scar on the wall where I threw the jamjar. *That was smart, O'Meara, wasn't it?* I find two quarters and a few dimes scattered in the glass. There's an Irish fivepenny piece on the floor too, an anachronism, a memory.

I flick a tiny shard of glass off my finger and Enrique tosses again in bed. He is continually thinning, like the eggshell of a falcon, and soon the sheets will hardly ripple. I move to the bathroom and take a quick piss in the sink. Enrique has always said that it's a much better height and there's no risk of splashing the seat. Not too hygienic, but curiously pleasurable. My eyes look bloodshot in the mirror and I notice the jowly look in my face. When I wash I can still smell yesterday's fish on my hands. We are down to the last bar of soap and the water that comes through the tap has a red iron colour to it. Back in the bedroom I pull on my jeans, a heavy-checked lumber shirt and my black-peaked hat.

71

I search in the pockets of my jeans and find three more dollars, then check my watch. Another hour late won't really matter. My coat hangs on the bedpost. I lean over him again and tell him that I will be back in a few moments. He doesn't stir. *Ah, isn't that just lovely, O'Meara? Out ya go and get breakfast for Enrique.*

The wind at my back hurries me along, down the carheavy street, past a row of saplings, over a child's hopscotch chalkmarks, to the deli, where Betty is working the counter. It's an old neighbourhood shop, the black and white floor tiles curled up around the edges. Betty is a large darkhaired woman – capable, Enrique jokes, of owning her own zip code. She often wears tank tops and the large flaps of flab that hang down from her underarms would be obscene on anybody else, but they seem to suit her. There's a barker on the other side of town, near City Lights bookstore, who shouts about the shows of 'Sweaty Betty', but I've never had the guts to go in and see if it's her up there, on-stage in the neon lights, jiggling. Betty negotiates the aisles of the deli in a crabways manner, her rear end sometimes knocking down the display stands of potato crisps. When she slices the ham the slabs are as thick as her fingers. There is a bell on the inside of the door and when I come in she looks up from the cash register, closing the newspaper at the same time.

'The Wild Colonial Boy,' she says. 'What's the rush?'

'Late for work. Just gonna grab a few things.'

'Still working down at the abattoir?'

'The warehouse. Gutting fish.'

'Same difference.' Her laugh resounds around the shop. The tassels on the bosom of her white blouse bounce. Her teeth are tremendously white, but I notice her fingernails chewed down to the quick. The bell clangs and a couple of elderly Asians come in, followed by a man whom I recognise as a bartender down on Geary Street. Betty greets each of them with a fluttering wave.

I move up and down the aisles, looking at prices, fingering

the $3.80 in my pocket. Coffee is out of the question, as are the croissants in the bakery case, which are a dollar apiece. An apple tart might do the trick however. Walking down the rows of food, other breakfasts come back to me — sausages and rashers fried in a suburban Irish kitchen with an exhaust fan sucking up the smoke, plastic glasses full of orange juice, cornflakes floating on milk, pieces of pudding in circles on chipped white plates, fried tomatoes and toast slobbered with butter. In the background Gay Byrne would talk on on the radio, while my late mother draped herself over the stove with a patterned apron on, watching the steam rise from the kettle. Mornings spinning off on my Raleigh to lectures at UCC, a bar of Weetabix in my jacket pocket. Once, champagne and strawberries in Sausalito with a lover who clawed his brown moustache between his teeth.

I reach for a small plastic jar of orange juice and a half-dozen eggs in the deli fridge, two oranges and a banana in the fruit stand, then tuck a loaf of French bread under my arm. There is butter and jam at home, perhaps some leftover teabags. Betty sells loose cigarettes at 25 cents each. Two each for Enrique and me will do nicely. Tomorrow night, when I get my wages from the warehouse — Paulie will be there with his head bent over the cheques morosely and some stray old fishermen will be coughing in from their boats — I will buy steak and vegetables. Not too much, though. Enrique has been having a hard time keeping his food down, and the blue bucket at the side of our bed sits, an ugly ornament.

Carting the load of groceries up to the cash register, Betty cocks an eye at me.

'How's the patient?' she asks. 'Haven't seen hide nor hair of him in the last three weeks.'

'Still holed up in bed.'

'Any news?'

'None, I'm afraid.'

She shakes her head and purses her lips. I reach into my pocket for the change. 'Can I get four of your smokes please?' I ask.

Betty reaches up above her for a box of Marlboros Lights and slides them on the counter, towards me. 'My treat,' she says. 'Don't smoke 'em all in one place, hon.' I thank her profusely and tuck them quickly in my shirt pocket. Betty leans over the counter and touches my left hand: 'And tell that man of yours I want to see his cute little Argentinian ass in here one of these days.'

'He'll be up and at it in a few days,' I say, putting the groceries in a white plastic bag and hooking it over my wrist. 'Thanks again for the smokes.'

The door clangs behind me and the street seems to open up in a wide sweep. Small acts of kindness smell generously of hope. Twenty cigarettes can make a man's day. I skip badly through the chalk marks – it's been years since I've hopscotched – and sit down on the curb, between a green Saab and an orange pick-up truck, to light up. Looking down the street I can make out our balcony, above the tops of the cars, but there's no sign of Enrique.

.

Last night he almost cried when the cocaine coagulated in his sweat, but when I scooped some off his belly and onto the mirror he pushed it away and turned his face to the wall, looking up at a photograph of him rafting the Parana River. The photo is fading now, yellow mustering around the edges. The way he leans backwards in the boat, through a rapid, with his paddle about to strike the water, looks strange to me these days, ineffably sad. He hasn't been near a river in years and hasn't ventured outside for almost a month.

In the apartment we have unrolled our sleeping bags and use them as blankets over the bed sheets. Our television set is in the front window of the pawnshop, beside a hunting bow. The trust fund is dry, but Enrique is adamant that I don't call his father. The insurance people are gentle, but unyielding. There are times I imagine a man at the very tip of Tierra del Fuego reaching his arms out towards the condors that flap their wings against the red air, wondering where his son has gone. There's a mother there too.

Enrique sometimes talks to me of moving to the Pampas. More often his mind takes him there and we are building a wooden fence together along the back of a ranch house. The grasses sweep along with a northward wind. At night we watch the sun swing downwards behind a distant windmill.

Late at night he often wakes and babbles. It's always the same vision . When he was young he would go with his friends out on his father's cattle farm. They would have contests in the rapids of a strong river, swimming against the current, so that whoever stayed longest in the one spot was the winner. Sometimes he would still be there, swimming stationary in the current, flailing away, without noticing that his friends were already halfway down the river. After the competition, they would stand in the river and catch fish with their hands. Then they'd light a campfire and eat the fish. It was Enrique who taught me how to gut when I first got the job down in the warehouse. With one smooth sweep of the finger you can take out all the innards.

When scrambling eggs I always make sure to add a little milk and whisk the fork around the bowl quickly so that none of the small stringy pieces of white will be left when they're cooked. The only disturbing thing about my mother's breakfasts were the long thin raw white pieces. The kitchen is small, with only room for one person to move. I lay the baguette on the counter and slice it, then daub butter on the inside. The oven takes a long time to heat. In the meantime I boil water for the tea and put some teabags in the sunflower-patterned mugs.

I hear Enrique stir out of bed and move slowly towards the window. At first the noise startles me, but I'm glad he's awake. I hope he doesn't cut his feet on any of the stray jamjar glass – a doctor told us that the longer this goes on the more likely it is that something like a cut will bleed for a long time. The oven clock has steam gathered on its glass face. *You're late again O'Meara, were ya picking petals offa roses?* I peel the oranges and arrange them in segments on the plate. *Or maybe you were spanking the monkey, is that it O'Meara?* I hear the radio clicked on and a chair dragged out onto the balcony. I hope he's put his scarf on under his dressing gown or else the chill will get to him.

I wish I could have seen him when I was down on the street – just sitting there, looking out over the whitewhite city, his hair dark and strewn like seaweed, the tufts galloping up from his chest towards his neck, his face chiselled, the scar on his chin worn like the wrongly-tied knot of a Persian rug.

The eggs puff up and harden, sticking to the side of the saucepan. I scrape them off with a fork and then arrange the dollops on two plates. I've burnt the bread a little and the water is still not boiled. Amazing thing that water. The molecules bouncing off each other at a huge rate of speed, passing on energy to one another, giving heat, losing heat. If only we could do the same. In the warehouse I spend my time thinking about these brutally stupid things, whittling the hours away. *There's lots of people in this town'd be happy to gut fish, bum-boy.* I put the bread on a third plate and wait. When the water finally boils I pour it on the bags, making sure the little paper tabs stay on the outside of the mugs. I gather the three plates in the shape of a shamrock in one hand – I was a waiter before I met Enrique – and I grab the handles of both cups with my forefinger.

The door to the bedroom is slightly ajar and I push it open with my left foot. It opens with a creak but he doesn't turn in the chair. Perhaps the traffic is too loud. I see him cough and then spit into one of our flowerpots. He leans back in the chair again. It's a little more grey outside now, the sun blocked by clouds. On the bedside table I see that he has picked up all the last pieces of the jamjar. The pillow has been turned and there are no more visible blood spots, but on the bed sheets there is a cluster of stray black hairs. Twenty-seven is too young to be going bald.

I move as soundlessly as I can across the floor. He has his head laid back in the chair now. The curtains on the French windows swish against my leg and the rings tinkle against the rod. I sidle up behind the chair, lean over him, hand him the tea and he smiles. His face seems curiously weathered, the eyes delta-run into crowfeet, the brow heavy. We kiss and then he blows on the tea, the steam kicking up. *Why the hell d'you wear those goddamn bracelets anyway, O'Meara?*

'I thought you were gone already,' he says.

'In a few minutes.'

'I see.'

'Thought it'd be nice to have breakfast.'

'Wonderful.' He reaches out for the plate. 'I'm not sure if . . .'

'It's all right. Eat as much as you can.' I put my own plate down on the balcony floor and close the top button on my shirt to keep out the wind. Cars trundle along the street below. Some youngsters have taken over the hopscotch court. There is a tremendous freshness to the breeze coming up from the sea and it rifles through the trees. Enrique purses his lips, as if to speak, then lets them fall apart, and looks along the street again, a small smile crackling the edges. The stubble collects along his cheeks. The bags under his eyes darken.

'I have some smokes too,' I say. 'Betty gave them to me. And some orange juice if you want it.'

'Great.' Enrique stabs gingerly at the eggs with his fork and moves the pieces of orange around. Then he reaches for a piece of bread and slowly tears the crust off. 'Lovely day, isn't it?' he says, all of a sudden sweeping his arm out to the street.

'Gorgeous.'

'Radio said that the high would be in the sixties.'

'Grand weather for sitting around,' I say.

'Lows tonight in the high forties.'

'We'll sleep well.'

He nods his head and shifts his body gently in the chair. A small piece of crust falls down into the lap of his dressing gown. He reaches for it and lays it on the side of the plate. 'Nice eggs,' he says.

'Wish I didn't have to go to the warehouse.'

'We could just sit here and talk.'

'We could,' I say.

I sit there and watch him as he eddies the fork around the plate, but his eyes are drooping already. The cup of tea sits on the floor, by the edge of his chair. He leans his head back against the chair and sighs. His chest thumps like that of a small bird. The beginnings of sweat gather on his brow. I watch as the fork slides across the plate and nestles itself against the clump of food. I look down at the traffic passing beneath us and all of a sudden I understand that we are in the stream, Enrique and I, that the traffic below us is flowing quite steadily, trying to carry us along, while all the time he is beating his arms against the current, staying still, keeping in the one place. I sit and watch him as he sleeps and the breakfast grows cold.

In a few moments I will go to work and gut everything they bring me, but for now I watch this body of Enrique's, this house of sweat, this language of amino acids, slowly being assaulted.

Enrique once told me a story about starfish.

There was as an oyster fisherman down the coast from Buenos Aires who farmed his own little area of the bay. He hadn't listened to the generations of fishermen that went before him, their advice, their tricks, their superstitions. All he knew was that starfish preyed on oysters. When they were dragged up in his nets he would take them and rip their pentasymmetrical bodies in two neat pieces. He would fling them over the side of the boat and continue fishing. I imagine he was probably a bearded man with a rawboned laugh. But what he didn't know is that the starfish don't die when ripped, they regenerate themselves. For every one he tore, a second one came about. He wondered why there were so many starfish and so few oysters left, until he was told by an older fisherman. From then on the fisherman left the starfish alone, although he could perhaps have taken them to shore and dumped them behind some big grey rock, or in a large silver dustbin on the pier where the children, on the way home from school, would fling them like stones.

There are times these days, strange times spent amongst those idle thoughts of mine, when I wonder why the fishermen never ghost their way into the warehouse, cigarettes dangling from their lips, to stand by me, amazed, two fully-grown starfish in their deep hands, saying *look at this O'Meara, look, for Christ's sake, can you imagine this?*

MEMORY AND DESIRE

VAL MULKERNS

The television people seemed to like him and that was a new
feeling he found exciting. Outside his own work circle he
was not liked, on the whole, although he had a couple of lifelong
friends he no longer cared for very much. The sort of people he
would have wished to be accepted by found him arrogant, un-
friendly, and not plain enough to be encouraged as an oddity. His
wealth made him attractive only to the types he most despised.
He was physically gross and clumsy with none of the social graces
except laughter. Sometimes his jokes were good and communic-
able. More often they were obscure and left him laughing alone
as though he were the last remaining inhabitant of an island.

Sometimes, indeed, he wondered if he spoke the same
language as most other people, so frequently were they baffled if
not positively repelled. He liked people generally, especially
physically beautiful people who seemed to him magical as old
gods. Sometimes he just looked at such people, not listening or
pretending to listen to what they said, and then he saw the familiar
expression of dislike and exclusion passing across their faces and
he knew he had blundered again. Now for several weeks he had
been among a closely knit group who actually seemed to find his
company agreeable. When the invitation had first come he had
been doubtful. He knew nothing about television and seldom
watched it. But because his father's small glass-making business
had blossomed under his hand and become an important element
in the export market, the television people thought a programme
could be made out of his success story, a then-and-now sort of
approach which seemed to him banal in the extreme. He had
given his eventual consent because time so often hung on his

hands now that expansion had progressed as far as was practicable and delegation had left him with little to do except see his more lucrative contacts in Europe and the United States a couple of times a year.

The only work he would actually have enjoyed doing these days was supervising the first efforts of young glass-blowers. Two of the present half-dozen were grandsons of his father's original men. At a time when traditional crafts were dying out everywhere or falling into strange (and probably passing) hands, this pleased him. He tried to show signs of his approval while keeping the necessary distance right from the boys' first day at work, but this was probably one of the few places left in Ireland where country boys were shy and backward still, and their embarrassment had been so obvious that nowadays he confined himself to reports on them from the foreman. It had been different in his father's time. The single cutter and the couple of blowers had become personal friends of his father and mother, living in the loft above the workshops (kept warm in winter by the kiln) and eating with the family in the manner of medieval apprentice craftsmen. During holidays from boarding school they had become his friends too, gradually and naturally passing on their skills to him, and so listening without resentment to the new ideas on design he had in due course brought back with him from art school and from working spells in Sweden. Gradually over the years of expansion after his father's death he had grown away from the men. Now since the new factory had been built in Cork he knew very few of them any more.

The odd thing about the television people was that right from the beginning they had been unawed and called him Bernard, accepting that he had things to learn about their business and that he would stay with them in the same guest house, drink and live with them during the shooting of the film, almost as though they were his family and he an ordinary member of theirs. It had irritated and amused and baffled and pleased him in rapid progression and now he even found it hard to remember what his life had been like before he knew them or how his days had been filled in. Their youth too had shocked him in the beginning; they seemed like children at play with dangerous and expensive toys. The director in particular (who was also the producer and therefore responsible for the whole idea) had in addition to a good-humoured boy's face an almost fatherly air of concern for his odd and not always biddable family. What was more remarkable, he could discipline them. The assistant cameraman who had got drunk and couldn't be wakened on the third day of shooting had not done it again. When Eithne, the production assistant, had come down to breakfast one morning with a streaming cold and a raised temperature, Martin had stuffed a handful of her notes into the pocket of his jeans and sent her back up to bed, weeping and protesting that she was perfectly all right and not even her mother would dare to treat her like that.

Martin was very good with unco-operative fishermen, and with the farmer on whose land the original workshop still hung over the sea. A nearby hilly field had recently been sown with oats, and the farmer began with the strongest objection to a jeep laden with gear coming anywhere near it. He had agreed to it during preliminary negotiations, but shooting had in fact been delayed (delayed until more money became available) and that field, the farmer said, was in a delicate condition now. If they'd only come at the right time — Martin it was who finally talked him around with a guarantee against loss which would probably land him in trouble back in Dublin. But Martin (the Marvellous Boy was Bernard's private label for him) would worry about that one when he came to it and he advised Bernard to do the same about his fear of appearing ridiculous in some sequences. Not even half the stuff they were shooting would eventually be used, Martin said, and anyhow he'd give Bernard a preview at the earliest possible moment. Bernard stopped worrying again. Most of the time he had the intoxicating illusion of drifting with a strong tide in the company of excellent seamen and a captain who seemed to know his business.

The actual process of remembering was occasionally painful, of course. His only brother Tom had been swept away by a spring tide while fishing down on the rocks one day after school, and at first Bernard hadn't believed any reference to it would be possible when the script finally came to be written. Martin had come back to it casually again and again however, and finally one day of sharp March winds and flying patches of blue sky he had stood with Bernard on the headland near the roofless house.

'Let me show you what I have in mind,' Martin said gently, the south Kerry accent soft as butter. 'It will be very impressionistic, what I've in mind, a mere flash. A spin of sky and running tides, a moment. If you'd prefer, it won't need anything specific in the script. Just a reference to this friendly big brother mad about fishing, who knew about sea birds and seals and liked to be out by himself for hours on end. Maybe then, a single sentence about the nature of spring tides. The viewers generally won't know that spring tides have nothing to do with spring. You may say we're telling them about a successful glass industry, not about the sea, but the sea takes up a large part of your own early background and this piece is about you too. I'd write you a single sentence myself for your approval if you wouldn't mind – just to show you what I think would work – OK.?'

'"These are pearls that were his eyes" – you could end like that, couldn't you?' Bernard heard himself sneering and almost at once regretted it. The director actually blushed and changed the subject. In a few seconds it was as if the moment had never happened, but it seemed to Bernard that a kind of bond had been perversely established.

Two days later a spring tide was running and he watched a

few sequences being shot that might well be used for the passage he knew now he was going to write. He walked away from the crew when he found he could no longer watch the sort of sling from which the chief cameraman had been suspended above the cliffs to get some of the necessary angles. The whole thing could have been done better and more safely by helicopter but Martin had explained about the problems he had encountered after overrunning the budget for the last production. It wasn't of course that he wanted necessarily to make Bernard's backward look a cheaper affair; you often got a better end result (in his own experience) by using more ingenuity and less money: he thought he knew exactly how to do it. The somewhat unconvincing argument amused and didn't displease Bernard, who thought it more than likely that something less conventional might finally emerge. The last he saw of the crew was that crazy young man, clad as always when working in a cotton plaid shirt, suspending himself without benefit of the cameraman's sling to try to see exactly what the lens saw.

A fit of nervousness that had in it something of the paternal and something else not paternal at all made him walk the seven miles around to the next headland. He hadn't thought like a father for five years. For half of that isolated time he hadn't brought home casual male encounters either because nothing stable had ever emerged from them and more often than not he was put off by the jungle whiff of the predator and managed to change direction just in time. Now he tried to resist looking back at the pair of boys busy with their games which they apparently regarded as serious. The head cameraman was even younger than Martin. He had a fair freckled face and red hair so long that it would surely have been safer to tie it back in a girl's ponytail before swinging him out in that perilous contraption. Bernard turned his face again into the stiff wind and looked back at the receding insect wriggling above the foaming tide, man and technology welded together in the blasting sunlight. The weird shape drew back his eyes again and again until a rock they called the Billygoat's Missus cut it off and he was alone for (it seemed) the first time in several weeks.

For the first time as in a camera's framed eye he saw his own room at home. Tidy as a well-kept grave, it was full of spring light from the garden. There were daffodils on his desk. Spangles of light from the rocky pool outside danced on the Yeats canvas that took up most of one wall and struck sparks from the two early balloons which he treasured. Five poplars in a haze of young green marked the end of his garden. Beyond it, the sharp-breasted great Sugarloaf and eventually the sea. The room had been tidy for five years now. No maddening litter of dropped magazines, no hairpins, no shoes kicked off and left where they fell: left for the woman next morning to carry to the appropriate place in the appropriate room because she was born to pick up the litter of other people's lives, paid for it as the only work she knew. One night in a fit of disgust he had kicked into the corner a black leather clog, left dead centre on the dark carpet awaiting the exact moment to catch his shin. Uncontrolled fits of violence he despised. Recovering quickly he had placed the shoes side by side outside the door as though this were an old-fashioned hotel with a dutiful boots in residence. She had come in laughing later on, both clogs held up incredulously in her hand, laughing and laughing, tossing them finally up in the air to fall where they might before she left the room. As perhaps she had done last night and would do again tomorrow. Wherever she was.

A rising wind drove before it into the harbour a flock of black clouds that had appeared from nowhere, and when drops of rain the size of old pennies began to lash down he sought refuge in the hotel which had been small and unpretentious in its comfort when he was a child. His father's clients had often stayed here. He had sometimes been sent on messages to them with his brother. Now the place had several stars from an international guide book and was famous both for its seafood and the prices that foreign gourmets were willing to pay for it.

He sat in the little bar full of old coastal maps and looked out at the sea; alone for the first time in two weeks he was no less content than in the casual company of the television people. Their young faces and their voices were still inside his head. As though on cue, Martin suddenly came through into the bar, also alone. The wind had made any more shooting too dangerous for today he said, and the girls had gone off to wash their hair. He had his fishing gear in the boot, but he doubted if he'd do much good today.

'Have lunch with me, then, and eat some fish instead,' Bernard invited, and was amused to see a flash of pure pleasure light up the director's face. Beer and a sandwich usually kept them going until they all sat down together at the end of the day.

'This place has got so much above itself even since the last time I was down here that I expect to be asked my business as soon as I set foot inside the door,' Martin grinned.

'They wouldn't do that in late March,' Bernard assured him. 'Neither the swallows nor the tourists have arrived yet, so I fancy even people in your advanced state of sartorial decay would be encouraged.'

Martin took an imaginary clothes brush out of the jeans pocket (too tight to hold anything larger than a toothbrush) and began to remove stray hairs from that well-worn garment which had seaweedy stains in several places and looked slightly damp. The boy walked with a sort of spring, like a healthy cat, and there was no trace yet of the flab which his pint-drinking would eventually bring. He ate the bouillabaisse and the fresh baked salmon which followed with the relish of a child brought out from boarding school for the day and determined to take full advantage of it. He praised the Alsace wine which was apparently new to him and

Bernard decided that one of the great remaining pleasures of money was never to have to worry about the cost of anything one suddenly wanted to do. Bernard listened abstractedly to a little house politics over the coffee and then at the end of the first cognac he spoke one unwary line about buying all those bandy little boss men for a next birthday present for Martin should he wish it. The sea-reflecting blue eyes opposite him narrowed coldly for a moment before they closed in a bellow of laughter and the moment passed, like the rain outside. The sea was too uneasy, however, in the whipping wind to yield anything, but Bernard remembered one good story about his dead brother on a long-ago trip to Kinsale. Martin made a note in biro on the back of the wrist which held his fishing rod and Bernard knew it would be transferred to the mounting heaps of papers back at the hotel. More and more in the course of the programme he was being his own production assistant.

*

Mr O'Connor had carried in a mountain of turf for the fire and Eithne rather liked to listen to the rattle of the rain outside by way of contrast. Her hair was dry by now but spread all over the hearthrug and she swung it back in a tickling blanket over the recumbent John D who was still struggling with the *Irish Times* crossword.

'Give that over and sit up,' she said, fetching her eternal dice-throwing version of Scrabble which she had bought somewhere in Holland.

'I was just going to work out another angle for that last shot to put to Martin when he gets back.'

'Martin is probably half way to France by now on an ebbing tide. We'll find his pathetic little bits and pieces in the morning.'

'Stop that!' John D was superstitious as well as red-haired. He was nervous about things like that. 'All right, I'll give you three games and that's it.'

'Nice John D. Did you notice Bernard's face today when you were strung up over the cliff, by the way?'

'I had other things to worry about. Is "cadenza" allowed?'

'It's not English but I suppose it's in the OED like everything else — it's virtually been taken over, after all.'

'OK. it's allowed.' John D formed the word.

'But no *brio* or *allegro molto*,' Eithne warned.

'No *brio* or *allegro molto* — I haven't the makings of them anyhow. What sort of look did Bernard have on his unlovely mug?'

'A bit nervous for you, I think. I think that's why he walked away.'

'Arrogant bastard a lot of the time.' John D swept up the dice after totting his score. 'Are capitalists human? You should put that theme to Martin some time.'

'More a Neville sort of line, surely? But I think you're wrong. He's shy and he's only just stopped being uneasy with us.'

'Just in time to say good-bye then,' said John D with satisfaction. 'There's hardly a week in it, if the weather lifts a bit.'

'If,' Eithne said, scooping a single good score. It was her game, her thing, but the others always won. 'I think he's lonely, which only goes to show you money isn't everything.'

'You can be miserable in much more comfort though. He looks to me like a bod who'd have it off wherever he pleased with one sex or t'other, despite his ugly mug. He has the brazen confidence you only get from too much money.'

'I think you're wrong and the death of his brother is still bothering him after all these years. It's something I just have a hunch about. And then of course his wife walked out on him a few years ago. Prime bitch they say she was too. He came home one night and found not as much as a hair-clip left behind, and his baby gone too.'

'"Hunch" is not a permissible word all the same. Thirties slang,' said John D with finality. 'Why wouldn't she walk out on him when he's probably given to buggery?'

'It's much more permissible than "cadenza". How about to hunch one's shoulders?'

'Go and ask Mr O'Connor if he has a dictionary then.'

'You go. My hair isn't dry yet.'

'Your hair is practically on fire, lady,' John D said, settling himself comfortably on the hearthrug again. A car crunched in the sandy drive outside and Eithne gave a long sigh.

'Thank God. I couldn't have borne the smell of good country roast beef much longer.'

'There'll be frogs' eyes to follow.'

'At worst there'll be stewed apples, at best apple pie. Doesn't your nose tell you anything except whether a pint's good or bad?'

In out of the rain and the early dusk, Bernard was touched all over again by the sight of two apparent children playing a game beside the fire. He came over very willingly to join them when Eithne called and Martin went upstairs to look over his notes before dinner. He would call Evelyn on his way down, he said.

Later they all went out in the pouring rain to the pub and listened while a couple of local Carusos rendered songs like 'Two Sweethearts' – one with hair of shining gold, the other with hair of grey – or the endless emigrant laments favoured by local taste. Whiskey chasing several pints made John D a bit quarrelsome and he shouted for a song from Bernard just to embarrass him. To everybody's surprise Bernard was not embarrassed. He stood up, supported only by two small Jamesons (the second of which he was still nursing) and gave the company a soft-voiced but not untuneful version of 'Carrickfergus' which was vociferously applauded by the locals and earned him delighted approval from the team. Eithne thought they ought maybe incorporate 'Carrickfergus' into the soundtrack, and John D wanted to know why they couldn't all move up to Carrickfergus and let Bernard do his party piece with his back against the castle walls. This suggestion was received with the contempt it deserved but Bernard wasn't discomfited.

That happened only when they got back to the guest house and he heard Martin telling Mrs O'Connor that they would almost certainly be finished shooting by the end of the week and would hardly stay over the weekend. The sinking of the heart was like what came long ago with the necessity of facing back to school after the long summer holidays. He felt ashamed of his emotion and unsure how to conceal it, so he went up early to his room. Normally they would hang about for hours yet, reading the newspapers they hadn't had time for during the day, swapping stories, doing crossword puzzles, discussing the next day's work. Usually he didn't contribute much to the conversation; like a silent member of a big family he was simply there, part of what was going on, perfectly content to sit up as long as they did.

Now there was something symbolic about hearing the murmur of their voices downstairs. The script had still to be written and there would be consultations in Dublin about it, hopefully with Martin, but (give or take a few days from now) the thing was over. Next week they would all be busy taking somebody else through his mental lumber room. The little family would re-form itself around another fire, and it would have nothing to do with him. And soon it would be April, breeding lilacs out of the dead land, mixing memory and desire. Time perhaps to go away; he had promised himself a few weeks in April. On the other hand, why not stay on here?

He let down the small dormer window and looked out over the water. This house echoed, in almost exact detail, that other, roofless, house; the murmur of voices, even, was like his sisters' voices before they settled down for the night, all together in the big back bedroom. His own small room above the harbour used to be shared with his brother. The rain had stopped now and there was almost no sound from the sea and he wasn't surprised when Martin came to his door to say the weather forecast had been very good for the south-west and they might get in a full day's shooting tomorrow.

'Come in and have a nightcap,' he invited, and Martin said he wouldn't stay long but happily didn't refuse the brandy when it was taken from the wardrobe.

'What will you do next?' Bernard asked, just for a moment unsure of how to begin.

'A bit of a break before I join Current Affairs for a short stint,' the boy smiled. 'Yours is the last programme in the present series. No more now until next season.'

'You mean you're going to take a holiday?' He strove to make his voice sound casual, although he was suddenly aware of the beating of his heart.

'Unless something untoward crops up, yes.'

'Why not join me in Greece, then, since that's where I'm heading next week or the week after? The place I have on Ios needs to be opened up after the winter and there's plenty of room I assure you. Also two local women waiting to cook and clean for us.' Bernard saw the refusal before it came; it was only a question of how it would be framed, how lightly he would be let down.

'It's a tempting offer, and there's nothing I'd enjoy more, all things being equal. Never been further than Corfu as a matter of fact. But my wife has organised a resident babysitter for the two boys and we're off on a busman's holiday to Canada as soon as I'm free. Laura is Canadian you know. I met her when I was training in London with the BBC. When we get back, maybe you'd come over for supper with us some evening? Laura's an unpredictable cook, but you'll agree that doesn't matter too much when you meet her. Is it a deal?'

He drained his glass and got up off Bernard's bed with the same catspring which was noticeable also in the way he walked.

'It's a deal. Many thanks. And maybe you'll both join me some time in Greece?'

Martin made the appropriate noises and didn't go at once, but started talking about a painter called Richard Dadd who (somebody had told him) had probably given Yeats his Crazy Jane themes. He hadn't seen the paintings himself at the Tate but Bernard had, so this kept them going until the door closed behind him, and on his youth, and on the hollow promise of knowing him as one knew every line of one's own hand. There was a lot of the night left and, fortunately, a lot of the brandy too.

The weather behaved as the weathermen said it would and the rest of the shooting went without a hitch. During this couple of weeks the year had turned imperceptibly towards summer, primroses in the land-facing banks, sea-pinks along the cliffs and an air about the television people that Bernard had seen before and couldn't quite place. Only when he went with them for the final day's shooting did he pin it down; a fairground the day after the circus. The television gear was more easily moved, of course; no long hours were needed for the pull-out. But the feeling was the same. They didn't believe him when he said he was staying on and they seemed shocked, which amused him, when he determinedly heaped presents on them the morning they were going; his Leica for Eithne who (incredibly) had never owned a camera of her own, a sheepskin jacket for John D because his own was in flitters from the rocks, a silver brandy flask (circa 1840), a cigarette lighter and a gold biro scattered apparently at random among the rest. The vulgarity of the largesse amused Bernard himself because such behaviour was not usual and he didn't entirely understand his impulse. But he understood perfectly why he gave Martin his signed first edition of *The Winding Stair*, a volume which for a year or more had lived in the right hand door-pocket of his car for no better reason than that he liked to have it there. He had bought it somewhere along the quays in Cork.

> *'Fair and foul are near of kin*
> *And fair needs foul,' I cried,*
> *'My friends are gone and that's a truth*
> *Nor grave nor bed denied*
> *Learned in bodily lowliness,*
> *And in the heart's pride.'*

A former owner had marked that with a small star in the margin, and Martin smiled slightly as he read it aloud in gratitude when the book fell open.

'I often have a disturbing feeling when I finish a job like this that I know —' he searched patiently for the words he wanted and his hesitation seemed to Bernard like comfort consciously-given for some loss he could understand. 'That I know almost enough to being all over again. Properly.' He didn't smile at all when they shook hands so that the handgrip seemed warmer. 'Until soon, in Dublin,' were his last words, a rather childish farewell which would have left a pleasant glow behind if Bernard had not known by now that they would not meet again. The vanful of technology went on ahead of the boy's unreliable little red sports car, and watching from the drive of the guesthouse, Bernard had the feeling of the fairground again after the circus caravans have rolled away. It was peaceful, though, with the blue sea breathing quietly all around him and a few mares' tails of cloud slowly unravelling in the sky.

He was leaning over the wall considering how he would fill his remaining time when the guesthouse owner strolled by, indicating the blue boat which bobbed at the end of its mooring rope below them. 'You could take the aul' boat out fishing any day you had a fancy for it, Mr Golden. You're more than welcome to her any time though I wouldn't recommend today, mind you.'

'I'm much obliged to you, Stephen. I have all the gear I need in the boot of the car so I might do just that. But why not today?'

'She'll rise again from the south-west long before evening,' his host said positively. 'And she'll blow herself out if I'm not mistaken. 'Twould be a dangerous thing to go fishing out there today.'

'The weather men last night didn't mention any gales blowing up.'

'The weather men don't live around this Hook either,' O'Connor said drily. 'I've caught those same gentlemen out once or twice, and will again with the help of God.'

'You might be right at that, I suppose. But if I do go out, I'll only fish for a short while, I promise you.'

A pleasant man, Stephen O'Connor, a retired Civic Guard with an efficient wife to make a business out of the beautiful location of their house and her own hard work. Bernard remembered him vaguely from childhood, pedalling wet and fine around the coast roads, stopping here and there for a chat, missing nothing. It was he who had brought the news that Tom's body had been washed ashore somewhere near Kinsale. It was he who had in fact identified it. On remembering this Bernard toyed for a moment with the idea of having an actual conversation with this kindly man whose memories touched his own at one black juncture. The moment passed however, and Stephen made a little more chat, lingering with natural courtesy just long enough for a guest to make up his mind whether or not further company would be welcome, and then he ambled contentedly in the direction of the greenhouse for the day's pottering. Old man, old man, if you never looked down again at a drowned face of my father's house it would be time enough for you. Forgive me, Stephen O'Connor.

The first warm sun of the year touched Bernard's eyes and he smiled, sitting up on the sea wall. No more Aprils, no more lilacs breeding out of the dead land, no more carnal awakenings. He felt peaceful, then a little surprised that the image behind his closed eyelids was not of his brother or of the young Martin or even of the caravans pulling out. It was the small wilful face of his daughter in the act of breaking away when one tried to hold her. He didn't know where she was, or even how she looked now, whether she still mirrored her mother in every gesture. He had a perfect right to know for the mere trouble of enforcing it. He hadn't done that, at first put off by the refusal of maintenance, by the eternal sound of the phone ringing in an empty flat and by two or three unanswered letters. He hadn't made a very energetic effort to keep in touch. As one year became two or three and now five, it had always seemed too late, but it would be untrue to pretend he greatly cared. It was just that, not being able to understand why the child's face should be so vivid in his mind, he was bothered by it as by some minor irritation, a door that slammed somewhere out of sight, a dripping tap. It wasn't until he was actually aboard the boat starting up the engine in a freshening breeze that he realised why he couldn't rid himself of his daughter's face today, of all days.

TABERNACLES

PADRAIG ROONEY

I was in the choir, *basso*, I think, but perched among the other singers, the boys left of the organ, the men to its right, I felt soprano, king of the architecture – vaulted, imitation gothic, pinnacled above me and falling away from the carved balcony into the body of the church. It was a simple concession on my part and a testing of the vocal chords with the aid of a blue, minutely-throbbing tuning fork which had brought me to this perch. I don't think my voice was particularly good – there were no solos to test me – but it was the tremor of having penetrated behind the scenes which activated me. The ceremony lost some of its mystery by my participation and, like adolescents in that limbo between belief and disbelief, I looked with nostalgia upon the heads below which were caught up in the fiction of transcendence. My illusions about them were so much more intact than their lip-service. I extracted from the mystery, Sunday after Sunday, its life-blood of cant and majesty. It was here that I was vampire extraordinary, among these stucco facades and plaster saints, in the groined neck of the edifice, the organ-pipes its vocal chords. They towered above me in ranks of different dimension and height and emitted a drone of air which struck me as more infernal than celestial. At their roots, the organist – spectacled and stooped over his knobs and keys, a Brother who, despite admonition and gossip, persisted in wearing an atrociously stained soutane – controlled this monstrosity at his fingertips and in the deft footwork which I scrutinised below his skirts, lifted for the purpose above his knees and betraying equally threadbare trousers. He got his cues from a mirror in which, in miniature, the nave and the altar with its celebrants were reflected like the *mise en abime* of a Dutch masterpiece. And we in turn got our cues from a nod of his spectacles, the poise of his delicately-shaped fingers over the keys. He would pull out stoppers, press down levers on which were written, in elaborate lettering, words in a language beyond my puerile comprehension. It seemed as if so much up there was beyond me, but balancing this I felt tingling in my bones and in the region of my neck a suspicion that this was my proper place in the cathedral. A moment would come in our hymn-singing when my throat was no longer my own – I imagined wings fluttering from it, a sure uprising in the neck, and the positioning of our bodies on a stepped rostrum in this fragile, carved balcony, up among the beams, the bones of the church, increased the feeling of suspension. The ceiling was a stretched vellum of painted stars edged with stone heads of saints, prophets – who knows? devils maybe – which peered blind into the rows of worshippers.

We would amuse ourselves from time to time by spitting on the heads of those below, discreetly but accurately. My fellow voice was a boy who vied with me for the high notes. His favourite hymn was 'Hail Queen of Heaven'; mine was 'Tantum Ergo'. The hymn-singing brought us close in the arched thorax of the cathedral. There was something expressed in our merging voices which our bodies held back. His white shirt was loose at the neck and a dark tie-knot slung almost casually round it like a sailor's. When descending to Communion he seemed always to be directly in front of me down the narrow, steep steps at the back of the cathedral, and my view of him was a fine, thin neck sloping out to equally slender shoulders surmounted by a head of blond hair. The steps wound, coiling round a single iron bar which went from the bowels to an invisible zenith among the gods. On the right, thick ropes knotted to metal rings in the stonework underlined the resemblance between the houses of God and dungeons, castles, places of torture. The stale air and rude trappings suspended us choirboys in timelessness, in a stopped history.

My hand, once, was descending quicker than my feet and met his hand on the sling of rope, momentarily, and I stumbled onto him, breathing in a smell of fresh shampoo and talcum powder. There was something well-kept about him: in descending it was his neck I focused on; in remounting after Communion, my eyes and thoughts blasphemously turned to the round buttocks which, exerted by the stiff climb, moved deliciously under the grey wool of his perfectly-pressed shorts. So my period of grace was of necessity short-lived and framed between these enticing gymnastics in the stairwell. I began to feel his convenient placing before me, every time without fail, was contrived on his part and, to outwit him, equally contrived to reverse the positions so that in the nave, before and after Communion, we held a comical, farcical race for positions while all the time inwardly hurrying our after-Communion prayers. A new communion, a forerunner of an inversion which would quickly make the cathedral our flaunting ground, was growing in us. Our descents, normally a clatter resembling released carrier-pigeons, were slowed to a slouch along the stairwell, gripping the guide rope with our frail fists. Coming back up we dawdled, as the others, full of grace and agility, shot by urging us on, and their voices echoed strangely down the gyres of that stone well like lost souls.

We stopped going to Communion. It was inevitable. We were among the few choir members left – some weekend alcoholics and adulterers – under the hissing pipes of the organ. The organist's seat was vacated but the instrument seemed to throb with an energy all its own. I ran my hand along the ivory-plated buttons with their strange lettering in gold and mother of pearl and looked up at the forest of shafts which was outlined against the stained glass of a rose window, filtering through a strange, unreal daylight. They had told us in school that gothic was inspired by the tall, heavenward trees of the North, those old forests long

since slaughtered for heat, the remnants of which we learned —
then with green crayon patches on our copybooks, later by flying
through them in fast cars — hugged the edge of our island and
the land masses of Northern Europe. The instrument sighed and
puffed like wind through trees. My earlier brush with the piano
faded to a sepia weakness beside the strength and bold outline of
the organ.

The boy I had discovered sacrilege with — his name was Ander
(recherché names were all the rage then) — was not content with
this dawdling, this admiration, at least not at that level. His qualities
of leadership did not sweep me off my feet; some quiet, private
part of me was asking for it. Our behaviour followed the mould of
previous initiations, a gentle concessional falling, a sundering. This
time my falling was inverted. Ander knew the ropes, the right
doors to open. It seems now his neatness and quietness was the
perfect disguise, whereas I was all jeans and tennis shoes, the
loud marginal type.

'Have you ever been up the spire?' he asked me.

'No,' I said, knowing it was out of bounds for us choir boys.

I knew then I would go up.

'Let's go then,' he said. 'It's this way.'

It was Communion time. We would be missed for the hymn
afterwards, but the service ended shortly and our absence would
be forgotten when next Sunday came about. I had admired the
spire, but always from the outside, and now was my opportunity
to rise higher and higher above the worshippers and the organ
loft.

Ander led me to a door which revealed another, ascending
stone staircase, narrower than the one which led down to the
nave. It was dark; a little light seeped in from slits in the wall,
through which I saw the pipes of the organ close up, and some of
the rose window. I was on my hands and knees, my upturned
face bumping against Ander's behind. This double humiliation,

and the lack of light, fresh air and space, defined a world of non-qualities or inverted qualities. It was dirty, my hands and exposed knees were black, and when my guide turned he grinned down at me like some chimney sweep which illustrated one of our schoolbooks, or a grotesque *putto* from the nether world. My excitement was rising. I could hear far down the voices of the others going through the Communion hymn, a ghostly echo of some dimension left behind, forgotten almost. Were it not for these voices, rising into muffled Latin, the men undercutting the clear sopranos of the boys and, at this height (how high were we anyway?), the rhythm of the organ, we would have lost all sense of where we were. I imagined it as a descent more than a mounting, into some well or cellar, where the sky was reflected in the still pool of water at its base – an underground Babel where all was echo and refraction, dissipation, in the end silence. Even then I ran away from referents to their images. My god of the ladders, in whose steps I followed, suddenly appeared against light, his limbs etched out of sunshine, gesticulating. He pulled me up the last steps and we approached a wide slit in the stonework to look out and down. The roofs of the cars in the carpark sent back a whitish glare and beyond them the gardens of the cathedral led to the town, minuscule, cowering in the valley. A fresh breeze blew. Behind us, in the chamber of the spire, two bells hung on a crossbeam, and through the floor the bellpulls led to their other extremity in the church porch. I thought of all the space below us, not outside the spire, but inside, the ever-widening cone of stone and slate which supported these bells, and the organ pipes so far down, even here audible through the floorboards. A wave of responding voices and the intoning voice of the celebrant wafted into our hutch – this was the logosphere of the edifice, where, because of the coiling of the steps, the antenna-like structure, the voices were magnified and distorted, became the ghosts of themselves. Whatever God there was would receive them as such, from this transmitter, restored to babble, a mesh of crossed voices, broken voices, almost tribal.

Ander seemed more interested in the view, the world theatrically miniaturised by our one-upmanship, while I hunkered round the centre of the platform, a relay between the voices and the invisible stars. I paced its dimensions, its circularity, a beast in a cage. On the wall or shell of the spire I deciphered the names of others who had climbed, some joined by hearts, some by crude, obscene messages. On the edges of the floor dried human turds and sweet papers littered the weathered wood. Ander was looking at me curiously, his hair caught in the bright sunlight. Was he god of the ladders or demon of the snakes?

'Well, now we're here,' he said. It was the first thing spoken since we had arrived. Its banality, at the time, didn't strike me, but his look, as he approached one of the big bells, warned me to be on my guard.

'Mass must be nearly over,' I said, by way of a move to descent. But it was only my voice talking. The magnetism which had dragged me up here, out of the orbit of the organ-pit, now sent me spinning round after him, or him after me, the bells, heavy copper and tin with pendant tongues in their orifices, always between us. The campanile spun and the sky slid sideways as I breathed in a fragrance of shampoo, felt his tight hands on my shoulders, steadying me.

'Look above you,' Ander whispered.

I looked up. A small wooden rectangle squared the circle, or almost. I felt a sharp pain in the groin, then a swift caress and his little knuckles against the skin of my thigh.

'Heaven or bust,' he said, releasing me and going to the slit.

The voices from below started up again as though to mock me. I didn't feel cheated or cornered. I had wanted it this way. They were singing 'Hail Queen of Heaven', which only now I can imagine seeping through those high floorboards with a twinge of irony. I felt surprisingly at home in the belfry. Ander started to join in with the singing from the impatient congregation but, though I laughed, his sarcasm seemed several levels below my Olympian stance. I saw myself as some Hercules rising up to a seat in this logosphere, this throne where time and death, the old constants, were rung out methodically. This was where Nimrod wept, at the pinnacle of his house, his last hunt futile, among those lofty trees, this foliage of words.

'Well . . . ?' Ander threw at me, slightly mocking or peeved.

'You want us to go up further?'

'There's only room for one,' he said.

'How do you know?'

'I tried; it's easy.' He softened. 'You climb the bell cross-bar and push your way in. There's a tiny porthole.'

He had come closer, as though in supplication. I felt myself tested and yet, having come so far . . . I was afraid of the bells. What if they started ringing?

'What time is it?' I asked.

'Twenty to,' he said. 'They ring on the hour only, and it's not a funeral mass, so we won't be disturbed,' he added, sensing the direction of my thoughts.

An aftertaste of intimacy hung there, and a hint of complicity and danger at once erotic and sacrilegious, which had been with us all along. The reversal of direction I had felt when mounting in the dark, through the spire, now operated in this chamber with its ropes and turds and graffiti. My unconscious flicked back and forth between the genital and the guttural. These bells, traditionally the *vox populi*, the town crier, the boys who cried wolf, the rhythm-maker, the unseen mouth. And several feet below us, surely, was the clock face by which I had checked my new tenth birthday watch. This clear space was the logical extension of the rumblings from the organ loft below, where until so recently I had been content. And they were genital too, these clappers; we had stroked their smooth cold metal and Ander's increasingly suggestive presence, his leading me on all along, the shadow of their metaphor, the echo of their tolling. His slight though agile body had brought me to this threshold, the end of the well in which we cowered. The shadow of the spire was thrown across the white-lined parking spaces in front of the episcopal palace by the bright morning sunshine, like an ink-stain, or a long, slim pen on dark paper. It seemed such a nice peaceful world outside in the exterior air. Already the people were going to their cars. And the cars would go to the newspaper shops. Our daring held us, funambulists without nets, and reduced these phenomena to insignificance. The real world seemed miles away. The real world was here: these bells, these ropes, these wind-dried shits and Ander in his Sunday best playing discreet pocket-billiards to my waiting. Though we were in under the heavy skirts of time it did not exist for us then. There was an interior space which had re-belled against her machinations, her solar and lunar rhythms, as against the congregation in its neat rows, the choir too perfectly in tune. I imagined ourselves as having been chased to the spire. I imagined, point blank. *This* point, the here and now. And all the rest a kind of panlogism which the spire was the centre of, I its inhabiting spirit, a *deus in machina*, endlessly inverting myself into existence.

The pinnacle, however, remained to be scaled. Ander had been there before, in the loft above the loft, and again it was his foot-steps I was retracing. I was the neophyte. He pinned me in this role, had doubtless seen me docile, sissy-like in the schoolyard and had chosen me from among the others for such a rite of passage. His maliciousness pleased me, his guarding of the silence. I couldn't help but admire his courage in coming up here alone. Or had he come up here alone? Had there been others before me whom he had put to the test? Had this belfry been their room apart where, like a coven of sorcerers, they performed their spells, their acts of cruelty, their immoralities?

'I'll help you,' he ventured, interlocking his hands at his groin and offering them to my foot. I put my weight into this cradle and swung up to the bell-beam. The rectangular lid was heavy and I needed all the strength I possessed to shift it sideways. From the gloomy hole a shower of dust descended, and I coughed. Ander below joined me in the coughing and told me there was an electric switch in the cubby hole to my right.

I swung up again and sat at the edge, looking round for space. The cone was, surprisingly, several yards wide – plenty of room for a second person. I switched on the light and immediately my attention was caught by a tiny altar, a table on which a metal box with a glass front reflected the light, protected by a transenna of gold, or so I imagined.

'What do you think?' Ander shouted up from below.

'What's in the box?' I asked.

'Look and see,' was his reply.

I approached on my stomach. A white host in a tiny monstrance at the rear of the box emerged from the dirty glass. Below it in a glass case there was a lock of thin hair, not at all wasted or faded-looking, and some substance which resembled dried peel, blackened, frizzled. I was looking at a reliquary. But the relics of whom, of what? I deciphered the lettering above the box, embossed in the metal – on closer scrutiny it was some alloy, bronze perhaps. It was in Latin, predictably.

Pange, linqua, gloriosi Corporis mysterium.

My knowledge of Latin, at that time, was strictly ecclesiastical, so I hadn't much difficulty in translating these five words. But still they didn't give me any clue to the origin of the hair, the nature of the shard of peel. I was overcome by a sense of extreme coldness, solitude. I realised with a shock where I was, the highest point for miles around, and that beyond the thin layer of slates there was only sky. The little reliquary magnetised me. I was afraid to crawl upwards to a glass porthole, covered with dust, at my back, and look out. I could hear the wind round me, as though I were in the centre of a cyclone, in the eye of a storm, calm, unmoving. Perhaps the relics had been brought here from Rome, Jerusalem? Was it the divine hair? One of the dozens of divine prepuces? They had instructed me in the various remains venerated throughout the world, in religious knowledge class – the holy nails, fragments of the cross, Veronica wiping the face of Jesus. I dismissed my speculation as far-fetched, but wasn't this the place for such ideas? And I knew such relics, or reputed relics, existed somewhere. I had written in my copybook: *that which is left after loss or decay of the rest*, and *gloriosi Corporis mysterium* referred to whose body, what body? The more I stared into the reliquary the more it entranced me. I could see my face in the glass, faintly, a child's face, haloed by the round window set into the tip of the spire. The hanging bulb began to give out a faint heat. I was no angel; hadn't I fallen dramatically and wilfully again and again only to reach the light eventually. This reliquary I looked into reflected my own face: *that* was its message, *that* centre might hold. And the Latin hammered out by some artisan in an unknown century referred to all bodies and to no body, but for the moment to mine. My sacrilege from the beginning had been a dance with inversion, a dance with my own decay: the climbing, the voices, the endless rising an crawling through the body of this church – its nave, its organ loft, its spire. Hadn't they taught us at school that each and everyone was the house of God, a divine sanctuary, a tabernacle. The host seemed to float out to me on a silver paten and hover in the air. The hair was hair of my hair, the black, exsanguinous matter was skin of my skin. I venerated them as I had venerated the face of the child among the high clouds who had transubstantiated them, made them live and tremble with life. And who else would have ventured up here for such a mutation, such folly? I was wearing my witch's hat, hatching spells under it in some fable, some fairy tale.

Ander started to shout. I saw him over by the slit, his back to me, doing something with his hands. A shift below of the dark bulk of the bells forewarned me. I stiffened for it. A slow toll shook my eardrums and reverberated inside a tiny skull. The face on the tabernacle shook like a face on rippled water. I braced myself for the next beat. There was nothing more. It was one o'clock. 'You're as white as a sheet,' Ander told me, helping me down. 'And freezing cold,' he added. He seemed flushed.

'It's spooky up there.'

'Did you see the tabernacle?' he asked. 'Imagine, anyone could steal it – the gold, I mean.'

'What's the hair and stuff?' I asked, knowing he would be none the wiser than I.

'Tell you later,' he threw at me, enigmatically. 'We've got to get out of here before they lock the organ loft door.'

We proceeded downwards. Ander was keeping something back. I wondered what he had been doing all the time I was up in the loft above the loft, and the split-second glimpse of his red, surprised face just before the bell tolled gave up only a half-notion.

The dark stairs were more treacherous descending than they had been ascending. Ander followed me. It was my privilege, I supposed. I felt I was shedding all that had happened up there, it had become part of the clouds, atmosphere only, not tangible. Through the slits I again saw the town, surfacing this time, and the leaves of the cemetery trees flying by in the breeze. The normal world. Sunday dinner. The newspapers. Then Ander stumbled and landed on top of me in a mass of limbs and clothing, whether deliberately or by accident I don't know. We were lying flat on our backs on the steps, laughing, and covering our mouths for fear of being heard, now we were so low.

'You know that hair?' he said, whispering close to me, in my ear.

'What about it?' I asked, sensing him teasing me in the half-light, testing me.

'Guess whose it is.'

'I don't know,' I said, knowing, remembering its fine blond hue, its brightness.

'It's mine,' he said, leading me slowly by the hand down into the porch.

INTRODUCING NESSA

MARY DORCEY

The traffic light had changed to green but she sat still, her foot pressed to the brake, her hands gripping the steering wheel so tightly the knuckles showed white under the skin. She looked at the telephone kiosk. A bulb in the ceiling filled it with light. She saw the beige paint peeling from the door, the tattered directory on the shelf, the black receiver gleaming on its metal cradle. Her fingers reached into the pocket of her coat and played with the smooth rim of a tenpenny piece. She had only to cross the street. In a few moments she might hear Nessa's voice again. But supposing it was not Nessa who answered. Supposing she was not in Leeson Street after all? Supposing it were to wake Sheila instead? What excuse could she give for calling at two in the morning? She would look ridiculous and start them talking.

She pushed the car into gear and swung the wheel roughly to the left, down the sharp incline of Ardmore Avenue to darkness and the sea. The road emptied behind her, speeding back between the smooth lawns of Hillside and Beech Heights, the houses staring after her blank and unseeing. At the foot of the hill she turned onto the seafront; drove past the station and the coal harbour until she reached the carpark. A row of cars was drawn up by the grass verge. As she pulled in, her headlights illuminated the windscreen of a blue Cortina. She glimpsed for a second a young woman's face, her eyes wide and startled; her head pressed between the seat back and her lover's shoulder. Saturday night and all over the city in locked cars men and women were clutched in one another's arms. She switched off the ignition and rolled down the window. The sea blew up to her: the small, nudging sounds of water against rock. As on that first night. They had walked here arm in arm along the dimly lit pier, the blue-black water heaving beneath their feet. Why else was she here now, if not clinging to the memory, as though it was already all that was left her? If she had guessed then how short the time ahead was to be, she would have tried to impress on her mind every moment, every last detail. As it was – drunk on cheap wine, careless – she had talked too much and whole hours of the evening were lost to her.

She lit another cigarette, gripping it between tight lips, sucked warmth from it. She was tired now, weary of pain, of anger, of self-pity. She knew there was no one to blame but herself. Not even Ben and Karen. Least of all them. She had seen them off tonight with presents and kisses – set them on the plane content in their image of her: good old Anna, never changes. She had given them a last pleasant evening, the one they wanted; one fit for retelling in Vancouver to any old friend who might ask, and to Harry. Was it for Harry she had done it? Was it for his sake she had lied? A lie no different from the others; one she would scarcely have noticed except for the mischance of it being overheard. And even tonight she had gone on with it, having nothing more to lose; gone on lying to make them happy. Ben had sat in front, his arm draped over the gear stick to fondle Karen's knee – smug and boastful in this new role of contented family man. Would it have pleased him to know what havoc his visit had caused? But he had no inkling of it. Shrewd, worldly wise, he noticed nothing. He made only one comment on Nessa, and that on the night of the dinner as she drove them back to the hotel. 'A nice looking kid,' he had said, 'but a bit of a wall banger.' And Anna had smiled as though in agreement.

She took a pair of leather gloves from the dashboard and, turning up the collar of her coat, stepped out of the car. As she locked the door, she heard a stifled grunting from the Cortina beside her. She walked down the wet slope of grass, the dank acid smell of shore rose to meet her. She could see in the distance the glassed dome of the lighthouse, the shaft of white light flung out on the black bay of sea. She walked close to the wall past the ferry with its yellow portholes shimmering on the oily water. Nothing stirred: even the gulls were silent. It was dangerous to come here alone – asking for trouble. But what did she care? Physical danger was a comfort to her; the clear, undemanding fear it aroused; distracting. She wanted the night and the wind in her face, the great blank emptiness of sky, it could not be dark or cold enough. She walked quickly, head down, hearing the ring of her heels on the granite paving stones. She remembered Nessa saying that she hated the sound – the vulnerability of it – a woman's footsteps leaving a trail through the darkness. Nessa! She felt the old constriction come back into her chest like a steel band tightening around it. What did she want of Nessa? Forgiveness? She could not ask for that. What then? Understanding – was that it? The newly discovered luxury, the last thing she could bring herself to give up? But how could she explain to Nessa what she did not understand herself. There were no words left to them; they, who once had so many, thousands of words written in love, strewn on paper about the house: on table tops and pillowcases, in drawers between the folds of a shirt, pinned on the inside of a cupboard door, hidden in the pages of a book – my darling – my lover – my only one. What could she call her now? Every phrase was bankrupt. She could no longer tell even where it had begun. The love and the lying were bound inextricably together, so that to surrender one was to lose the other. And yet there had been a time when they were not. A time before fear and caution; at the start, whenever that was.

The night of the party, that first night when I kept you in conversation for hours by the fire while other women danced. Afterwards persuading you to come here with me, to walk by the sea in darkness and silence, a windblown, starless night.

We walked as far as the old boathouse, the invisible water beating against the flags of the pier. I remember our talk – dreamlike; fluid and luminous as dream. My voice predominating, in wandering anecdotes, telling the secrets of years and more than that. Discovering places I had not known – the gaps between one event and the next that are the real happening. You said we remember the past like a street seen at night; the pale, globed lamps strung in orderly procession behind us. But it was not in the light we lived, but in the spaces between – in the darkness. You seemed most at home in those unlit spaces.

You walked with your head down so that I hardly noticed how intently you listened. Smiling every now and then with that ironic, worldly wise smile of yours. At the end of the pier we climbed down the narrow stone steps to the water's edge. Standing one lower than me, the black fronded seaweed washed lazily at your feet, you looked up:

'You have set a lot of store by sincerity, haven't you? It's going to be hard for you when they start demanding lies.'

I did not know what you meant then, and did not ask because you had retreated a step to stand beside me, and I wanted only to preserve this moment of intimacy forced on you by the erratic gushing and seepage of the sea.

I remembered it later when you teased my trick of easy confidences; the innocence of my face – a privileged habit you called it – the careless, unthinking response of respectability.

And enjoying it as you did, this 'old world charm', you could hardly have foreseen how easily I would lose it. How quickly I would trade one habit for another; how soon the pattern would build; one deceit leading to another until at last they were stacked like bricks around me.

Was it I who invited you back for a drink, or did you suggest it? Either way you came home with me. You were impressed by the house, and critical because it was elegant and suburban or because my salary alone could not pay for it? You wandered about the kitchen while I made coffee, running an eye over the shelf of cookery books, fingering gadgets on the sideboard: the blender, the juice extractor, the electric breadknife — the remnants of middle class marriage. I chose the old brown earthenware mugs from the rack and set them down on the table, the milk still in the bottle.

'Harry pays half the mortgage,' I told you, 'it's no more than fair while I am bringing up Sally.'

'Sure, why not?' you answered, your voice coming to me from the sitting room where you were putting a record on the stereo, 'you have worked for it after all.'

I do not know why you made me feel I should find excuses. Perhaps it had nothing to do with you.

You stayed the night because I was too tired to drive you home; in my bed, because it was too late at that hour to make up another. The light off, it was I who reached out a hand, saying 'goodnight', to ease the tension I felt lying so close to a stranger. The rough wool of your hair startled my touch, the curls springing back from my fingers. You stretched your hand to mine and drew it to your mouth. I felt the warm deliberate pressure of your lips. We might have fallen asleep that way, side by side, our fingers interlaced, but at that moment a car drove by, sweeping a yellow arc about the walls. I saw your face lit for an instant; your eyes glittering like a cat's; wide with alarm. It was you, Nessa, who first showed fear. Was it that gave me courage? Or was it a caprice; arrogant in its naivety — did I want to show you how little I was disturbed — how broadminded? I kissed your mouth. After that there was no turning back and no stopping place.

We slept for a few hours after dawn, light returning, the sounds of morning rising from the street, and it was the first time, Nessa, in almost three months that I slept without dreaming of you.

But that was not the real beginning was it? For me at least it started somewhere else entirely, long before that night. In those shabby unheated rooms beside the river when I went to my first Thursday meeting. You hardly remember that afternoon, I suppose, a cold wet day towards the end of December. I had read a letter from one of you in the *Times* advertising a debate on the divorce campaign. I do not know exactly what prompted me to go — curiosity in part, wanting to see for myself how women at the centre of so much controversy behaved among themselves, and the half acknowledged feelings of anger and frustration I had known since coming home. It was a shock coming back after five years of married life in Canada. I had forgotten how women were treated here: the patronage and contempt that were a part of daily life, how the smallest social exchange could become a set battle. It infuriated me to have half grown boys call me 'dear' and 'love'; to tolerate the gauntlet of innuendo and abuse one had to run ordering a drink in a pub or simply walking down a city street. I had forgotten all this. I had not realised that I could be made to feel a schoolgirl again because I had taken a ring from my finger.

We were halfway through the meeting when you came in. You stood leaning your back against the door jamb, hands sunk in the pockets of your jeans, smiling with that curious, upward, catlike tilt of your face. And your eyes were feline too: brilliant and wary as a cat's.

We were sitting on the floor in a circle discussing welfare discrimination against married women. When you spoke, the first emotion you roused in me was resentment. You accused us of trading in power by association, quoting Shaw: 'Any woman who reads the marriage service and goes through with it deserves all she gets.' You said we collaborated in our own oppression. Of course, you were being intentionally provocative but I felt injured, aggrieved. As a single mother, working to keep myself and my daughter, I had expected support and sympathy from feminists, not denunciation. As you talked on, developing your theory of right wing women policing each other to win male approval, I recognised a depth of feeling that eclipsed mine completely: an anger carried so long it had been honed to a smooth, gleaming weapon. My hostility evaporated. Listening to you, I felt restored to my old self-image of balance and moderation. In a strange way (and this should appeal to your love of irony) that was the origin of your fascination for me – you made me feel safe, normal again.

From then on I went to the meeting every week. Sitting in that cold draughty room in the company of women who were self-sufficient, self-directed, who took each other seriously and who, in the intensity of their conflicts, bestowed on each other an authority nowhere else given to women, I felt an amazed elation, the sense of coming home, though it was a home I could not have imagined. Experiences I had thought too private, too petty to be spoken of, shared in that room became politics so that I lost the burden of them and found them transmuted into tools of liberation.

So many marches and meetings, so many drunken debates afterwards in pubs up and down the city. And always for me, your voice passionate and eloquent: inspiring, provoking. Anyone familiar with these things could have predicted, I suppose, that I would fall in love with you. But what was it that drew your attention to me? You have given me many reasons, but I still do not understand it. Was it just the old pull of opposites? Or was I a challenge to you, or perhaps even a kind of reassurance?

I thought twice before going to Sheila's party. It would have been easy to find an excuse. I think I knew, without allowing myself to know, what was likely to come of it.

Do you remember how awkward I was at the beginning, visiting your house in Ranelagh? Five women living together, sharing one another's clothes and bedrooms, walking about the kitchen half-naked, rolling joints for breakfast, making love at all hours of the day and night: shamelessly, as though it were the most natural thing in the world, Robyn and Joan so loud they could be heard from the back garden. I had not realised how many women were in on this extraordinary secret I shared with you.

It took me a while to work out who was lovers with whom. I imagined communal orgies. I thought that, living as you did, you would have a total disregard for the usual romantic conventions. The day you introduced me and we sat in the kitchen drinking bottled Guinness, with photographs and posters from the movement staring down from the walls, I felt ridiculously out of place; for the first time what I suppose I looked: a suburban housewife. But if I did, no one else seemed to notice. None of you was puzzled by me. Not even when I began to call four or five times a week. You went about your lives blithely unaware while I shed my orderly habits as so many superfluous clothes at the end of winter and no one asked questions or showed the least surprise. Had you seen it all before?

You must have, of course, and must have been through it yourselves at some time. You said I was coming clear from years of camouflage. Out of the closet, as you all called it. But to me when I forgot to be self-conscious, it felt more like emerging from a chrysalis – a slow, laboured, sensuous process of self-discovery. Every day casting off layer by layer the outworn pretences: weakness, passivity, dependence on men – centuries of artifice sloughed away – the quick, vital core released.

In your room on those long March afternoons, the window looking onto a jumble of small gardens and the yellow brickwork of the old bakery, in bed together: the strangeness was only that there was none. Where had I learnt my knowledge of you? In what hidden part of my being had I stored it? Each nerve woken by your touch remembered you. Your lips on my skin were my own, or yours in some other life. My hands became the flesh of your thighs, the arc of your spine. Our names came spilling from some source more secret and magical than childhood. And when

I reached inside you and felt the push and suck of your womb, it was as if my own body was birthed again, hurled through the singing flesh and bone.

How long was it before I persuaded you to move in with me? That was the first mistake. I should have left things as they were, spontaneous and undefined. But I could not bear to be parted from you, not for a morning or a night, I wanted you near me and all to myself. I had no way of reckoning the cost even if I had wanted to.

One night driving back to my place from a party at Barbara's, you asked if I did not mind living alone after so many years as one of a couple. You knew only too well how much I missed Sally. There was no need to go into that. But I had told you very little about Harry. I had not talked much about him to anyone since the break up. Perhaps it was because I had felt none of the expected things: no guilt, no fear of the future, no half regrets. So I told you then what I had not dared tell the others, that for weeks afterwards I had been conscious only of a sublime relief – a shameless rejoicing. I woke in the mornings an hour earlier than usual, my heart pounding with excitement, and I would lie there not able, for a moment, to remember the cause. And then it would come back to me – flooding my nerves – the realisation that I was alone – free. Free of the exhausting games of reproach and self-justification I had played for years with him, arguments that were incapable of resolution because they had no starting point. I would get up at once without waiting to dress and hurry down the cold uncarpeted stairs of my new house, wanting to sing with pleasure because there was only myself to make breakfast for – no one waiting to be served, no complaints, no disputes over the newspaper, no disputes at all, not even the need to make conversation.

And you smiled and said you knew exactly: 'Going into the bathroom – dry towels and no hairs in the basin.'

You named it with your usual mockery — the bliss of recovering solitude after years of submergence in another life. Yet, seeing it so clearly, you did not wonder at my impatience to surrender it again.

You moved in with me, it must be said, under duress. You had fallen behind with the rent because Robyn had lost her job, and the landlord, to whom you had been suspect from the start, seized the chance to get you out. It was a temporary measure, we told each other, until you found another flat in town. That was three months ago. How long would it have continued, I wonder, if Ben and Karen had not come to dinner?

Our life was nearing a cross-roads anyway with Sally returning home in two weeks' time. Not that you thought so. You were looking forward to it. You seemed to imagine she could be slipped into our world with no more disturbance than a dog or cat. You loved my stories about her; you encouraged me every time I talked about her, which I did far too often: all the hilarious times and the sad ones. You dragged them all out of me, and we laughed ourselves awake in the morning, drinking jugs of black coffee and swapping stories of our own upbringing. It was as if you returned me, briefly, in those hours to the simplicity and spontaneity we think of as belonging naturally to childhood, but is perhaps only experienced, recalling it, years later, when we have escaped its captivity.

Part of me longed to introduce you to Sally. I wanted to show each of you off to the other. But when I thought of the questions she would ask, what she would say when she found a stranger sharing my room, little hooks of ice seemed to fasten themselves about my heart. Was it only coincidence that she had stayed so long with her father, a month more than planned, or had she detected something in my letters already, some unconscious signal that deterred her? I tried to explain to you, but you said that at eleven years of age she was no longer a child and would understand my need for a life of my own. I said that eleven was exactly the worst age. They understood enough to be vulnerable but not yet enough to be understanding. She would not begrudge me a life of my own, she was used to that. But it was the kind of life that was the problem – something she had never encountered before. 'How on earth was I to explain you?' I asked. And you said that there were no words, only actions. That she would see for herself when the time came – see my happiness and be glad of it. And then you would kiss me and we would make love again. I would forget my doubts, forget just what it was I needed to make clear.

So it was always: the hunger of our bodies subverting us, distracting us from all necessary discussion. And so it was that I never got around to telling you about the dream.

You said she would see my happiness. It was true, she would have. No one with eyes in her head could have missed it. I was absurdly, immeasurably happy. I would catch sight of myself in a mirror and, with astonishment, see my brilliant eyes, my cheeks flushed like a schoolgirl's, and think: so this is what they mean when they say radiant with happiness! All the clichés made true. All that my mother, in her innocence, had thought I would discover in marriage and motherhood, I discovered in those weeks with you. I would stare back into the glass and slowly shape the words: love, lover, in love, rehearsing them as though they were not the most commonplace in the language, but rather phrases of initiation to some secret rite.

In those first weeks I lost altogether the usual sense of human separateness, of being a single, self-contained entity in the world. When I think of that time, I think of our bodies – our hands, our mouths. Every nerve in my being fused with yours so that we were like one creature, drawn taut with desire, and love was something that moved over us, air or fire, and we trembled together in its force. Away from you, my flesh hurt as though cut from your bone. Spasms of longing might grip me at any moment: having a drink with friends, leading a prayer in class, standing at the checkout in a supermarket, and the thought of you — the smell, the taste of you, would overpower me so that it seemed my heart would batter its way from my chest. On such days when I got home to you at last it was with a kind of desperation we made love. I felt possessed by a deadly fever; felt I must be consumed utterly, burnt to ashes before I could regain sanity, self-possession. It frightened me. I had not known such desire was possible. With men sex had been effortless — like the pleasures of food and drink. Once gone from their bed, I lost all memory of them, except for a certain satisfied ease that gave me more energy, not less, for the things of the world. With you, lovemaking carried me so far I feared the struggle it cost to return. There was no end and no beginning. Only longing. I could not have enough of you. I remember the first morning, lying in your arms I asked was it always like this? Like what, you said. So sweet — so devouring? And you smiled your mischievous, enigmatic smile and said why else do you think they hide it from us?

I wanted there to be no more hiding. I wanted to announce it to the world, I wanted to run through the streets calling out my love for you. But I did not. Oh no — from the first day I learned to conceal it. The first time I was tested — back at school on Monday. That morning, after two days and three nights in bed with you, I went into work and felt like a sleep walker who wakes from some marvellous dream to find herself at the open window of a tower block. It was Peggy Keogh who woke me — Peggy with her red, greedy lips opening for gossip. Peggy bringing me over a mug of coffee and asking in that tone of lazy curiosity:

'What did you do for the weekend — anything strange or startling?'

I felt my heart beat, the blood coming into my cheeks. How was I to answer her? Only a second's hesitation but she caught it.

'Well,' she said, running her eye over my face. My stomach tightening, I snatched at an answer.

'Yes, as a matter of fact,' and I gave a quiet little laugh of mockery, 'I met the love of my life.' That was it. As simple as that. She looked away at once, ladling sugar into her cup.

'Is that all,' she said, 'I didn't have such a great time myself.'

I had hit on it quite by accident – the perfect strategy – to lie by telling the literal truth so bluntly they could not believe it!

After that it came with frightening ease. I discovered a hundred ways. I lied to everyone and everywhere. Inventing stories that nobody asked for – imagining suspicion where there was none, and forestalling it with every trick of dissimulation. I learned with amazing speed. I found that lying was something that engaged the whole body, eyes, mouth, hands, even the way one stood could be put to service, and that its skill depended less on what was said than on carefully chosen silences. You would not believe how many opportunities came my way.

It hurt most to lie to my mother, who loved me, who had faith in me, who only wanted my happiness – who had said it so often I had almost come to believe it. The Sunday I went to visit her – the Sunday after the first week spent in bed with you, I had a wild fantasy of confiding it all; of taking her in my arms and telling her that I was happier than she could ever have imagined possible. The instant she opened the door to me I was returned to reality. She wore her sad, wistful look when she greeted me – a smile that conveyed all she wanted for me; the depth of her disappointment and her determination to go on hoping, in spite of all. We sat in the dining room for dinner. My father carved the joint at the head of the table. He talked about the mess the country was in; the new bill they were introducing to give an allowance to unmarried mothers. It would make a laughing stock of us he said, every whore in the place paid by the state to raise her brats. I lost my temper.

In the kitchen later on, doing the dishes with my mother, she put a hand on my arm and begged me to be patient with him; to remember his age, that he did not mean half of it anyway; it was only that he was annoyed with them for taxing his pension.

They were the usual words, but there was a special tenderness in her appeal. She had picked up, of course, with her unfailing eye, the change in me. she saw the new energy, the excitement I was trying so hard to suppress which had burst out in my heightened aggravation with my father. She wanted the reason. I would not help. So at last she had to ask. I raised my eyebrows and gave a look of perfect surprise. And she gave back a small knowing smile — a smile that would not be denied.

'It's Harry, isn't it? Is he coming back with Sally this time? I knew it would only be a matter of time before you two got together again.'

I turned my back on her. I told her not to be so foolish. That it was nothing of the kind. And she changed the subject and went on with the dishes for my sake, but the pleasure stayed in her eyes.

It wounded me that, ridiculously. That she could be so wide of the mark, wilfully, almost. I saw that she would never let herself confront the truth, even if it was staring into her face. It would take a battering ram to break down her defences, her dreams for me. And I had not the strength of one word.

She asked, as I was leaving, if I would be alone on Wednesday — would she come over as usual after her golf? I heard the pause that I left between us, as if it was the noise of something opening. I felt the shabby pretence of struggle with myself before giving in and with eyes down, telling her, yes I would be alone — to come over as usual. She kissed me. She had got the reassurance she wanted.

I began then, on the way home in the car, to think of an excuse. Some way, that you would not notice, to get you out of the house for the night.

And so it started – hiding you like a stray dog I had brought in from the streets which had to be kept from polite company. They compelled me to lie, Nessa. They forced me to conceal my love for you as though it were something contaminating. Every name I had heard used against women like you – like us – came back to me. Every insult that made us seem corrupt or pathetic. Away from you I had no guard against them – no dam to keep the poison from my heart. It shamed me to hide you: to deny you, every hour of the day, if only by keeping silence – silence when they asked how I had spent the weekend or what was it that had me looking so pleased with myself? For of course they all nosed it out. At work, even those I hardly knew sensed something, felt the presence of some private source of happiness hidden from its rightful place in their gossip. I lied, Nessa, for both of us; I cut myself in two, but what did it matter, it was a superficial thing, was it not, no more than a social tactic? I lied to them, and I lied again to you so that you would not know how I betrayed you. I denied everything I had discovered, denied it to strangers so that they might allow me a little corner in their world.

And all the time I was haunted by the fear of exposure. The more I concealed our relationship, the more I dreaded its discovery. There were dangers everywhere. Do you remember the day we went to Wexford and, imagining myself safely miles from anywhere, I was kissing you languorously in the car park of White's Hotel when, over your shoulder, I saw John Fogarty walking towards us up the street. I tried to pull you into the car out of sight but you stood obstinately staring back at him. You wanted to know who he was and when I told you, asked did I not think he looked suspiciously macho for a music teacher. You forced me to wait, and then he had seen us and I had to speak to him. I blurted out some rubbish, blushing, about a change being as good as a rest which made everything worse. You began to laugh helplessly and he looked at you in bewilderment and did not notice that you were not introduced.

You thought it all a great joke. I tried to make you see the seriousness of it. What if he had seen us? What if he went into school on Monday and told Peter Walshe, or, worse still, Peggy Keogh? And you said he would just think we were nice affectionate girls and if he thought anything else it was because he knew too much and could not afford any gossip. Needless to say, no one *I* knew could be gay – nobody normal – so that did not persuade me at all. I think you felt I was playing it up to amuse you. Whatever it was, you were strangely patient.

How often did we go through my check list of fears? And, after a show of dissent, you would acquiesce reluctantly when I said that, being a teacher in a Catholic school, I would certainly lose my job if anyone in authority knew I had a woman lover; that I could not tell any family friends or relations because they might tell my mother; and that I could never, in any circumstances, let my mother suspect it because the shock might kill her; but you would not agree, whatever I said, that if she knew, she was capable of going into court to testify against me if Harry ever tried to get custody: you would not think so little of her. And when it came to acquaintances and strangers, you said I had run out of excuses.

You teased me – made me see the absurdity of it. You said I was going through a phase – growing pains – that every girl had a difficult period between adolescence and maturity. And I agreed, yes, it would all come right with time.

You loved sending it up, reversing all the usual saws about sexuality. You made a game of the elaborate stratagems to which I resorted to allay the neighbours' suspicions: making sure that they saw curtains drawn in two bedrooms, that we did not always leave the house together, that we had a record playing when we made love. It seemed a novelty to you. Like a child's game of making secrets, lending a thrill of the illicit to every ordinary activity. Was that the source of your patience? Did you believe your own jokes, believe that I would in time develop your courage and self-confidence, become at home in this underworld? I think you must have.

That was why I could not tell you about the dream, a pathetic trivial thing, brutal in its lack of subtlety. I am embarrassed even now to confess it. Night after night – almost from the first day you came to live with me – I have been haunted by the same predictable little fable. I am taking Sally to school. Her hand is in mine, warm, soft, confiding. We walk as far as the cloakroom door. Children are playing on the lawn to either side of us. Birds are singing, the sun falling on our upturned faces. Images of spring. Mother Ignatius is standing in the doorway. As we draw near her, she does not greet us, or step back to let us pass. Her white plump hands are clasped together across her black apron, she stands rigid, barring our path. She looks at me, and her eyes are two hard blue stones that will not meet mine, but have fastened themselves to my breast. 'I must ask you, Mrs Munro,' she says in her clear, thin voice, 'to take yourself and your daughter away from here and not to return again. We have the other children to consider.' And as I stare at her, bewildered for a second, I see that the pale stiff face under the white veil is my mother's and the eyes confronting mine now are my mother's eyes, staring in dull horror. 'There is a word for your kind I will not sully my lips by repeating.' And I hear the word she will not speak banging inside my brain. I turn without answering and pull Sally alongside me away down the wide gravel path to the gates. We walk with our heads lowered, Sally's quick stumbling footsteps following mine, her cheeks flushed, afraid to run. The children on the grass are laughing, pausing in their game to call after us. And Sally lets go of my hand.

That was the dream, Nessa. You see, it was too tawdry a thing to confide to you. You who stopped to meet me on that cross-roads from another existence. You who asked always why we should cripple ourselves to protect their ignorance?

It was that foolish secret that has destroyed us.

You know well my love of parties. I do not suppose we missed one in those weeks. Crowded, noisy rooms full of dancing, drink and music; strangers cheek to cheek, or small intimate celebrations; a familiar group around a table. I loved them all. Even more than going to them, I liked to give them − to draw people together; to share my friends; to bind them in an atmosphere of candlelight, good food, wine and conversation, in a room that might be anywhere. To bind them to one another so that they forgot themselves and talked of things they had not intended and might regret when remembered.

So that when Ben called, his voice bouncing across the line to announce their arrival, wanting to meet right then, my first thought was come over to dinner, I cannot wait to see you. Thinking how you would enjoy them, the laughter and talk we would have, sharing you with old friends at last. It was not until I put down the phone and you called to ask who it was that I remembered: remembered who you were, and what I had become, and knew that they would see only the common image of the thing and pity me or sneer. Oh, to my face they might be pleasant enough, after the first stiff shock, careful, polite liberal words. But they would begin immediately to withdraw from me, to hide their lives from me as they would from a stranger. For this is what they do, I know, if you will not lie to them; if you force them to acknowledge it, they begin to lie to you. They conceal themselves behind good manners; seeing in you a threatening, unpredictable outsider who had rejected their standards, their common life − an outsider with an ugly name.

There was no way to ask them not to come and no way of

asking you to leave. The next day, all through the preparations with you, shopping, cleaning, cooking this special meal for my oldest friends, I made a show of excitement. Knowing that if you guessed my thoughts it would be worse, wanting at all cost to avoid your questions, your anger: rightful anger. I bought four bottles of wine, food enough for ten, and rolled joints in advance to last the evening. You took it all without comment, noticing nothing strained in my high spirits, not curious, not wanting to know what they were like, these emissaries from my husband for whom I was taking so much trouble. It is one of the things I like most about you: your unself-consciousness, your way of taking things as natural and uncomplicated. So in your easy trust of me – wanting to share my pleasure – you did not notice, did you, that an hour before their arrival, while you were bathing, I took down from the wall the picture you had given me: two Victorian ladies on a balcony, bows in their hair, long flounced skirts, their arms about each other's waists, one turning her head to stare in arch defiance at the camera? I took it from our bedroom wall, and the photographs of the two of us lying drunkenly in the garden on your birthday. I took your clothes and books too and made up the bed in the spare room, putting your things about it as though it was lived in. I made these alterations with a thief's stealth, checking a mental list of precautions to make certain that I removed every trace and hint of our relationship. I would not have believed myself capable of such furtive caution.

When I went into the bathroom I carried a bottle of champagne, wanting you drunk early so that you would be unwary; wanting to make you happy with me in this last hour alone. And you drank to the success of the evening, understanding exactly my need to impress these friends, to show them how well I had done; how much I had achieved since leaving Harry. You kissed me, the wine spilling warm from your mouth to mine. Lightheaded with fear I caressed your shoulder and the soft fall of your breast. Lying across the bed on the woollen counterpane, we made love. Stretched on the white cover, I held your dark head between my hands and was glad that your eyes were hidden from me while your mouth drew its path of fire across my skin. And then, for the first time, the dream came to me, filling my mind with its spiteful image. I wanted to break from you and, calming us both, confide my dread so that you might dispel it. But our bodies moved us beyond consciousness and when at last words broke from me, they had nothing to do with guilt or fear but a fierce, sweet joy.

And so it was that at eight o'clock, when we went downstairs dressed and groomed to greet our visitors, it was as two lovers that we opened the door. They should have seen it. Our eyes were bright and full with it. But people only see what they have heard of.

A middle-aged man held out his arms to me: a man with hollow cheeks and a greying beard. Karen beside him, thin, nervous as ever, smiling at me. Standing in the hallway, we all said how good it was, how long it had been, how little any of us had changed. And then you stepped forward. And they waited hesitant, a little surprised, for the introduction. Was that my chance? Was it in that second I should have made everything clear? Should I have taken your hand and said I would like you to meet Nessa – my lover? Is that what you would have done in my place? And I suppose then they would have kissed you too and smiled while I took their coats. But I cannot ever know what they might have done because I did nothing like that. I stood a little to one side and, without looking at you, said, 'Nessa: Karen and Ben,' and they shook your hand in turn and said how pleased they were.

And so we sat together around the sitting room fire and I poured out the drinks. And they were so easy, flattering and humorous. I showed them around the house and they said how lovely: the space, the light, envying me the garden, the lawn, the roses, the little glimpse of hills behind the roof tops. And you, setting the table, lighting candles, did not guess that I showed them the spare room and said Nessa likes to sleep at the back, it's quieter.

We gathered about the long table with its flowers and embroidered cloth, and Ben talked, and I talked, and mostly you listened, knowing none of the people or places. And I filled every glass to the brim before it was emptied and ladled out dish after dish against all protest. And they said delicious, marvellous, a feast, a banquet: I had lost none of my touch. And Ben, sinking his small sharp teeth into cream filled pastry, said that Harry had been crazy to let such a paragon out of his kitchen. And we all laughed, except you, but then you did not know Harry and no one found it odd that you did not laugh. And I poured brandy over the crêpes, and the flames leapt from the centre and ran blue and yellow round the pan, and they cheered and called bravo and said how wonderful it was to be together again, it had been much too long.

I passed round the joint as we sat by the fire and Ben said that Harry was off it completely; did not drink or smoke, had taken up jogging and healthfoods; and I said how extraordinary, Harry of all people! And Ben chortled, and looked knowing, and said, yes, Harry of all people; he is an utterly changed man. And I poured coffee into the blue-grey pottery cups you had given me. And Karen exclaimed how lovely they were and demanded to know where I had bought them. And I told her the name of the shop and the street, but not that you had given them to me for my birthday, spread them on the sheet between us, spoils of love, and, choosing one, running your fingers along its rim, had said: 'The colour of birds' eggs, the colour of your eyes.' Lounging by the fire, legs stretched to the heat, his hands cradling the broad base of his glass, Ben began to talk politics, about the left in America and the women's movement. And you saw at once how I steered him off with irony and wit and a sudden impassioned eagerness to know how Karen's exhibition had gone in the fall.

But Ben saw nothing and did not notice that I had been selecting the talk all evening; nudging and shunting us from one topic to another. He did not see how my eyes reached for yours across his shoulder and begged you to be patient; saying I love you, trust me, say nothing. But you did, and dropped your gaze from mine. You took the bottle of brandy, and filled up your glass again, and sat, watching and listening, and kept silence. And were you waiting, confident I suppose, that sooner or later I would say something real, while my nerves were stretched taut, my eyes straining to catch the least gesture, to anticipate danger and draw us from it? And you had never seen me so gay, so frivolous, my conversation so insistent. You know you have changed after all Anna, Ben said, so laid back, and Karen agreed. My heart raced, my hands shook as I poured more coffee. And so it was I made my first mistake letting Ben take hold of the talk, sucking at his pipe, his tone suave; a long wandering monologue of his travels in North Africa and Asia, with self-satisfied indignation telling us of the oppression of women in these countries; the barbarous system they subjected themselves to. And I listened, tired suddenly, and thought how much he had altered, even more than myself in three years. Or had he remained exactly as always and it was only my vision that had shifted, transforming him, opening up a chasm between us? I listened, waiting for the word or phrase that must inevitably come, the question or joke that would shatter my defences, pitch us into territory from which there could be no retreat. And you were bored, unheeding now, and perhaps you thought that when the time came I would stand my ground, assured, uncompromising, and say what needed to be said.

But it was not Ben who crossed the line at last. It was Karen, almost at the end, while we washed dishes in the kitchen and I had started to relax a little, imagining we had passed safely to the last half hour, to the last drinks, the last drowsy words of thanks and then bed and your body and a thousand ways to explain, to apologise. Karen stood by the sink, drying the coffee jug you had given me too, and, as if by instinct, spoke your name and asked so casually, with such lack of emphasis, her voice a little husky from smoke and alcohol,

'When did Nessa move in?'

I could not have willed myself to move or speak, though my hands went on mechanically scouring cheese from the pan.

'You know in Canada,' she continued, 'if two women of our age live together, everyone thinks they are queer. Isn't it absurd?' And she laughed that pleased chuckle of the sophisticate at the credulity of others. She laughed and I heard myself laugh too, a kind of high pitched rasping noise made into a laugh, and our joined laughter seemed to run about the walls, rattling the plates and cups, shaking the flowers in their vase, quivering the candle flame, and I said, 'Yes, that's Canada for you!' my words linking with the laughter, 'we do things differently here. In Dublin, if two single people live together it's only to halve the electricity bills!'

My back was to the door and I heard nothing above the shrilling of the kettle but I knew, the blood beating at the base of my throat, I knew in that second you had come into the room and that you were standing in silence behind me. I knew that you had overheard every word spoken. I bent forward over the sink, my hands plunged in the soapy water, and waited for someone else to speak, for someone to lift the burden from me. Karen turned, opening her lips, and then closed them again because you had gone, left us without so much as a goodnight. I heard your footsteps across the hall and up the stairs muffled by the carpet and the door of the spare room opened and shut. I stood rooted, gripping the rim of the sink. Then Karen spoke again, her voice flung into the vacuum as one in fear rushes down a darkened passageway sensing but unable to locate the danger.

'Well, what was that about?' And then, with a quick brightening smile, 'I guess it must have been the dope,' she said, 'I guess it got to her all of a sudden.'

'Yes, I suppose it did,' I replied, seizing at once on the brilliant simplicity of it. And when we went inside for a last coffee she told Ben and he agreed with her – the dope, the drink – all of it suddenly too much. And we laughed again and had another drink ourselves.

And lying upstairs alone, Nessa, perhaps you heard us. And if you did, was it that final cowardice that decided you?

Shortly after that I drove them back to their hotel. When I returned an hour later, the house was in darkness; and checking the rooms, I found them all empty. You had taken your bike, a few belongings: clothes and books in a rucksack, and without bothering to leave a note on the table, you had left my house.

She had reached the pier's end, the water, the glowing glass dome of the lighthouse.

She leaned against the stone parapet and looked out to sea. She watched the waves break in the harbour mouth; break and, turning, beat their way out again through the incoming swell: each white bank jostled by another. She looked past them towards the open bay, the dark waste of water that lay beyond. She thought of all those compelled to live at sea. She wondered how they endured it; to live for months on end in exile from land. There were even some who chose to – who set out, voluntarily, on lone voyages of discovery. Harry had envied them – the last great adventure left to man, he called it. Well, man could have it and gladly, as far as she was concerned. The sea, to her, was no more than an immense vacancy; a glittering mirror, which no matter how far travelled could give back nothing but one's own reflection. But that was perhaps just what they sought in it.

She was cold. Her hands in the pocket of her coat, she drew it close about her and rocked herself gently. She should go home. In a few hours it would be time for work.

She turned from the sea, from its cold and dark, from the repetitive noise of it, the white froth left clinging to the rocks.

She turned her eyes towards the shore; the houses flung like an arm around the bay, the neon signs of the seafront hotels, the yachts at anchor; each one moored rattling to its buoy, the metal bridges arching over the railway. This was what she loved – this was her security: where the amorphous wash and spill was given shape and meaning by the grip of the land. The reassurance of the everyday: the solid human world; her world, of work, friendship, family.

How often had she tried to explain it to Nessa? With no success. How could she have hoped to? Nessa had faith in people – she believed in good intentions, the power of conviction, the capacity for change. She could never understand women like Anna, anymore than she could understand cowardice or admire hypocrisy. Anna had said often enough, that it was easy for Nessa to confront the world – she had so much less to lose. But that was only half the truth. Nessa was brave; to a fault at times, careless of opinion, and above all sure of her cause. But for Anna there was no cause – no lofty vision, no banner, no battle cry – nothing to fight for but love – the right to give her heart where she pleased. And in all the world was there anything less free than love? Anything more subject to social coercion, more vulnerable to envy and malice? She had known this before ever meeting Nessa but in the last few months with her she had learnt more. It was this very love that had stripped the veneer from things, shown her people as they really were; the rage and vindictiveness that lay just beneath the surface, in wait for anyone guileless enough to break rank. And once seen it was not easily forgotten.

Nessa had mocked her middle class privilege, her complacency, but even she did not see how deep the roots went – cut them, it seemed, and the whole structure toppled.

For two days now Anna had put off calling Nessa. She had told herself it was because she feared her reproaches, her anger, but there was another reason, deeper than this and less easily acknowledged. She had been aware of it in the first second of waking, of finding herself alone. Something even a few days ago she would not have believed possible. Shocked, she had pushed it below surface. But there it was again. She could not deny it. Relief was what she had felt, then and again tonight, a shabby, reluctant dawning of it, but unmistakable nonetheless. Having lived for so long on a precipice, it was an immense release from pressure to have reached an end; to know that one way or another, the struggle was over.

At the rim of the sea, light was creeping into the sky, staining the grey a muddy yellow. Seagulls set up their harsh wail along a line of black weeded rocks. Nessa would be in bed still, wherever she was; in Leeson Street, at Sheila's or Claire's, in whatever household she had taken refuge: sprawled across the sheets in the fierce abandon she had in sleep, her dark head pushed into the pillows, her skin breathing heat and fragrance. If Anna could go to her, she would steal in beside her, and without waking her, draw close; kiss her neck, her shoulders, the long indented path of her spine, she would whisper some of the old words – my darling, the most precious thing in my life, nothing I would not do for you – some soft loving lie to add to all the others.

But she knew, even as she imagined this, what it was she feared in appealing to Nessa, what had made her postpone calling her all these days. She was afraid not of obduracy but of forgiveness. Yes, she was afraid that she might be pardoned but on condition. Forgiven but asked to change; to begin again but differently. And which would be more painful, which would take more courage in the long run? To live without her, or to live with her – without the lies? Had she the strength for either?

She turned from the sea and began to run; running towards the shore; the dim outline of houses huddled about the bay, the clatter of her heels echoing in the waking silence. She ran without stopping until she reached the carpark. The Renault stood alone on the black sweep of tarmac, the courting couples, hours ago, gone home to their separate beds.

As she drew close to the car she noticed a door opening in one of the terraced houses on the far side of the road. A man in grey striped pyjamas stood in the hallway, stretching his arms, yawning, the white drawstring of his trousers dangling under the sagging wall of his belly. She watched him bend and lift four milk bottles from the step, scratching at the seat of his pants as he straightened up. She looked at his worn cloth slippers, the ashen stubble shading his cheeks. A woman appeared behind him cradling a crying baby on her hip. Catching sight of Anna, watching from across the road, she stepped back hurriedly, pulling her husband after her, and closed the door; not wanting to be seen in her nightwear. What hypocrites people were, Anna thought, with their petty decencies and respectability: with their right times and their wrong times, their shaved lawns, their concrete walls; their little censorious minds set straight. And their furtive pleasures behind lowered blinds and closed curtains; on Friday nights and Saturdays, the thin partitions of their rooms shaken with it; in the name of God and country, spawning babies. Shamefaced in the morning. How absurd it all was. She stared at the door of varnished teak that had closed opposite her, with a strange fascination, as if beholding something never seen before. Was it for these people – these solid citizens and all like them, was it for their good opinion she had sold herself? Was she prepared to trade everything she had discovered, to keep a little corner in their world? Private, safe, accepted?

She got into the car and started up the engine. She drove quickly along the seafront and turned into Ardmore Avenue. The phone booth on the corner was empty. She parked the car, stepped out and walked across the street. When she lifted the receiver and placed the coins in the slot, it was Sheila's number she picked at random. For thirty seconds the phone rang uninterrupted. They must all be asleep, she thought, after a late night or perhaps had left early. And then, abruptly, the ringing tone stopped and Nessa's voice took its place; sounding muffled, half asleep, as if she were still in bed. Of course – she would be in Sheila's room with the phone beside her.

'Hallo?'

Anna wondered if Sheila was there too, listening, or would she be on her way to work by this time? What was she to say now, she asked herself. She could not think of one solitary thing she had planned; she could think of nothing at all, but to say stupidly, forlornly:

'Nessa.'

'Oh . . . it's you.' The voice was cold; indifferent. Or hostile? She could not tell which.

'Nessa . . .'

'Yes?'

She wanted to say, I have missed you, but she did not. She wanted to say, I am sorry, but she did not. She only said them in her head, deliberately, as if counting the words, assessing their suitability for some other occasion.

'I am sorry if I woke you,' she said at last, to say something, anything before the silence hardened to stone between them.

'Oh, it doesn't matter.'

'Is Sheila there still? I'm sorry if I woke her.'

'No, you didn't,' the answer came out flat, merciless, refusing to give her any help at all. So she was not going to be forgiven then. She would not be asked for explanations, apologies. This voice was not going to ask her anything whatever. It would go on replying in polite, bored monosyllables until she put down the phone.

'You left your dole card in the house. I thought you might need it.'

'Oh yes, I will. I'll want it on Tuesday.'

The next step obviously was to offer to bring it over. Anna could do it now, before work, if she hurried. But it would have been as easy at that moment to grow wings as to suggest it. Her right hand was gripping the receiver that smelt of stale aftershave, her left hand was picking at the directory open beside her. She had torn the first three 'Murrays' from the top of the page when Nessa spoke. Anna was so startled she gave a little nervous jump the way her mother did when the doorbell rang unexpectedly.

'By the way, I thought you might like to know . . . ' Was the tone reproachful now or scornful? 'That one of your friends thinks we seem very happy together.'

'Who?'

'Karen.'

'Karen?' What was this about? Was Nessa taunting her, or was this intended to be funny?

'What do you mean, Karen?'

'Just what I said. Karen thinks I must be good for you. She said you seem altogether different.' Anna felt a cold anger rising in her. But whether it was towards Nessa, Karen or herself she did not know.

"When were you talking to Karen?'

'That night. She came up to the bedroom before leaving.'

'I see,' Anna said, though she saw nothing. She could not follow any of it. She did not know how she was supposed to respond. And she did not know why she felt angry.

'Why?' she asked at last.

'Why what?'

'Why did Karen go up to you?'

'Oh, she just wanted to apologise.'

'Apologise? For what?'

'Because of Ben. She thought it might have been something he said that offended me. She was worried when I left so suddenly.'

'And what did you say?' Anna could hear the irritation just barely suppressed in her voice. She was angry with herself for asking these questions. She felt they were drawing her into some trap she should be able to see but could not. But neither could she prevent herself from speaking them.

'I told her it had nothing to do with Ben, or nothing of any importance anyhow. I said it was you who was being offensive.'

The detached, controlled cool of Nessa's voice struck a little flame of fear through Anna. What else had she told Karen? If she could not manage to stay absolutely calm herself she might never find out.

'And what did Karen say to that?' she asked, at last, when she felt herself ready.

'She said yes, she saw what I meant. She said it was a pity you seemed to think it necessary to hide our relationship. She said there was nothing Ben would have enjoyed more. It would have capped everything.'

Anna was slammed into silence: a tense, angry, humiliated waiting. There was nothing she could say. She had absolutely no words for this. It was beyond her wildest fears.

After moments of suspense, Nessa spoke again:

'Poor Anna,' she said, 'all that hard work for naught. You see, it seems there was something they wanted to tell you. It seems that, along with health foods and jogging, there's something else Harry has taken up. But neither of them knew how to tell you. It's quite a crisis for him.'

'What, for Godsake?'

'Men.'

'Men?'

'Yes . . . men.'

And then Anna heard the last thing in the world she had expected. A sudden explosion of sound came through the phone so that she had to hold it out from her ear. It was a second before she realised that Nessa was laughing. And not in derision or scorn but a giddy whooping and bubbling of mirth.

'Men,' Nessa said again, the single word struggling clear to be engulfed once again by a wave of laughter, so that after a moment Anna found she was laughing too. And so there they were, no more than five miles apart, in the early hours of the city; holding tight to their receivers and carried over the distance; bouncing, gushing like water, unstoppable, laughter ran along the wires that joined them.

BLOOD BROTHERS, SOUL SISTERS

TERRY PRONE

One afternoon, he decided to go home.

He tried the sentence out for size. 'One afternoon, he decided to go home.'

But it was not quite true, he reflected. The sentence sounded as if he were in charge of his life. It suggested the tough decisiveness of a bodybuilder benchpressing three hundred pounds, face varicosed in the agony so visually reminiscent of orgasm.

He tried that phrase out too. 'Visually reminiscent of orgasm.'

He could not pinpoint when he had begun this commentary on his life as he lived it, articulated in his head but unspoken. In the morning when the alarm clock gave its throat-clearing noise preparatory to ringing, he would lie on his back in bed and the commentary would start up. It was a way of observing his life and yet distancing him from it, so that he frequently had to pull his concentration back to reality, the way you pull your eyes back into focus when tiredness has diluted the precision of your gaze.

In theory, his commentary acknowledged, it was undoubtedly he who had made the decision to go home. In practice, the decision had possessed him. Not as a demon. More as a car is possessed on foot of non-payment. One afternoon a decision had made him . . .

But then, the earlier decision had made him, too. The decision to leave the flat in Rathmines and go to London. For a year. Or two.

'It may be for years and it may be forever,' his father warbled at the time, to distract his mother. Clemmie Hogan was like a natural steam eruption. Her emotional pressure built up, usually over a period of an hour, and resulted in regular ear-splitting

137

explosions of hysteria. Her husband had learned early in the relationship that a well-timed laugh could abort the purgative cycle, and had subsequently worked to make himself a master of the one-liner. The two of them were definitively happy, although most people outside the family found Paul Hogan's rapid-fire jollities as wearing as long-term hiccups.

It had not been for years. It had been for eighteen months. In Chelsea. In a group of pre-War apartments overlooking a garden so darkened by the tall surrounding buildings that it looked like the bottom of an ill-lit aquarium, dark green spiky foliage ever-present, yet never growing further from the darker soil. On the second floor of the apartments was an excellent restaurant visited by the inhabitants.

'Relics of oul dacency,' his father had said on his lone visit, looking around at the cardiganed and bent old men and women, closer to Rattigan characters than to life.

They had liked him, the genteel old inhabitants. They had liked him because he was soft-spoken. Courteous. And unhurried.

That was happening to him more and more, he noted. Even his thoughts were breaking into staccato phrases, in time with his breathing.

This is a long, long corridor, his internal commentator observed. Why? Concentrate, now. Oh, yes. On the other side is the duty free, the brown bottles of Baileys and the twinned white and black of Sheridans and the sillier tourist trap tripe-drinks all competing in two prices for favour.

He paused to look out of the window, letting the other passengers pass him by. Small commuter planes on the parking area. Shortts? Perhaps Fokkers. From somewhere in the ill-sorted files of his memory surged the open-pored fat face of a TV comedian.

'So this war hero is telling the story of how he was shot right out of the sky, and he's telling the interviewer, "These fokkers came from nowhere, three of them, and dey go bang bang and I lose de ving, and I know I go down —" and the interviewer says to the camera, "I suppose I should make it clear that Fokker is the name of a wartime plane", and the war hero says, "No, no, you don't understand. Dese fokkers were Messerschmidts!"'

When he had first heard it, he had been a teenager, in a home where bad language was not approved of, and he remembered the exhilaration of telling it to his parents, knowing that the laughter it provoked would allow him to get away with the 'dirty words'. Smiling at the memory, he resumed his walk down the long corridor, a group of sleek young executives beaming knowingly at him from an IDA poster at the end of the corridor. They were young, those IDA faces. Young. Glowing. Eyes unaccustomed to fear or compromise. He hated them.

No, he amended, as the moving staircase took him down to the baggage retrieval area, he didn't hate them. His reaction to them was the same reaction Irish people have when visiting France the first time. Aren't the children clever. To speak French so well. Aren't the IDA kids annoying. To have such notions of immortality. Or worse. To have no need for notions of mortality or immortality.

The customs officer ignored him as he pushed the trolley carrying his two old cases through the blue channel. The grey glass doors opened as he approached, and he turned the wheels to bring him into the fenced-off square outside which the welcomers were supposed to sit. As always children had invaded the square and arrivers with trolleys full of luggage were blocking the two exit areas. He stood, momentarily, his eye caught by an airport feature new since his last visit: angular miniature rostrums. Lit up from inside. Red, white and blue. Five of them. With poles linking them to the ceiling and, a foot above head level, a dotted red electronic sign, always moving to the left, saying Welcome to Dublin in high-tech repetitious parody of the clutchers and kissers around him.

His sister nodded and rolled her eyes up to heaven at the new arrivals who were preventing the two of them from meeting. When the traffic unjammed she surged at him, her unmade-up face soft and cold against his cheek. She hugged him long and hard. Eventually he gently disengaged from her.

'Think you'd hold on a bit longer,' she muttered cheerfully. 'Best looking man in the airport giving me a hug. Some of us are not that well endowed in gorgeous hunks, you know.'

'Probably compensation.'

'Mmmm?' She was feeding her parking card into the machine. Neatly, he thought. Neatly and surely. She would have the right change, he knew. She did. And would want a receipt. She did.

'For being well-endowed elsewhere,' he finished. She gave the quick token laugh she always did. A laugh that said, 'Not funny. But we'll go along with it.' A habit of preoccupied motherhood.

She stumped ahead of him, her every footfall self-assured and overt, as if making a point. The hatchback swung up and he hoisted the luggage into the boot. Ramps everywhere, these days, for invalids. Oops – for People with Disabilities. He wondered about the freedom of the disability badge, the stick figure with the wheelchair wheel. The freedom not to have to pretend to be well and strong and vigorous. The freedom of childhood, when an adult hand pulls the curtains against the noisy brightness of the day and tucks the bedclothes firmly in around the fever. When there is permission to let go and sink softly into the sweaty half-comfort of midday dozing.

Marion drove badly, as she always had. She never seemed capable of seeing further away than ten yards, so when other cars braked or when traffic lights turned red, it came as a surprise to be coped with, rather than a logical inevitability. His luggage shifted in the boot and he wondered if he had padded the oversized framed Mapplethorpe sufficiently. On the other hand, his internal commentator observed, there would be certain circular aptness to arriving home on this occasion with a framed

Mapplethorpe half-visible behind shattered glass.

'. . . so I've just given up. You can do so much, and then you have to let whatever happens, happen.'

His sister was in full flow, he realised, and he had missed what the subject was. But the questions to cover his failure to listen came with the custom of years.

'Not an easy lesson?'

'No. But there comes a time. Thanks for the signal, buddy.'

This is to a Fiat which had cut in ahead of her. Feargal had been watching the Fiat for some time. Its driver had been indicating his intent clearly for at least a minute and a half.

'Derek is living with some bright girl in Dublin and she's going to leave him in due course, because she's doing very well and she'll get a scholarship and go off to Moscow or somewhere. She studies Russian.'

The car surged out onto the N4 and Feargal consciously relaxed his legs, willing himself not to push against non-existent brakes on his side of the vehicle.

'And Padraig?'

'Padraig is still at home. Applying to all the RTCs, now it's clear he'll never get into a university. He doesn't have his uncle's capacity for getting his head down and studying.'

Feargal smiled.

'His uncle probably studied hard for the wrong reasons.'

She looked at him sideways and he fought down the desire to tell her to watch the road ahead.

'I think I studied because I had nothing else to do. I never really fitted in at UCD. I wasn't a great sportsman and I wasn't a debater and I hated most of the social life. So what else was there to do?'

'Yeah, well I wish my pair had less interest in sport and social life. Derek had the bloody nerve to say to me recently that I was being rigid and that what he wanted to be was a Renaissance man.'

Feargal laughed until a bout of coughing stopped him. Marion turned off the heater in the car as if it was to blame.

'A Renaissance man!'

She suddenly pulled out to pass an articulated lorry and Feargal's internal commentator began to pray, in the language of his childhood. O Jesus Mary and Joseph, save me in this hour of danger and I will never, ever, as long as I live, I swear to God, ever again . . . The lorry was successfully passed and Feargal pondered the realisation that he had run out of bribes for God. This must be some rite of passage into middle age, he thought, since up to now he had always had a plethora of self-deprivations he could offer in moments when panic slammed him past reason and back into the babbling bargains with the Almighty which had seen him through childhood.

'. . . that Renaissance men were educated to within an inch of their lives and were producing *disciplined* works of art by their early twenties, because they had been ferrying pots of red ochre or whatever for Old Masters since they were in nappies.'

Feargal reached out and patted his sister on the back of her head.

'I thought it was yellow ochre.'

'Ground-up eggshells or some bloody thing.'

'And they had to grind the eggshells by hand, probably, too.'

She looked huffy at the mockery. So he went further.

'In fact, if the truth were known, Renaissance man probably served an apprenticeship that involved him standing with his hand cupped underneath the hen, ready to catch each emerging egg.'

'Oh, shut up, you. I've missed you, you know.'

All in the same tone of voice. That very aggressive affection which made her such a good mother. She could TCP a cut, pull off a dirtied Elastoplast, or cut through a tantrum like no other mother he had ever seen. Fifteen years ago had probably been her best time, he thought, when she had babies and theories and nobody around her of an age to slide away from her tightly packaged precepts.

'. . . the thought of it. I'd rather be dead.'

He had no idea what the alternative to death was, in this instance, but it was the idea of death that attracted his attention. His raised level of sensitivity to comments of that nature reminded him of times when Brian, who was blind, had visited the Chelsea apartment. Everybody would say things to Brian like 'Did you see so-and-so?' then realise what they had said and be disturbed by it, even though Brian, with a lifetime using as valid currency the language of the sighted, was completely undisturbed.

'. . . I would. I'd rather be stone dead.'

Stone dead, he thought. That would be a good kind of dead. The kind of dead he dreaded was a seeping, suppurating, putrefy-ing dead, with damp decay and sweet-scented rottenness and waxy strips of flesh sagging away from strait of bone.

'Sing to me.'

'Sing what?'

'"Drink to me only".'

For a second he needed to think of where to pitch it so she could take the melody and he could improvise around the light soprano voice. Throat-clearing. More throat-clearing. Faltering start and then the two voices filling the car. They had always sung the songs of a generation before their own, the commonplace of a family where every party was a sing-song.

Now, his sister's voice came out of her, innocent and un-inflected as when she was twelve. Innocent, uninflected and soaring to the high notes without shrillness or stridency. The middle-aged face of her and the speckling of unaltered grey in her hair, and this voice, untouched by time, experience and proudly-claimed moral certitudes.

They finished the song and were silent. She looks upset, his commentator nudged. Better not to ask why. If you ask why, other people's problems seep into the fabric of your time like dye leaking from a garment. You can never get it out of your life, and you can never get it back into their life, so do not invite the sharing of miseries.

A wave of terror, unrelated to her driving, washed over him, and he wanted to scream. Except, said the commentator, scream-ing don't achieving nothin'. As a child he had daydreamed on the swing in the back garden. Always nightmares. Nightmares playing out behind his round face. Nightmares running like a film in his mind, in the hope that if he replayed them enough, he would find a solution to each of them. There was the death-by-drowning nightmare. The holding of the breath and praying for a hand to reach down into the water and pull him up, his face swelling, blood pounding in his ears as the lungs fought the sphincter of his throat. At ten, at twelve, he had sat on his own and imagined the unspeakable sensation of thick water bloating into nose and mouth. He had read the books that said you would die quickly. Five minutes. But five minutes was not quick. All hell could be experienced in five minutes. Five minutes would go on and on into eternity.

Unknown to him, his father had watched his only son and been thankful for the apparent tranquillity of the child. So much better, his father had thought, than if the boy had picked up his mother's nerves. Unknown to his father, the calm-faced child, dreaming in the garden, had all the while been bargaining with terror. Dear God, let me not die by drowning, let me die any way but not by drowning, preferably by a tree falling on me and knocking me unconscious straight away or maybe in my sleep. Dear God, I will give you ten years of my life if you'll just show me now how I'll die. Dear God, I wouldn't mind having both legs amputated and bleeding to death, because bleeding, you would drift away from the pain. But not drowning, please God.

Marion's voice pulled at his attention.

'Do you hate the thought of going back to the Department?'

'Not really. I've learned a lot. It'll be different.'

'Do you go back to the same job?'

'Probably not. Just to the same level.'

'Could you have stayed away longer?'

'Probably could have got another extension. That's the beauty of career breaks.'

'Not to mention being able to get back in without a medical.'

It winded him like a head-butt in the stomach. For a moment he looked straight ahead, reading the specifications off the back of the artic ahead of their car. Then he looked at her. Then back at the artic.

'Oh, let's be clear, everybody at home will decide you're fitter than you ever were. You don't have to worry about *that*.'

His mouth was fluffily dry, and, abruptly he was as disconnected, mentally and physically, as when he had first learned to drive and had been unable to coordinate pushing in the clutch and changing the gear. He had learned to drive on a Mini, and all other cars thereafter had felt crowded in their interior – crowded by contrast with the bare-floored front of the Mini.

'Who was the man who invented the Mini?'

'Alex Issigonis,' she said without skipping a beat. It was one of the reasons she had done nearly as well as he had in exams, their eerie capacity to retrieve stored information.

His breathing slowed to near-normal in the aftermath of the answer, and he flexed his fingers to unclench them, waiting for her to fill the silence.

'How far is it gone?'

'Pretty far.'

'I figured it was hospital, not holidays. You always sent cards when you went on holidays.'

She passed the artic and he found he missed the little block of figures from its back. Tare something, it had said.

'How did you know?'

'I've always known.'

No, no, his commentator muttered. That wasn't what I was asking you. I was asking you how you knew I was sick, not how you knew I was gay.

'I wasn't good enough to be *told*, but I've always known.'

The bitterness of the reproach hung between them: unprecedented apostasy. The gentle collusion of long-accepted pretences bleached out in a headlong harshness. Feargal sat, mulled and dumb, no longer fearful of the road.

'I wasn't good enough to be *told*,' she repeated.

Feargal made a noise without meaning.

'I was too goddamn provincial and smalltown and *limited*, wasn't I? I mean, you always need someone to make the tea, but your only sister isn't good enough for anything more than making the tea.'

The car was now travelling so fast that even the soft sleety rain hitting the windscreen was splattering. Her hand slashed at the windscreen wiper wand and the wipers came on at their fastest speed, flailing at the spreading drops.

'*That* only happens in Dublin and London, dopes from our little neck of the woods wouldn't be able to cope with it. Wouldn't have the sensitivity. Wouldn't *realise*.'

The white letters on the speedometer indicative of one tenth of each mile traversed were leaping upwards in jerky movement, the black letters indicative of each complete mile moving more sedately. But not much more sedately. One mile. Another mile. A third mile passed. And another decision made itself for Feargal.

'I'm sorry,' he said.

First time in your life you've ever made an unconditional apology, his commentator observed, resuming its discourse without emotion. Up to now you've always hedged your bets with apologies. 'If you understood me to mean X, I'm sorry, I really meant Y.' That's the kind of apology you used to make. 'I'm sorry if I hurt you', you used to say. As if the hurt was a matter for debate and you were just issuing a credit note, drawn on your sensibilities, to cover all eventualities.

'I'm very sorry.'

The speedometer continued to chop up the miles.

'The day Roger died, I rang you. You were in Dublin, that time. This male voice answered and then you came on and Jesus, you started explaining him *away* . . . As if I *cared* . . . I rang you in desperation. My brother would know what to do. Roger was sitting with his legs crossed in the goddam deckchair, *dead*, and you're at the end of a telephone pretending to be not gay, I mean who gave a shit?'

'In the deckchair?'

'Mmm. Going out to tell him his tea was ready and he not moving. Not moving. And not knowing for sure, because the sun had kept him warm. Imagine that. The sun kept him warm. Thinking stupid things – like how could he die on me and me after putting scallions in his salad. Half the time I didn't put scallions in his salad because I didn't like the smell. How could he die on me withoug saying goodbye. I shouted at him. I begged him not to be dead. Anything for him not to be dead. I held his hand so tight I left these dents on it. But I couldn't *affect* him, you know?'

Feargal nodded, facing the road, not looking at her.

'It's surprising how few people you can ring up to say, "Would you mind taking over, my husband's just died in the deckchair."'

The sureness had been washed out of her voice by tears. Feargal gestured towards the hard shoulder

'Pull over. Go on, pull over.'

The car drifted, almost of its own volition, over the yellow line and onto the gravel of the hard shoulder. It moseyed aimlessly along the hard shoulder until he pulled up the handbreak and joggled the gearstick into neutral. She held the top of the steering wheel and her face went down on the back of her hands.

'Even the doctor. Hanrahan's locum. More or less said why was I bothering him. Obviously thought I should have said, "OK, Roger, you're dead, we'll get the police or the movers or somebody." I expected him to carry Roger in. I really did. But he didn't. It was important, to get him in. I was afraid flies would settle on him.'

It came out in a howl, and the weight of her head on her arms depressed the centre of the steering wheel, so that the horn bellowed too. Feargal tried to gently pull her off the wheel and onto his shoulder. She resisted fiercely.

'You came home for two days. Two days. You visited me like a stranger. I needed you to be my pal, my brother, my supporter, but you were so damn busy getting out and away and back to anonymity, you just left me alone, in the dark strung out between here and eternity with nothing but stale cake and the deckchair and the two little bewildered boys. You weighed me up against your privacy and you found me wanting. And you put it down to sensitivity.'

She leaned her hot face against the window beside her and cried as if Roger had died yesterday, not eight years before. Gradually the explosive sobs subsided.

'You know, someone brought over his clothes from the golf club. You know that? Dumped them out in the porch. So when I went out to put the milkbottles out, there they were, a pile of his clothes, not washed, smelling of him. Five weeks after he died.'

Passing juggernauts were rocking the car on its wheels. Feargal got out of his side and walked to the driver's door. Marion scrambled across the middle of the car and huddled in the passenger seat. He got in, fastened the seat-belt and made to put the key in the ignition. Glanced at her. Waited.

'I don't know how I knew you were sick. Or when. I just knew.'

'Me, too.'

'Sorry?'

'Before I had symptoms, I knew. One day, I just knew. The test was no surprise.'

'You're on millions of pills.'

It wasn't a question.

'Yes.'

'I've been reading up about it. Night sweats and stuff.'

'Why?'

'Why what?'

'Why would you be reading up about it?'

She looked at him as if the answer was so obvious that the question must be facetious.

'Because I'll have to look after you.'

He was suddenly furious.

'Says who, for fuck's sake?'

'Says me.'

It was said with such simplicity that a blanket of calm and inevitability fell.

Feargal looked out at the darkening sky. The rain had stopped. Except when the big lorries were passing, it was quiet. The inside of the car felt clammy to him.

'I'm good at it and you don't want to be among strangers. Among *professionals*.'

She's right, his commentator told him. Absolutely right. She's as strong as a little bull. With neither revulsion nor pride in the wiping and debriding. It must be done, therefore she must do it. That's the way it's always been. Duty follows her. She is someone to make the tea. Someone to manage the dying.

'Manage the dying,' he said aloud, and the terror washed in again, but at a lower level, like the incoming wave of a receding tide.

'Easier than Roger.'

'Because I'm not your husband?'

'No. Lord, no.' She was surprised. 'You'll be able to go through the rage and the fear and the pain and get through to a peaceful place where there's no hope. Not hurled into it like being driven into a wall.'

He considered this for a moment.

'You may be a natural nurse, but as a saleswoman you're crap, you know that?'

She laughed unsteadily.

'Don't discourage me. I'll have to sell it to Ma and Da in due course.'

He started the car and turned the lights on, moving off the hard shoulder and onto the main road again.

'D'you know what I'd like?' she asked. Her tone was back to normal.

"What would you like?'

'Chips. There's a takeaway in the next town.'

'You never lost it.'

'Nah. Everybody but me knows where pubs or churches are. Me, I know every chipper and Chinese in this country.'

He drove steadily and skilfully in the gathering darkness, watching for the bright red Coca Cola signs over the chip shop. Its window was sweated with condensation.

'What do you want?' She was rooting in her handbag for her purse.

'A single. No vinegar.'

'Rubbish. You need protein. You're having a burger.'

The door slammed behind her and she stumped into the shop.

It was ever thus, his commentator observed. Kindness and coercion. Blood brothers. Soul sisters.

He examined the proposition and was content with it.

THE WIDOW'S BOY

JULIA O'FAOLAIN

When her husband was reported missing on the Russian front, Nino's mother bore up and went to work to keep shoes on Nino's feet and bread in his mouth: two things which his father must have needed sorely at the end. Cardboard boots, according to what you heard now, were what the Italian soldiers had been issued. Boots of smartly blackened cardboard or, at best, stiffened felt which melted to nothing in the snow. Thin coats. Inadequate rations. Nino imagined his dying father losing his toes and gnawing thirstily at an icicle. The gnawing face was the one in the photo-portrait on his mother's dressing table because Nino could not be absolutely sure of how his father used to look.

For a while he had confused him with Jesus who, in *his* portrait, was suffering from severe blood-loss. Nino's grandmother begged Jesus to bring Nino's father home, but Nino reasoned that a man so afflicted could not be of much assistance – and was proven right when a letter came confirming his father's death.

His mother cried then and so did Nino, though his father was by now a mere smudge in his mind, fading along with Jesus who, said Gianni the cobbler, had been promoted by priests and Fascists to make us toe their line. "'Blessed are the poor in spirit",' sneered Gianni and added bits of mock-Latin, "'for theirs is the Kingdom of Heaven!" Thanks Lord, but we'd sooner have the Kingdom of Here. *Gratias agimus tibi*!' Maybe it was real Latin? Gianni had been to school to priests, though he was now a Communist and had heard Russian comrades confirm the story of the cardboard boots. The sign swinging over his shop was a golden boot and that too seemed like a confirmation. Nino ran messages for him, picking up worn shoes and delivering mended ones to customers who sometimes gave him a tip. Being a widow's boy had advantages.

It had drawbacks too though, and Nino wondered how their life might have been if his mother, instead of losing a husband, had lost a leg or been disfigured just enough for there to be no need to worry about her honour. As it was, she was the prettiest widow around — which was not the advantage you might think. Widows are fair game. Jokes about them made fellows leer and dig each other dreamily in the ribs while taking deep drags at forbidden cigarettes in the school bog. Girls, it seemed, were different. They were shy and if you went too far with one you had to marry her. But widows wanted it — whatever 'it' was. They longed for what they'd once enjoyed, and when Nino's father was freezing his arse in the Russian snows, his young wife had surely been suffering the fiery frustrations of passion in her lonely bed.

When the other kids talked this way their words had such a zing that Nino was ready to join in their secretive snigger and let himself dream of sinking into soft, embracing snow. Glittering, he thought. Gaudy. Like rainbows on ice. Then he remembered his mother looking tired in her cotton pinny and grew confused. He looked at the shoes which she had polished for him last night, after working a ten-hour day. Snows and fires were magic and so, it seemed, was the 'it' that everyone wanted. Well, let them find it in some other family, decided Nino, who should have put a stop to all this before.

'Alone, all alone in her feverish bed!' repeated his best mate, Pippo, who lived in the same *palazzo* and walked to and from school with him every day. 'That's if it *was* lonely and not occupied by some randy draft-dodger.'

And though he knew that Nino's mother lived a hard and blameless life, Pippo let blue cigarette smoke snake insinuatingly from his nostrils. He loved romancing and his older brothers had given him a taste for smut.

'Shut your face, moron!' Nino had to say then, though he knew Pippo would enjoy giving him a bloody nose which, sure enough, he did, for he was big for his age and his brothers had trained him to box. The worst of it was that, from then on, Nino's friends grinned whenever the word 'widow' was pronounced. Sometimes it was only the ghost of a grin – or maybe, as they claimed, Nino was imagining things, having grown suspicious and nervy like a scalded cat? What was undeniable was that the word 'widow' cropped up everywhere. In church the priest talked of the widow's mite, and at night in the piazza there was a drunk who sometimes started yelling that Italy had been widowed by the death of Mussolini and whose friends had regularly to make him pipe down. Then a poster for an operetta called *The Merry Widow* was put up all over town and it was months before the last copies were overlaid by electoral notices – 'Vote for La Pirra and De Gasperi!' – and by ads for films featuring Fabrizio, Totò and the alluring but worn-looking Anna Magnani. Maybe the reason she was so popular in those years was that she looked as if, like so many others, she had seen bad days but managed, pluckily, to survive. *She* looked like someone's widow – oh, why did he have to keep thinking of widows?

And why did he have to have a widowed mother? She was a good one in every other way: neat, sensible and not too strict, and her pasta was never mushy or underdone. Somehow, though, her niceness, like her prettiness, could be turned against her – *them*. As if it were bait.

'A nice Mamma you've got there!'

You could sift that for smutty meanings and, even if you didn't, the words twisted in your mind. 'Nice' how? In what way?

The most embarrassing thing happened in, of all places, the English-language class which the school had introduced because the British Institute was lending it a teacher with a pre-paid salary. He was Mr Williams, a lanky, long-haired man who read English poems aloud from a book. One was about a boy who worried about his mother. Mr Williams threw back his long hair and recited slowly so that the boys could study his accent.

'James James
Morrison Morrison
Weatherby George Dupree
Took great care of his Mother,
Though he was only three.'

The class fidgeted. The poem struck them as odd. Or silly? No:
odd.

'James James
Said to his Mother . . .'

Finding that his audience wasn't with him, Mr Williams switched
to a funny, fluting voice:

'Mother,' he said said he,
'You must never go down to the end of the town . . .'

Baffled, the class heard him out as he explained about the English
sense of humour. 'Come on,' he pleaded jovially, 'laugh, chaps! This
is a funny poem.' And read:

'James James
Morrison's mother
Put on a golden gown,
James James . . .'

As it dawned on them that the joke was about concern for a
mother's good name, the boys grew indignant. Good names were a
sore subject and had been so ever since the Fascists said we had
tarnished ours by betraying our German allies – only to be told that
Fascism was what had tarnished it. Either way, hard feelings were
hard to shake off, and of all people the English – who had egged on
the betrayal – should be treating us with kid gloves. Instead, here was
Mr Williams trampling on sacred values like motherhood and
committing *oltraggio alla patria*. An insult to the nation, a major
offence! The class looked ready to riot.

Then Pippo created a diversion. He explained why, for us, the
poem wasn't funny. 'Here,' he told the Englishman, 'if there's no
father, the son takes his place and if the boy is a widow's son like

Nino here, then . . .'

Pippo meant no harm. Intent on enlightening Mr Williams, he forgot his earlier teasing of Nino – who, however, did not. The poem had caught him on the raw and Pippo's words pricked and prodded at his mortification.

'If Nino's mother brought men to the house,' elaborated Pippo, 'or if she wore a golden gown and went . . .'

It was pedagogic. Pippo was enjoying teaching the teacher and Mr Williams was enjoying being taught. He smiled encouragingly at Pippo whose response – a raised eyebrow, the ghost of a grin? – caught the tormented Nino's eye and precipitated his attack. Hurling himself at his friend, Nino hammered his face with his fists. Pippo, after a stunned pause, drew back his own large fist and punched Nino – who was spindly with match-stick-legs and wrists – so hard that he fell backwards into a desk. Pippo then leaped on him, blacked one of his eyes and began pulling the noose of his tie so tight that he might have strangled him if Mr Williams had not pulled him off.

'You see,' Pippo taunted instructively. 'Widows' sons end up crazy. They have the worst of all bargains. They're like cuckolds who don't even enjoy what's on offer themselves!'

Again the maddened Nino lunged and again Pippo punched him. The *bidello* or school porter, a big, muscular fellow, had meanwhile been attracted by the noise and in two ticks cleared the room. Pippo was sent to the headmaster and, while the rest of the class went home, Mr Williams loosened Nino's tie, took him to the bathroom, washed his face and examined him to make sure he wasn't badly injured. Then he gave him a lift in his car to the nearest chemist's shop where the chemist, a friendly man, was just pulling down his shutters. He drew the two in, patched Nino up and produced brandy which Nino took for medicinal reasons and Mr Williams from good fellowship, and the upshot was that the two men took Nino home to his mother who, in gratitude for their concern, invited them to partake of a plate of pasta.

Afterwards Nino, packed off to bed and muzzy from the brandy, heard them singing as the chemist picked out a tune on Nino's father's old squeeze-box. Both he and Mr Williams liked opera and were soon talking of coming back on another evening with a guitar. Nino groaned from fear of scandal and of what the neighbours must think. Here was the widow entertaining not one man but two, while her guardian and chaperone — himself — was out of commission. This no one must ever know.

English class, after this, became a Purgatory. Mr Williams' marked friendliness towards himself was, Nino felt, compromising, but an outright coldness between them could, on the other hand, arouse worse gossip, since it was known — everything was — that Mr Williams and the chemist had been back twice to the house and that the two had taken Nino and his mother rowing on the Arno, followed by dinner at a trattoria.

He tried talking to his mother about the dubious propriety of this but she laughed, saying that there was safety in numbers and that the two men were lonely, living as they did in noisy boarding houses where they enjoyed no privacy and were fobbed off with coffee made from toasted barley and sauce made from offal. It was only Christian, she insisted, to make them welcome in her large, pleasant flat. In these tough times. Besides, they kicked in something to pay for the food. Then she pinched Nino's ear playfully and kissed the top of his head. She didn't take him — or life — seriously at all.

Some time after this she started travelling around Tuscany, selling cosmetics and doing demonstrations in small towns where ladies came to learn how to apply and remove make-up and to have massages and facials. She did this in *profumerie* and in the sort of small chemist's establishment which sold cosmetics as well as drugs. Maybe her friend the chemist had helped her get the job? She would, she explained, sometimes have to be away overnight and so Nino was going to have to stay with his grandmother. Yes, Nino, no arguments please. This was a promotion and we needed the money.

'I don't want to hear any more of your nonsense and I sincerely hope you'll give up fighting and settle down to your studies.'

Nino's grandmother lived a train-ride outside the city and it would have cost too much for him to travel back and forth to his old school, but luckily it was now the summer vacation and who knew what the autumn would bring? His mother hoped to get a job back in town before long.

Being with his grandmother wasn't all bad. It got him away from the treacherous Pippo, into whom he would otherwise have bumped every day in the lift and on their shared stairway. He spent the first weeks of his holiday reading and his mother came by every Sunday.

Then he and his grandmother had a tiff. She was stricter than his mother – more old-fashioned – and wouldn't let him go to the race track with some boys he had met. Nino decided to ask his mother for permission and, as his grandmother had no telephone, went out to ring from a café. There was no answer at first, but as it was still very early in the morning – he had got up specially – and his mother might still be asleep, he let the phone ring and ring. Finally someone picked it up. A man's voice spoke. It was Mr Williams'. 'Hullo,' it said, 'hullo. *Pronto.*'

Nino hung up and left the café. Without thinking, he headed for the station, took the first train which was full of commuters, dodged the ticket collector, and reached the city just about the time his mother usually left for work. When he reached her flat, though, his key didn't work. Someone inside had drawn the bolt and when he knocked they didn't open.

Walking like a sleep-walker – there was, he knew, no sense to what he was doing but he did it anyway as if he was a wind-up toy which someone had set in motion – he went downstairs and round to the back of the house, where he began to shin up the drainpipe which, three floors above, ran past the balcony of their flat. It was a mad thing to do. Useless. What did he want? A scandal? Or to show her that he couldn't be fooled? Just to show her. Just . . . No, it was crazy. Foolish! He was on the point of giving up when someone hailed him from the second-floor balcony. It was Pippo.

'Hullo. What are you doing?'

'I forgot my key,' Nino lied.

It was months since their fight and Nino found that he wasn't angry with Pippo any more. He was angry with *her*! Let Pippo see her, he thought furiously. Let everyone! Maybe that would teach her!

'I thought you were a burglar.'

'No.'

'Come in the front door,' invited Pippo. 'I'll let you in and you can climb up from here. We have a step ladder.'

Nino, not knowing what to say, let himself drop into the yard then, reluctantly, went round to the front and slowly up the stairs to Pippo's flat. This, he told himself, was a bad mistake. Maybe everyone in the palazzo knew already, and if they didn't, what was the point of his letting them know? Pippo must know. Maybe he, Nino, was peculiarly half-witted and lacking in common sense? Maybe he should turn around and take the train back to his grandmother's? By the time he reached Pippo's door he was crying and had smeared dirt from the drainpipe all over his face, though he didn't know this until Pippo commented on it.

'Your mother's not in,' said Pippo. 'The couple is, though. I think she lets them have the flat when she's away.'

'What . . . ' But he couldn't bring himself to ask. What couple? Who?

'Don't feel bad about it,' said Pippo unexpectedly. 'I think it's just from friendship. Not for money or anything. I don't think that. Nobody does. Your Mamma's just lonely. She likes the bit of music and their company.'

By now he had pushed Nino out onto the balcony and up the stepladder, so that he could see in the window to his own sitting room where Mr Williams and the chemist were naked as truth itself and lying in each other's arms.

HE LAY DOWN ON ME

JOHN JORDAN

On a fine Saturday morning in May, when students were released in flocks on St Stephen's Green and Grafton Street, hummingbirds, starlings, crows, a crow called Sean Mahony paid for a Peter Cheyney at the counter of Shay Adams. Shay said casually, 'Come up and see me some time.' It had been in the National School and Shay had passed Miss Mae West's invitation to Sean on a scrap of paper, which immediately Sean had brought to their teacher. The Master, sniffing moral turpitude, had, in his own words, knocked the hide off Shay.

Now Sean turned geranium. 'Ah, Jay, Shay, you don't still hold that against me?' His peaked face, still pimpled, cringed. And Shay remembered Sean reciting the parable of the Prodigal Son and how he convulsed the class when he came out with 'And he fell *into* his neck and kissed him.' Across the years that seemed so many but made barely a decade, the whoopings of small boys rose above the traffic in Dawson Street, and almost with love Shay said to Sean, 'No Sean, I don't of course. We were all eejits in those days.'

These days he would be at pains, usually, to say 'idiots.' Their juvenile vernacular would not go down well at the dinner-tables in Jammet's and the supper parties in County Dublin where his unpimpled face gained his access.

'Oh Jay, Shay, that's terrific. I could of wet me knickers when the Master . . .'

'Forget it,' Shay interrupted. The mood of love was passing.

'Say, why don't we go out and have a jar some night — just you and me, no mots — and we'll have a chat about oul times.'

'Well, I don't know . . .'

'Ah come on. You're only young once. What about tonight?'

Usually Shay spent Saturday nights in a pub that catered for a stew of actors and writers and painters, and professional men who paid for most of the drinks. Those soft-faced men who had done well out of the War paid in drink for the whiff of palette and greasepaint, and the odd, trite, literary allusion. He could not go there with Sean Mahony. He settled to meet him in a faceless lounge where Bohemia was an unknown country.

'Game ball,' said Sean, 'we'll have a rare old gosther.'

The lounge was full of young men who glittered with cigarette lighters and cases. When a light was offered with conjuror's dexterity, the recipient would say 'Terrific,' with intense admiration. If a case was flashed around, there would be cries of 'Signs on you' and 'Oh the hard men,' in unconvincing proletarian accents.

'Effin' young business-men,' said Sean, who had just failed Pre-Med.

'Well, they seem to be enjoying themselves.'

'Shaggin' messers.'

They were drinking rum-and-coke, just becoming fashionable, and it seemed to go to Sean's head very quickly, Shay thought, and he had a sigh for his usual Saturday night company, for even the blancmange-faced men who had done well out of the War.

'Ah Shay, do you remember Bill Maguire?'

'I think so.'

'I saw him the other night, drunk as a lord, friggin' pissed.'

'Is that so?'

'Yeah, he could hardly stand. I got him a taxi and — d'you know what? — he told me to eff off when I tried to help him in. Bloody alco if you ask me.'

'I didn't ask you.'

Across the years the whoopings of small boys rose above the roars of the young businessmen. Shay said, 'I'm sorry, I didn't mean that.'

'That's all right.'

'We all have our own problems.'

'Sure.'

'Same again?'

'Game ball.'

Six months after he'd left the National School, when he was working for an old woman who snoozed among empty sweet jars and fly-brown advertisements for plug tobacco, he had met Bill Maguire again. He remembered him from a year when Maguire came in as a relief teacher. And Maguire remembered him and tried to use him, Shay thought, as an excuse for wheedling cigarettes, still scarce at the end of the war.

'Only for regular customers.'

'No harm in trying. You're Adams, aren't you?'

'Yes.'

'Good name that. Ever hear of Nick Adams?'

'No.'

'Hemingway. Great stuff. Put hair on your chest. Well, *slán leat*.'

'*Slán leat*.'

A few months later when the old woman died and he had to quit the shop and was at a loose end, he met Maguire on Portobello Bridge. The week before he'd seen his picture in the *Evening Mail*: gallant rescuer of some kid who'd nearly drowned at Seapoint. A naked torso, fleshy and hairy, rose to a homely face with twinkling eyes and a rakish grin: the kind of face to be seen all over Dublin, devil-may-care, confidential, reassuring. Your father as you would like him to be. The kind of face to go with a man who would as well rescue cats from rooftops as kids from the sea.

At school Shay had sensed, and perhaps the other fellows too, that Bill Maguire was no great shakes as a teacher. There would come a time when he perceived that the heartiness and the dash camouflaged an uncertain rebel, the routine thorn in the flesh of clerical managers.

'It's young Adams isn't it?' boomed Maguire when they met on the bridge. And Shay answered 'Yes, sir,' as he had not done in the old woman's mouldering shop. Maguire leaned back against the balustrade in a familiar cruciform position and quizzed him with twinkling eyes.

'Ah well now, how are you gettin' on?'

'Well, sir, I'm out of work now.'

'That's tough now. How old is it you are?'

'Goin' on sixteen.'

'You should have gone on and done your Inter, yes, and, by God, your Leavin' too.'

A woman in a mackintosh stared back as Maguire's voice rose to a reverential shout.

'My father died.'

'Do you tell me that. I'm sorry to hear it. Yes. Still, you're a bright lad. You should get on.'

There seemed no more to say. But the man and the boy stayed on, in the dying amber light, Shay drawn uneasily by the quizzical twinkle and its message of comradeship. Maguire heaved himself straight. 'Come on,' he said. 'Come on up to the flat and we'll have a gosther about the old place.' Maguire had taught in Shay's school for less than a year.

'Thanks very much, sir, but I . . .'

'Oh I won't keep you late. I'm feeling in need of a bit of company tonight and you're a bright lad, Adams, a bright lad.'

He still hesitated. He had not forgotten the man who a little while before had approached him in Stephen's Green where he sat reading Dorothy L. Sayers.

'Ah yes, Lord Peter Wimsey. Do you not think he's a bit of a sissy?'

'I don't think so . . .'

And then in a rush the man, about Maguire's age, with un-twinkling eyes, asked, 'Did you ever read the beautiful sonnets of William Shakespeare?'

He said he had not and moved away when the man made to clamp his hand on his knee. Then the man got up quickly but walked slowly away. Shay had sat on and later wondered why he had felt both sad and afraid.

'All right, sir,' he said to Bill Maguire, 'I'll come up just for a bit.'

Maguire's bedsitter, which led to a kitchenette, smelt of tobacco, gas, stale stout, and the sea. He glimpsed bathing-trunks and a towel on a bracket of the sink in the kitchenette where Maguire made water without closing the door. The trunks were still dripping. Maguire must just have come from swimming, perhaps at Seapoint where the boy had nearly drowned. He was the kind of man, thought Shay, who would swim all the year round.

'Sit down now, sit down,' he said, fastening his fly. He turned on the light although the dusk was only beginning to shadow the unmade bed near the curtainless window, the hillock of dirty clothes at its foot, and the stacks of books on the floor. Shay had not ever seen so many books in one room.

He sat in a squeaky basket-chair by the gas-fire while Maguire sat on the bed and lit a pipe ritually.

'Pardon the mess,' he said, 'all bachelors are the same.' He scrabbled from his pocket a crushed packet of Drumheads.

'I don't smoke, sir.' He did not know why he lied.

'Would you take a bottle of stout?'

'I don't drink, sir.'

'Ah well you've plenty of time. And for the girls too.'

He was aware that Maguire, very softly, had passed wind. Soon he was puffing like a train, talking about someone called 'Prowst'.

'I'm gettin' through him at a fierce rate. Friend of mine in the Board of Works got me the ones that are banned. *The Cities of the*

Plain. Pretty hot stuff, mind you, but not dirt. I can't stand dirt.'

The monologue went on until after six bottles of stout Maguire had to go to the kitchenette. When he came back he plucked up a book and waving it at Shay said, 'I'll tell you what Prowst is about. Prowst is about memory. That's what he's about. *This* is what he is about.' And he began to read in a low tone, soft as butter:

'When to the sessions of sweet silent thought

I summon up remembrance of things past . . . '

By the time he had finished, Shay had forgotten the smell and the dirty linen at the foot of the bed, but when Maguire pronounced, 'Shakespeare's sonnets. Bloody great stuff,' with extreme unction, he remembered again Lord Peter Wimsey and Stephen's Green and the man with the twinkleless eyes and that strange mixture of fear and sadness . . .

'You read that grand, sir.'

'Do you think so? I always fancied myself as a bit of a reader. And man alive, for God's sake don't call me "sir". Why, you're as tall as I am. A skinny-melink, the same as meself at your age. But you'll fill out. What's this your first name is?'

His face had become rhubarb and he produced a Baby Power from under the bed.

'Shay they call me, sir.'

'Shay, Seamus, James, Jim. My own da was called Jim. Dead, poor man. And the mammy too, poor soul. And,' he sounded suddenly furious, 'for Christ's sake don't call me "sir". From now on it's "Bill" old son, make no mistake about it.'

Maguire became his tutor in books. Much later he discovered that his flatulent tutor was not quite literate in some departments. Yeats was 'Yeets' and Synge was 'Singe', just as Proust was 'Prowst'. But he was generous with his books, many of which he had borrowed from shadowy friends in the Board of Works and the Electricity Supply Board and the Gas Company. Twice a week for months and months of stout and gas and often the canal scaly from the moon, Shay would come to return the books and listen to the monologues of Maguire as he smoked his pipe and drank stout and every so often, very softly, passed wind.

On a Saturday evening in late September, just after he'd started in the bookshop, at thirty shillings a week, on the recommendation of the PP who'd met him reading in the street — it was, fortunately, *Great Expectations* — Shay arrived later than usual at Maguire's. He'd been caught in the Saturday night Confession rush at the Carmelite Church in Whitefriar Street, where the confessionals had popular appeal because of their absolute darkness and the confessors because of their supposed leniency. At last his turn had come . . .

'Anything else my child?'

'I read a bad book . . . and . . . ' The sticky euphemisms came out.

'Say three Hail Marys, especially for the grace of Purity, and try to avoid that kind of book.' He had said his penance lightly but went through the Hail Marys a dozen times in an effort at concentration. He might have been atoning for, not himself alone, but for Maguire, dispenser of 'the bad book' that had provoked his seed at a café-table in Grafton Street.

He had in the end crossed himself quickly, just avoiding the scrabble between the breasts common among the most devout of his contemporaries, genuflected in a scurry, by-passed the green-bottomed font where Holy Water looked like the water of the canal untouched by the moon, and rushed to meet Maguire, clutching *Appointment in Samarra,* Sartre's *The Age of Reason* and a selection of Lorca's poems in translation. John O'Hara, Jean-Paul, and Federico, had been with him to Confession.

The lounge had become a strident gabble. The young businessmen had become either boisterous or maudlin and had to be restrained from singing. When Shay went to the lavatory one of them was getting sick with the help of another who assured him that once he'd got it all up he'd feel better. 'Me tie,' said the sick one, 'me tie,' he moaned, 'I got it at Christmas from the ma.'

Back in the lounge, Shay asked suddenly, 'Was Bill Maguire very bad?'

'Jaysus, Shay, I told you, he was footless.'

'Was he . . . shabby?'

'Well it was dark and I didn't notice. Anyway, he's only an effin' messer.'

'I suppose so.'

That Saturday night three years ago when he arrived late at Maguire's, his load of culture like a baby in his arms, there was no answer to his bell. But there was a light in his curtainless window. After five minutes' ringing, the hall-door was opened. It was a woman.

'He's not in,' she snapped.

'Well, will you tell him Shay Adams called?'

She swung the door wide open and in the weak electric light he had a full view of her. She was a kind of woman he'd read about in books: uncertain age, frizzed and peroxided hair, unnaturally white teeth, cruddled make-up.

'Are you a friend of him?'

'Well, yes.'

'So that's it,' she said, viciously, 'that's why he upped and left me waitin' upstairs in that kip of his for four hours. It's the like of you he wants.'

Suddenly she became agreeable.

'Why don't you come up and have a dropeen with me? He *might* come back yet, the dirty scut.'

She laughed, almost girlishly.

'Fancy a great big fella like that after the likes of you.'

She was already half-way up the stairs, laughing joyously and he followed her, fascinated, only dimly sensing the cause of her brazen ascending trills.

The first thing he noticed in the room was that the bed had been made and the grimy sheets turned over.

'Yes,' she said. 'You can keep on lookin'. We didn't even get into it. Don Jew-an with no knackers, that's him. Have a drink?'

She poured from one of a row of spirit bottles on the mantelpiece.

'I declare to me Aunt Fanny fellas like that should be locked up. Bringing home decent workin' girls and then runnin' out to the bar he says and not comin' back and me without a make in me pocket.'

She gulped whiskey. 'But out of here I shall not move' (she had become ladylike) 'until he returns and gives me my due.'

She swallowed more whiskey and her mood changed again.

'I mean . . . he will come back, won't he? I mean he has to. He lives here doesn't he?'

She began to cry and was very ugly.

'Tell me he'll come back. You look like a nice lad, not one of them pansies on the quays. Tell me he'll come back.'

He was addled by the unaccustomed whiskey. He heard her story, in a half-dream. And then she suggested he go with her under the grimy sheets. She'd make a man out of him . . . And he might have gone if the bell hadn't rung.

'You go,' she said. 'I must be a sight.' In thick whiskey tenderness he said, 'Oh no. You are lovely.'

The bell rang again and he half-lurched downstairs to the door. When he opened it, Maguire fell in and Shay almost missed seeing in the shadows a little man who piped out indignantly, 'I'm the driver and he owes me a quid. I'd the divil and all tryin' to get him out of the car and then, d'you know what, he lay down on me.'

'He what?'

'He lay down on me. A big slob like that. Couldn't budge him.'

Shay turned Maguire and managed to get a pound from his

pocket. His shirt was open on that naked torso, fleshy and hairy, he had first seen in the pages of the *Evening Mail*.

'Here you are,' he told the taximan, who went away still muttering about how Maguire had lain down on him. By this time the woman – she said her name was Daphne – was swaying down the stairs.

'Oh the beast,' she said. 'The dirty beast.'

Together they got Maguire to his feet and propped him up the stairs. Instinctively, eyeless among his books, his own and those borrowed from the faceless men in the Board of Works and the Electricity Supply Board and the Gas Company, he reeled to the bed. Once he opened his eyes wide, and took in Shay and the woman. He went asleep as the gas-fire popped out. When she thought it safe, the woman extracted three pound notes from his pocket.

'Three feckin' notes,' said Daphne, and ladylike again, 'After all I've been through!'

She powdered her nose, repaired her mouth, and put on a sad fur-coat. She drank another whiskey and looked pityingly at Shay.

'Go home, sonny, to your ma,' she said and left him with Maguire.

The big man tossed about and once extended a craggy hand. 'When to the sessions,' he choked out. 'Don't mind that bitch, old son, come here.'

Shay left, putting out the light.

Shay and Sean stood together outside the emptying pub. The centre of the city was still booming with traffic and spangled with neon.

'Well,' said Sean. 'How about a chipper?'

'I think I'll catch the bus if you don't mind. We've had a busy week at the shop.'

'Sure, sure. But we must have another night soon. It's great to have a gosther about old times.'

'Well, so long.'

Standing in the bus queue, Shay wondered if he would ever see Mahony again, the first in three years to name his flatulent mentor. Where was Maguire now? With shadowy friends from the Board of Works or the Electricity Supply Board or the Gas Company? All men, no doubt, who had got their Leaving Certificate, perhaps even taken university degrees since they read Proust and the like. Did these men go with women like Daphne? Women who wore sad fur-coats and had false pearly teeth and who when they cried were very ugly?

Next Saturday night he would be back among the actors and the painters and the writers and the pudding-face professional men who would never need to lie down on diminutive taxi-drivers.

OPENING NIGHT

RITA KELLY

E mily arranged everything. It suited her fluid programme,
rehearsals, costume-fittings, previews and the press. They
would open on Tuesday; something new from one of the more
traditional dramatists, she didn't comment, never does in fact, a
breach of integrity. Just the ticket, *G One*, on the edge as usual,
and a hurried note on the back of a disappointing reproduction
of the *Duchess of Cumberland*!

> Anne, I've been missing you so much. I've booked a
> room for Opening Night, about an hour's drive,
> nicely situated. Why not come to Dress, it's been so
> long, we could have supper out and . . . but it's so
> difficult to drag you away from your hermitage. Hope
> you got my letter. I took the train back from Leitrim,
> frightful journey, were it not for your absorbing letter
> I should have found it interminable. In case you
> don't make it to Dress — sorry for being impatient,
> but I do look forward — wear the amethyst pendant
> and when I give the coiffure (wait until you see it!)
> two pats you'll know that I've seen you. Hurry love.
> The rest I shall whisper as we overcome the vast
> waste of the night. As always.

Anne read it again before the mirror, smiled and took the
pendant from her jewellery-box. Turning the card in her hand,
she paused. Certainly disappointing, too pale. The colour drained
out of the face, then the character gone too. An indelicate process,
only a ghost of the original. Curious lack of taste or she must
have been hurried.

Her hair had lengthened nicely. Keep it to the shoulders,

nothing dramatic. A ray of sunshine lightened the dark mass. She needed some sun to improve her own colouring, but later. As yet there were only the first stirrings of spring. Through her window the bare fruit-trees, the tired and ragged grass. Only the primulas, glowing by the road wall, tough and tender. Thin branches, twigs and twitter against the blue washed reaches of the sky. A tractor with a wake of gulls crossed and recrossed the elevated distance. Linear equations, slowly and steadily plotted; the crust torn and the soil exposed.

She returned to her eye make-up. An interest in appearance because of Emily. Despite the three years, it was still incredible that beyond this stretch of land fingering the foothills, there was someone locked in the rush of her own life but needing Anne as no one ever needed her before.

Some gift for Emily. Something pertinent? The little urn, the first satisfactory piece she had succeeded in doing from the local clay, gleaned from the riverbed. Emily would like it. But it looked bare, of course. She was on her knees digging up a bunch of primulas. She set them in the urn, tucking the roots in beneath a layer of moss. The clay clung to her fingers, cold.

The foyer was filling, the usual first-night faces and furs. A hum of animated conversation, chocolates, cigars, perfumes. Men making themselves busy about little nothings: 'Your programme, dear, your coat, shall I order coffee or would you prefer . . . ' Nice people all of them, come in out of the dark and so aware of their accessories.

Anne was glad to have missed dress rehearsal; the tension, stagehands shouting abuse at the lightsmen, the ASM arguing about cues in a nervously adamant tone and the director abusing and loving everyone simultaneously!

'Dress that bed, you charming imbecile. Hold everything, we'll take that again starting with Phillip at the window. What's that bitch doing? Send her back in here. Hurry darling or this shower will want time-and-a-half.'

A fissure in the crowd, the dramatist, his wife, little whispers and barely-held elbowings.

'It's him.' That light in their eyes, liquid, looking on fame and hoping that some tiny shred might come their way dispelling the drab. The welcoming party, loud kissings.

'Darling, you've come. Allow me. Nice house. Booked out for the week in fact. Everything *en train* for the London production. Wish me luck, you ravishing creature.' And there is a gentle surge in the wake of the dramatist's group.

'Good evening, Miss Browne. *G One*, she's expecting you. Enjoy the show.' Anne took her seat, pleased yet again by the particular atmosphere, the movement, the continuing conversations a little muted now; soft house-lights, wafts of warm air, scent, colour and glitter. She felt herself part of a gathering excitement, little flutterings and tensions of muscle, a flush beneath the make-up, internal secretions which seemed to run the length of her body causing a slight shiver. Emily would have the primulas by now, they survived the journey well, and enhanced the urn. She will leave them before her in the dressing-room, the dressers in ecstasy.

'Aren't they gorgeous.'

Anne had a sudden fear. Perhaps there was a taboo about uncut flowers in the theatre. Difficult to remember all the taboos but it was too late now. A group passed in by her, one of the disadvantages of an end-seat. As the house-lights dimmed, an usherette came with a package. A smile, nothing more, and in the reflected stage-light Anne extracted a crimson rose from its wrappings.

A heavy, drawing-room set. Even the opening dialogue sounded rather cocktail partyesque. Emily is on, in evening dress, green velvet, delightfully cut, the blonde wig, such a transformation. She quickly gives the wig two pats. Can she possibly have seen? But she must. That imperceptible quickness, part of the long experience. In spite of the secret sign Anne begins to doubt, is it really her, the Emily she knows intimately, and has held to her, nestling against the night and letting the outside world slip behind the curtains. No, it can't be and yet underneath that strange persona lurks the real Emily; the thin shoulders, and the tired girl wrapt in sleep long after dawn. She catches it in the eyes, the tone of voice, the features in certain poises, certain movements and gestures. But the effect is rather disturbing as if the real person were constrained beneath the wig, behind the mask and speech.

Anne sees less and less of the play, only Emily, hears her only. She has leaned forward in her seat without being aware of it as if to catch every syllable, every nuance, more clearly. She feels herself inundated by the complexity of the real person seeping through the character as if she were playing to Anne alone. Not knowingly, because Emily keeps insisting that the actress forgets, forgets everything but her part. *Methinks the Lady doth protest too much.* Even when she exits, her sparkling presence haunts the retinae and all the senses; a piquant afterglow.

The drama dives into some deep recess. Night, scant scene, scant costume. A sudden stillness as if the audience were holding their breath. Strange and subtle lighting. Emily sits, stylised foot-position, layers of chiffon trailing gracefully from the thigh. The breasts are draped but the light catches the pale cleft. A certain intimacy, some melting of the mask perhaps.

The house-lights are up. The audience stirs itself into motion and speech, a little unsteady, a little brittle. Anne rises and allows herself to be floated towards the exit. The slight pressure of bodies against her, polite society, so close and so utterly distant.

She takes her coffee to a corner and fingers through the programme. It gives colourful biographical details, previous parts. Again another Emily, the conscious photograph. The ghost of her intrinsic charm under the professional gloss. *Déjà vu.* Already dead. She opens her handbag. The rose lies in its white wrappings.

Its sharp sweetness pervades her, slightly intoxicating. A bell sounds calling her back. Cups and glasses are quickly abandoned. Seats regained. Shreds of speech hang in the moment of dipped lights before the curtain slides soundlessly back.

Anne dreams through the final act. The central conflict is passed and the extended solution is set in motion. The pieces fitted together and the action comes full circle. But something has been glimpsed, changed. Minute gestures have become enriched and ambiguous; haunting. Already seen and not seen, already buried. Emily's eyes are on her as she takes the final bow. The light is savagely extinguished. The face fades, glowing. The dark engulfs it.

She moves out in a daze, clear only about getting to the stage-door on time. People are slow to leave, feeling that all has not been seen, some reluctance to reassume the cold night air outside.

The figure comes from the stage-door to the first pool of light. Anne stops. How very ordinary it is. How gaunt, the hair short and ruffled. She moves from under the lamp and they meet in the half-light. A quick kiss, a long and anxious embrace, a smell of cleansing cream.

'The car is close by. Want to drive?'

'No Anne, you do. I just want to . . . watch you.'

'All right.'

They edge into the traffic and jerk from lights to lights, accepting the delay with badinage, pretending that there is no hurry to be out of it and away from the throbbing of other people's engines.

'I like the coat. Mock mink?'

'How can you, Anne, I had to succumb to TV ads to make the final payments.'

'You didn't, I thought . . .'

'Well, it's only voice-over, and one long-distance shot, you'll never see it anyway.'

'But that's not the point.'

'Of course it is.'

'What was it, underwear?'

'Nothing as scintillating as that, pain-relievers.'

'Really Emily, did you have to?'

'Darling . . . Forgive me, I know you hate the epithet. It slipped, but is it any wonder? A whole month without seeing you. It's so easy to adopt the tone when you're not about.'

'Next thing you'll have the junior lead losing a night's sleep over you.'

'That's about it; a night, nothing more. Things scarcely run that deep, though she is rather . . . '

'Yes?'

'Thought that'd move you.'

'Think I don't know what goes on? It becomes a habit, you can turn it on without thinking.'

'Not my line, Anne. Might be in a few years perhaps when she finally discovers her part. At the moment she is annoyingly transparent.'

'No defences?'

'No, and damn little to defend.'

'Therefore she's got the makings of a good actress, the negative capability and all that.'

'I don't like the implications. Besides, I think that is a common fallacy, as if we were all devoid of personality, blank, empty vessels through which the character might sound.'

'But you must allow, Emily, that some of them come rather close to that definition.'

'So hard to be certain. You've got to keep covering your tracks in this game; it becomes part of the propulsion after the initial years. However, Anne, it's to get away from all that I've booked this room.' And a hand reaches across the gear lever finding Anne's chill fingers. The lights etiolate and the city becomes scant. They climb steadily up the dark shoulder, spiralling about the overhang. There are glimpses of the spread of lights below; some dominant and some winking in the further distance. Clouds carry the glow. Hardly clouds, but a bright effulgence of light. A dreamscape; some glimmering nook of stageland that the sudden flick of a switch might black out.

Emily looks straight ahead following the lit road, a beam pushing its way through high hedges. Her face is grey and drained in the diffuse interior, softened profile, increased shadows. Above the mink collar, protectively rolled up, a few wisps glisten.

Something dashes across the road, a rat, a hare? Emily gasps:

'Did you kill it?'

'No, it just escaped.'

'Poor little bastard.'

A tension in the voice, or was there? Anne could not be certain.

Strangely, in the driving-mirror there appear hints of pale light, as if they were being pursued. Anne blinks and looks in the mirror again but the lights have disappeared, or have they? Dare not look again, perhaps it is a car in the distance, its stray beams, yet nothing solid comes, no further brightness. Out of the corner of her eye the little hints are there again. She feels her body stiffen as if there were something on the back seat; that close. Not just way back in the miles of dark, but immediately behind. Did she feel a breathing at her back?

'Tired Anne?'

'No, no — just a little bleary.'

The road, it must be concentrated upon, passed under arched trees, beech, the distinctive bark, and an undergrowth of richly browned leaves. Bare, thick trunks passing the light from one to the other; regular plantation. The white line comes in bits out of the gloom at the end of the light's range and is sucked under the car with hypnotic regularity and speed. Miles and miles of it.

Something uneasy about the silence, Emily resting her voice, of course, which she can do so unobtrusively. But she seemed so often on the point of speaking, and then all was shuttered. On quickly glancing across, Anne catches a hint of the stage-persona, breathing and rocking with the motion, slight and fleeting, and glancing again it is gone.

'You got my letter?'

'Yes, Emily. Why?'

'Nothing, just wondered.'

'You went down for the funeral.'

'Yes. Strange going back, pretending that the years haven't passed.'

'I know.'

'All those people expecting to be remembered and known. Though I don't know them and I never shall. It means nothing, "I'm John, mother often talks about you, saw you on television." Then you glimpse his mother across the room. Yes, you remember her; long-legged, cycling in from the country with eggs. And the woman across the room, her face a little puffy, is as distant from you now as that carefree girl on the bicycle.'

'But Emily, imagine how it feels for them. They, I imagine, regard you as someone very much out of the usual. They cherish glimpses of you at weddings and funerals. They remember the chocolates you brought to the children years ago and probably still keep needles and thread in the box.'

'Anne, you don't think they'd hoard an empty box, for goodness sake. If that's all one is allowed . . .'

'You're not allowing them very much else, are you?'

'Whose side are you on anyway?'

'And the flurry in some kitchen in Leitrim as they drop everything and gather around in an excited silence to watch you sell some useless pain-reliever.'

'I could be selling dope for all they'd care.'

'Yes you could. Because all they care about is that you're one of them, who has escaped the kitchen and the swamp of fields and the brown mud which clings to your shoes, all that, and yet you appear in it, sound through it, some rain-soaked night, bright and bedazzling.'

'"Tense, nervous headache . . . we have developed a formula . . ."'

'Sure we have. And that's all you've got to say to them.'

'And what would you have me say, "Sorry for your trouble"?'

'Emily, "The hungry sheep look up and are not fed".'

The conversation is ripped asunder by the rattle of wheels on a grid. Two white eagles face each other on the piers. Their car lights are reflected in the black windows of the gate-lodge. An undulating park, rich verdure. The car swings about the bends creating groves of trees, picking them out of the dark. A moment, and they have suddenly receded. A bank of reeds, lit and swaying. A glint of wave. All planned and landscaped to enhance the approach to the country-seat – time slips back, a barouche, horses' hooves, hair-pieces, whalebone corsets and the cold.

'Anne, I'm sure you're surprised that I went at all.'

'Yes. Where?'

'The funeral. She was an unusual person, odd, independent; father's sister. Some little mystery, her years in New York.'

'Did you know her well?'

'Not very. A feeling of difference. A certain fear, a fascination.'

A flood-lit entrance, an expanse of grey wall broken by granite-cased windows. Arrow-slits and castellations.

A porter opens a heavy door on ornate hinges. There is a gleam of granite in the door-surround. Cumbersome aperture. He will show them to their room and bring supper presently. Anne notes the empty reception area, no one, dimly lit, the unexpected at the foot of the stairway, a suit of armour, the grotesque helmet where the face should be. Sounds reverberate off the stolid walls and high ceilings. They find themselves in a bare stone silence.

In the hall an immense arched fireplace — hogs on spits, glowing hot claret, hunts — now black with old-fashioned cooking utensils grouped about the gate. Weapons hanging idle on the walls, heavy, wide-blade swords, rapiers, maces, lances. A glittering confusion of period; all relics of man's unmannerly, bloody make-believe.

The porter, slouched a little, leads to the deep-set carved door of the bedroom. Inside a cheerful log-fire; red the dominant colour. Twin beds of generous proportion. A quick glance from Emily behind the porter's back as he begins to fuss about the fire, enough logs for the night. She thanks him profusely and gently hurries him to the door. The stone silence and the armoury is closed out. They draw towards each other, finding each other in a long-awaited embrace. Lips seek lips. Emily breaks away in banter.

'I had to ask for twin beds, hoping that we might get something medieval. Well, not too bad are they?'

'What shall we do? Divide the night between the two so as not to upset the chambermaid?'

'Anne dear, you know the routine. Though I might choose to have a headache, the *noli me tangere* tactic.'

'But, we have developed a formula, have we not?'

'Think I'll have a bath. Or shall I wait until after supper? My feet are killing me.' She kicks off her shoes and throws the mink coat across a chair, a slim woman, ageing. Anne saw her, gone now the layers of chiffon, the stylised foot-position not needed. Anne lights the bedside-lamps and turns off the centre chandelier. Easier to bear the lesser light.

'Perhaps you should go straight to bed, Emily, and have supper there.'

'And you can tell me a story and tuck me in. "Last thing at night before we go to bed, Mum tells stories out of her head." Big, bloody thrill.'

'But you look tired, and besides . . . '

'Besides you're beginning to sound like old Warren at the Academy, ever tell you about her? "Allow me to impress upon you, young ladies, the importance of a good night's sleep, the organs of speech require adequate rest. And as to the intercostal diaphragmatic muscles . . ." Never mind. We grow old, we grow old.'

'You know that I didn't mean.'

'Of course you didn't, Anne, you never overstate the obvious.'

Emily strides about the room, stops before the mirror, regards herself wryly, pulls a face and turns abruptly.

'Just look, wrinkles, bags under the eyes, the lot. *That this too too solid flesh* . . . Without a face-lift I had better get myself to a nunnery or else be cast to mother a generation of Whiteheaded Boys. "A great manager she is. Such a pleasant way with her, not what you'd call a clever woman, hasn't got the book-knowledge. But she's a simple decent woman and what more do you want?"'

'And pray what role is this?'

'Want a drink? They've sent up our favourite fifteen year-old.'

'But there will be wine with the supper.'

'I know Anne. I just want a drink; opening night after all. A celebration of some kind is the custom. Besides, there might not be many more.'

'Bad casting, Emily, self-pity not quite your line.'

'Sorry love for being a nag. It's wretched of me. Come, tell me I'm forgiven.'

A knock upon the door draws them apart quickly. The porter enters, places the tray and withdraws, wishing them comfort in their sleep. Anne goes to the tray. It has been a long day since rooting up the primulas. She picks at things, prawns, chicken, french bread, camembert. She smiles, examining the wine.

'You don't forget, do you, Emily?'

'Can't afford to in my business.'

Anne quickly undresses at the bed. Emily is about to pour some whiskey but catches Anne's eye in the mirror and recaps the bottle. Anne goes towards the fire in a long pink nightgown, stretches along the rug, waiting for Emily to come and have supper. Firelight flickers in the brass fender. Above the mantelpiece, an eighteenth century portrait, a lady in riding habit, weighed down by the clothes and the heavy technique. Something pathetic in the pallor and in the attempt to look the part.

Emily comes in a satin peignoir and sits in an armchair. She has regained her panache, mastering the garment, aware of her place in the set which a slight relaxing of muscle might distort. They help each other to supper; Anne rests her back against Emily's knees, asking, 'Are you comfortable?' Between sips of wine, Emily nods her head. And they accept the silence. Only the timber sounds as it shrinks and burns apart or a gust of wind whirling in the chimney. The thick walls; an encapsulation. Nothing can penetrate to them but the ghost of a wind. It seems an age since they left the city and throb of theatre. It has become the dream that it is, this moment, this strange room on loan against the night, the only reality.

As it was on loan to all those pale people in riding habits through the ages; relaxed and insulated for a time, ready with cross-bow or sword to protect, defend. The unpredictable hordes which might form themselves on the nearest hill or come like spectres from among the trees, trampling the rich lawns. The eternal struggle of keeping the mystery at a distance.

'May I pour you a whiskey, Anne?'

'Please, and water . . . all right, I'll fetch it. Emily, why are you putting on more logs? We'll be in bed soon and it's not really cold.'

'Just . . . I hate to see it go down.'

'I'll never get through all that whiskey.'

'Course you will, Anne. Then we'll go to bed.'

'Promise?'

'Now you are being childish.'

'I don't mind if you're prepared to mother me.'

Anne's hair is tossed in an affectionate way and she leans back to see Emily's face, something unexpectedly remote in her gaze, as if her thoughts were elsewhere and the affectionate gesture merely automatic.

'Emily, forgive the reversion.'

'Nothing to forgive, love. It's one of your charms. I was thinking of you, alone in that isolated little house.'

'But you're equally as isolated in your flat.'

'It's not the same, I mean . . .'

'We have discussed it before, Emily, and you know that I'm not ready to move in with you.'

'You misunderstand me. I know perfectly well what the flat would do to you from day to day, and it's not even practical.'

'Then what is it, Emily?'

'Well, I was thinking of moving down with you.'

'Are you mad?'

'No, not yet at least. Give it all up, I'll have to sometime so why not now? I could, I'm sure, find work locally if speech and drama hasn't become extinct in our schools. And you could continue with your pottery.'

'It's not that. You know that I should so love to have you, but you can't after all the years it has taken, just throw it there and bury yourself in isolation. And you'd need to be a lion-tamer to deal with the classroom. I should feel that it was my fault, that you were doing it because of me.'

'Anne, what's wrong with that? Have I ever had such a positive and attractive reason for doing anything before?'

'But you mustn't begin to think like that for years.'

'How long do you think an actress's career lasts?'

'As long as she wants it to last.'

'Anne, what's the point in waiting for years, old age, blindness and an interminable fatigue? What matters then but the urge to stay warm, keep the blood circulating through tired veins, rave about the past and pretend not to be waiting for death?'

'Emily!'

'I mean it. When I think of my aunt, all those years alone . . . odd how one is inclined to feel suddenly close to someone hardly known.'

'Perhaps a touch of guilt for seeming to neglect them.'

'No, what could I have done? Besides, she would scarcely have welcomed the intrusion.'

'But can you be so certain, Emily? Perhaps the aloneness was a defence, a way of disguising a real need.'

'Yet to have ended in such a way —'

'Emily, it's inevitable. At least she died in her own house.'

'That's precisely it.'

Emily had slid down onto the rug and crouched. Arms about her knees, she stares into the fireplace, now a heap of glowing embers. She rocks herself slightly, backwards and forwards, muttering.

'"A heap of turf against the wall . . . oh, to have a little house, to own the hearth and stool and all . . ." Utter nonsense.'

'At least you'd be out of the wind's and the rain's way.'

'But it's so pretty, so . . .'

'It has its place, surely!'

'But it makes no allowance for the . . .'

'For the what, Emily?'

'For the absolute mess of things. For the stink and the savagery. For . . . Anne, the rats got in . . . her face . . . until the bone showed through . . .'

The body convulsed. Anne holds it close to her and feels the breasts tremble under the skin of satin.

TORRIDGE

WILLIAM TREVOR

Perhaps nobody ever did wonder what Torridge would be
like as a man — or what Wiltshire or Mace-Hamilton or
Arrowsmith would be like, come to that. Torridge at thirteen had
a face with a pudding look, matching the sound of his name. He
had small eyes and short hair like a mouse's. Within the collar of
his grey regulation shirt the knot of his House tie was formed
with care, a maroon triangle of just the right shape and bulk. His
black shoes were always shiny.

Torridge was unique in some way: perhaps only because he
was beyond the pale and appeared, irritatingly, to be unaware of
it. He wasn't good at games and had difficulty in understanding
what was being explained in the classroom. He would sit there
frowning, half smiling, his head a little to one side. Occasionally
he would ask some question that caused an outburst of groaning.
His smile would increase then. He would glance around the
classroom, not flustered or embarrassed in the least, seeming to
be pleased that he had caused such a response. He was naïve to
the point where it was hard to believe he wasn't pretending, but
his naïveté was real and was in time universally recognised as
such. A master called Buller Yeats reserved his cruellest shafts of
scorn for it, sighing whenever his eyes chanced to fall on Torridge,
pretending to believe his name was Porridge.

Of the same age as Torridge, but similar in no other way, were
Wiltshire, Mace-Hamilton and Arrowsmith. All three of them were
blond-haired and thin, with a common sharpness about their
features. They wore, untidily, the same clothes as Torridge, their
House ties knotted any old how, the laces in their scuffed shoes
often tied in several places. They excelled at different games and

were quick to sense what was what. Attractive boys, adults had more than once called them.

The friendship among the three of them developed because, in a way, Torridge was what he was. From the first time they were aware of him – on the first night of their first term – he appeared to be special. In the darkness after lights-out someone was trying not to sob and Torridge's voice was piping away, not homesick in the least. His father had a button business was what he was saying: he'd probably be going into the button business himself. In the morning he was identified, a boy in red and blue striped pyjamas, still chattering in the wash-room. 'What's your father do, Torridge?' Arrowsmith asked at breakfast, and that was the beginning. 'Dad's in the button business,' Torridge beamingly replied. 'Torridge's, you know.' But no one did know.

He didn't, as other new boys, make a particular friend. For a while he attached himself to a small gang of homesick boys who had only their malady in common, but after a time this gang broke up and Torridge found himself on his own, though it seemed quite happily so. He was often to be found in the room of the kindly housemaster of Junior House, an ageing white-haired figure called Old Frosty, who listened sympathetically to complaints of injustice at the hands of other masters, always ready to agree that the world was a hard place. 'You should hear Buller Yeats on Torridge, sir,' Wiltshire used to say in Torridge's presence. 'You'd think Torridge had no feelings, sir.' Old Frosty would reply that Buller Yeats was a frightful man. 'Take no notice, Torridge,' he'd add in his kindly voice, and Torridge would smile, making it clear that he didn't mind in the least what Buller Yeats said. 'Torridge knows true happiness,' a new young master, known as Mad Wallace, said in an unguarded moment one day, a remark which caused immediate uproar in a Geography class. It was afterwards much repeated, like 'Dad's in the button business' and 'Torridge's, you know.' The true happiness of Torridge became a joke, the particular property of Wiltshire and Mace-Hamilton and Arrow-smith. Furthering the joke, they claimed that knowing Torridge was a rare experience, that the private realm of his innocence and his happiness was even exotic. Wiltshire insisted that one day the school would be proud of him. The joke was worked to death.

At the school it was the habit of certain senior boys to 'take an interest in' juniors. This varied from glances and smiles across the dining-hall to written invitations to meet in some secluded spot at a stated time. Friendships, taking a variety of forms, were then initiated. It was flattering, and very often a temporary antidote for homesickness, when a new boy received the agreeable but bewildering attentions of an important fifth-former. A meeting behind Chapel led to the negotiating of a barbed-wire fence on a slope of gorse bushes, the older boy solicitous and knowledgeable. There were well-trodden paths and nooks among the gorse where smoking could take place with comparative safety. Farther afield, in the hills, there were crude shelters composed of stones and corrugated iron. Here, too, the emphasis was on smoking and romance.

New boys very soon became aware of the nature of older boys' interest in them. The flattery changed its shape, an adjustment was made – or the new boys retreated in panic from this area of school life. Andrews and Butler, Webb and Mace-Hamilton, Dillon and Pratt, Tothill and Goldfish Stewart, Good and Wiltshire, Sainsbury Major and Arrowsmith, Brewitt and King: the liaisons were renowned, the combinations of names sometimes seeming like a music-hall turn, a soft-shoe shuffle of entangled hearts. There was faithlessness, too: the Honourable Anthony Swain made the rounds of the senior boys, a fickle and tartish *bijou*, desired and yet despised.

Torridge's puddingy appearance did not suggest that he had *bijou* qualities, and glances did not readily come his way in the dining-hall. This was often the fate, or good fortune, of new boys and was not regarded as a sign of qualities lacking. Yet quite regularly an ill-endowed child would mysteriously become the object of fifth- and sixth-form desire. This remained a puzzle to the juniors until they themselves became fifth- or sixth-formers and desire was seen to have to do with something deeper than superficial good looks.

It was the apparent evidence of this truth that cause Torridge, first of all, to be aware of the world of *bijou* and protector. He received a note from a boy in the Upper Fifth who had previously eschewed the sexual life offered by the school. He was a big, black-haired youth with glasses and a protruding forehead, called Fisher.

'Hey, what's this mean?' Torridge enquired, finding the note under his pillow, tucked into his pyjamas. 'Here's a bloke wants to go for a walk.'

He read the invitation out: '*If you would like to come for a walk meet me by the electricity plant behind Chapel. Half-past four Tuesday afternoon. R.A.J. Fisher.*'

'Jesus Christ!' said Armstrong.

'You've got an admirer, Porridge,' Mace-Hamilton said.

'Admirer?'

'He wants you to be his *bijou*,' Wiltshire explained.

'What's it mean, *bijou*?'

'Tart, it means, Porridge.'

'Tart?'

'Friend. He wants to be your protector.'

'What's it mean, protector?'

'He loves you, Porridge.'

'I don't even know the bloke.'

'He's the one with the big forehead. He's a half-wit actually.'

'Half-wit?'

'His mother let him drop on his head. Like yours did, Porridge.'

'My mum never.'

187

Everyone was crowding around Torridge's bed. The note was passed from hand to hand. 'What's your dad do, Porridge?' Wiltshire suddenly asked, and Torridge automatically replied that he was in the button business.

'You've got to write a note back to Fisher, you know,' Mace-Hamilton pointed out.

'Dear Fisher,' Wiltshire prompted, 'I love you.'

'But I don't even—'

'It doesn't matter not knowing him. You've got to write a letter and put it in his pyjamas.'

Torridge didn't say anything. He placed the note in the top pocket of his jacket and slowly began to undress. The other boys drifted back to their own beds, still amused by the development. In the wash-room the next morning Torridge said:

'I think he's quite nice, that Fisher.'

'Had a dream about him, did you, Porridge?' Mace-Hamilton enquired. 'Got up to tricks, did he?'

'No harm in going for a walk.'

'No harm at all, Porridge.'

In fact, a mistake had been made. Fisher, in his haste or his excitement, had placed the note under the wrong pillow. It was Arrowsmith, still allied with Sainsbury Major, whom he wished to attract.

That this error had occurred was borne in on Torridge when he turned up at the electricity plant on the following Tuesday. He had not considered it necessary to reply to Fisher's note, but he had, across the dining-hall, essayed a smile or two in the older boy's direction: it had surprised him to meet with no response. It surprised him rather more to meet with no response by the electricity plant. Fisher just looked at him and then turned his back, pretending to whistle.

'Hullo, Fisher,' Torridge said.

'Hop it, look. I'm waiting for someone.'

'I'm Torridge, Fisher.'

'I don't care who you are.'

'You wrote me that letter.' Torridge was still smiling. 'About a walk, Fisher.'

'Walk? What walk?'

'You put the letter under my pillow, Fisher.'

'Jesus!' said Fisher.

The encounter was observed by Arrowsmith, Mace-Hamilton and Wiltshire, who had earlier taken up crouched positions behind one of the chapel buttresses. Torridge heard the familiar hoots of laughter, and because it was his way he joined in. Fisher, white-faced, strode away.

'Poor old Porridge,' Arrowsmith commiserated, gasping and pretending to be contorted with mirth. Mace-Hamilton and Wiltshire were leaning against the buttress, issuing shrill noises.

'Gosh,' Torridge said, '*I* don't care.'

He went away, still laughing a bit, and there the matter of Fisher's attempt at communication might have ended. In fact it didn't, because Fisher wrote a second time and this time he made certain that the right boy received his missive. But Arrowsmith, still firmly the property of Sainsbury Major, wished to have nothing to do with R.A.J. Fisher.

When he was told the details of Fisher's error, Torridge said he'd guessed it had been something like that. But Wiltshire, Mace-Hamilton and Arrowsmith claimed that a new sadness had overcome Torridge. Something beautiful had been going to happen to him, Wiltshire said: just as the petals of friendship were opening the flower had been crudely snatched away. Arrowsmith said Torridge reminded him of one of Picasso's sorrowful harlequins. One way or the other, it was agreed that the experience would be beneficial to Torridge's sensitivity. It was seen as his reason for turning to religion, which recently he had done, joining a band of similarly inclined boys who were inspired by the word of the chaplain, a figure known as God Harvey. God Harvey was ascetic, seeming dangerously thin, his face all edge and as pale as paper, his cassock odorous with incense. He conducted readings in his room, offering coffee and biscuits afterwards, though not himself partaking of these refreshments. 'God Harvey's linnets' his acolytes were called, for often a hymn was sung to round things off. Welcomed into this fold, Torridge regained his happiness.

R.A.J. Fisher, on the other hand, sank into greater gloom. Arrowsmith remained elusive, mockingly faithful to Sainsbury Major, haughty when Fisher glanced pleadingly, ignoring all his letters. Fisher developed a look of introspective misery. The notes that Arrowsmith delightedly showed around were full of longing, increasingly tinged with desperation. The following term, unexpectedly, Fisher did not return to the school.

There was a famous Assembly at the beginning of that term, with much speculation beforehand as to the trouble in the air. Rumour had it that once and for all an attempt was to be made to stamp out the smiles and the glances in the dining-hall, the whole business of *bijous* and protectors, even the faithless behaviour of the Honourable Anthony Swain. The school waited and then the gowned staff arrived in the Assembly Hall and waited also, in grim anticipation on a raised dais. Public beatings for past offenders were scheduled, it was whispered: the Sergeant-major — the school's boxing instructor, who had himself told tales of public beatings in the past — would inflict the punishment at the head-master's bidding. But that did not happen. Small and bald and red-skinned, the headmaster marched to the dais unaccompanied by the Sergeant-major. Twitching with anger that many afterwards declared had been simulated, he spoke at great length of the school's traditions. He stated that for fourteen years he had been proud to be its headmaster. He spoke of decency, and then of his own dismay. The school had been dishonoured; he would wish certain practices to cease. 'I stand before you ashamed,' he added, and paused for a moment. 'Let all this cease,' he commanded. He marched away, tugging at his gown in a familiar manner.

No one understood why the Assembly had taken place at that particular time, on the first day of a summer term. Only the masters looked knowing, as though labouring beneath some secret, but pressed and pleaded with they refused to reveal anything. Even Old Frosty, usually a most reliable source on such occasions, remained awesomely tight-lipped.

But the pronounced dismay and shame of the headmaster changed nothing. That term progressed and the world of *bijous* and their protectors continued as before, the glances, the meetings, cigarettes and romance in the hillside huts. R.A.J. Fisher was soon forgotten, having never made much of a mark. But the story of his error in placing a note under Torridge's pillow passed into legend, as did the encounter by the electricity plant and Torridge's deprivation of a relationship. The story was repeated as further terms passed by; new boys heard it and viewed Torridge with greater interest, imagining what R.A.J. Fisher had been like. The liaisons of Wiltshire with Good, Mace-Hamilton with Webb, and Arrowsmith with Sainsbury Major continued until the three senior boys left the school. Wiltshire, Mace-Hamilton and Arrowsmith found fresh protectors then, and later these new liaisons came to an end in a similar manner. Later still Wiltshire, Mace-Hamilton and Arrowsmith ceased to be *bijous* and became protectors themselves.

Torridge pursued the religious side of things. He continued to be a frequent partaker of God Harvey's biscuits and spiritual uplift, and a useful presence among the chapel pews, where he voluntarily dusted, cleaned brass, and kept the hymn-books in a state of repair with Sellotape. Wiltshire, Mace-Hamilton and Arrowsmith continued to circulate stories about him which were not true: that he was the product of virgin birth, that he possessed the gift of tongues but did not care to employ it, that he had three kidneys. In the end there emanated from them the claim that a liaison existed between Torridge and God Harvey. 'Love and the holy spirit,' Wiltshire pronounced, suggesting an ambience of chapel fustiness and God Harvey's grey boniness. The swish of his cassock took on a new significance, as did his thin, dry fingers. In a holy way the fingers pressed themselves on to Torridge, and then their holiness became a passion that could not be imagined. It was all a joke because Torridge was Torridge, but the laughter it caused wasn't malicious because no one hated him. He was a figure of fun; no one sought his downfall because there was no downfall to seek.

The friendship between Wiltshire, Mace-Hamilton and Arrow-smith continued after they left the school, after all three had married and had families. Once a year they received the Old Boys' magazine, which told of the achievements of themselves and the more successful of their school-fellows. There were Old Boys' cocktail parties and Old Boys' Day at the school every June and the Old Boys' cricket match. Some of these occasions, from time to time, they attended. Every so often they received the latest rebuilding programme, with the suggestion that they might like to contribute to the rebuilding fund. Occasionally they did.

As middle age closed in, the three friends met less often. Arrowsmith was an executive with Shell and stationed for longish periods in different countries abroad. Once every two years he brought his family back to England, which provided an opportunity for the three friends to meet. The wives met on these occasions also, and over the years the children. Often the men's distant schooldays were referred to, Buller Yeats and Old Frosty and the Sergeant-major, the little red-skinned headmaster, and above all Torridge. Within the three families, in fact, Torridge had become a myth. The joke that had begun when they were all new boys together continued, as if driven by its own impetus. In the minds of the wives and children the innocence of Torridge, his true happiness in the face of mockery and his fondness for the religious side of life all lived on. With some exactitude a physical image of the boy he'd been took root; his neatly knotted maroon House tie, his polished shoes, the hair that resembled a mouse's fur, the pudding face with two small eyes in it. 'My dad's in the button business,' Arrowsmith had only to say to cause instant laughter. 'Torridge's, you know.' The way Torridge ate, the way he ran, the way he smiled back at Buller Yeats, the rumour that he'd been dropped on his head as a baby, that he had three kidneys, all this was considerably appreciated, because Wiltshire and Mace-Hamilton and Arrowsmith related it well.

What was not related was R.A.J. Fisher's error in placing a note beneath Torridge's pillow, or the story that had laughingly been spread about concerning Torridge's relationship with God Harvey. This would have meant revelations that weren't seemly in family circles, the explanation of the world of *bijou* and protector, the romance and cigarettes in the hillside huts, the entangling of hearts. The subject had been touched upon among the three husbands and their wives in the normal course of private conversation, although not everything had been quite recalled. Listening, the wives had formed the impression that the relationships between older and younger boys at their husbands' school were similar to the platonic admiration a junior girl had so often harboured for a senior girl at their own schools. And so the subject had been left.

One evening in June, 1976, Wiltshire and Mace-Hamilton met in a bar called the Vine, in Piccadilly Place. They hadn't seen one another since the summer of 1974, the last time Arrowsmith and his family had been in England. Tonight they were to meet the Arrowsmiths again, for a family dinner in the Woodlands Hotel, Richmond. On the last occasion the three families had celebrated their reunion at the Wiltshires' house in Cobham and the time before with the Mace-Hamiltons in Ealing. Arrowsmith insisted that it was a question of turn and turn about and every third time he arranged for the family dinner to be held at his expense at the Woodlands. It was convenient because, although the Arrowsmiths spent the greater part of each biennial leave with Mrs Arrowsmith's parents in Somerset, they always stayed for a week at the Woodlands in order to see a bit of London life.

In the Vine in Piccadilly Place Wiltshire and Mace-Hamilton hurried over their second drinks. As always, they were pleased to see one another, and both were excited at the prospect of seeing Arrowsmith and his family again. They still looked faintly alike. Both had balded and run to fat. They wore inconspicuous blue suits with a discreet chalk stripe, Wiltshire's a little smarter than Mace-Hamilton's.

'We'll be late,' Wiltshire said, having just related how he'd made a small killing since the last time they'd met. Wiltshire operated in the import-export world; Mace-Hamilton was a chartered accountant.

They finished their drinks. 'Cheerio,' the barman called out to them as they slipped away. His voice was deferentially low, matching the softly-lit surroundings. 'Cheerio, Gerry,' Wiltshire said.

They drove in Wiltshire's car to Hammersmith, over the bridge and on to Barnes and Richmond. It was a Friday evening; the traffic was heavy.

'He had a bit of trouble, you know,' Mace-Hamilton said.

'Arrows?'

'She took a shine to some guy in Mombassa.'

Wiltshire nodded, poking the car between a cyclist and a taxi. He wasn't surprised. One night six years ago Arrowsmith's wife and he had committed adultery together at her suggestion. A messy business it had been, and afterwards he'd felt terrible.

In the Woodlands Hotel Arrowsmith, in a grey flannel suit, was not entirely sober. He, too, had run a bit to fat although, unlike Wiltshire and Mace-Hamilton, he hadn't lost any of his hair. Instead, it had dramatically changed colour: what Old Frosty had once called 'Arrows' blond thatch' was grey now. Beneath it his face was pinker than it had been and he had taken to wearing spectacles, heavy and black-rimmed, making him look even more different from the boy he'd been.

In the bar of the Woodlands he drank whisky on his own, smiling occasionally to himself because tonight he had a surprise for everybody. After five weeks of being cooped up with his in-laws in Somerset he was feeling good. 'Have one yourself, dear,' he invited the barmaid, a girl with an excess of lipstick on a podgy mouth. He pushed his own glass towards her while she was saying she didn't mind if she did.

His wife and his three adolescent children, two boys and a girl, entered the bar with Mrs Mace-Hamilton. 'Hi, hi, hi,' Arrowsmith called out to them in a jocular manner, causing his wife and Mrs Mace-Hamilton to note that he was drunk again. They sat down while he quickly finished the whisky that had just been poured for him. 'Put another in that for a start,' he ordered the barmaid, and crossed the floor of the bar to find out what everyone else wanted.

Mrs Wiltshire and her twins, girls of twelve, arrived while drinks were being decided about. Arrowsmith kissed her, as he had kissed Mrs Mace-Hamilton. The barmaid, deciding that the accurate conveying of such a large order was going to be beyond him, came and stood by the two tables that the party now occupied. The order was given; an animated conversation began.

The three women were different in appearance and in manner. Mrs Arrowsmith was thin as a knife, fashionably dressed in a shade of ash-grey that reflected her ash-grey hair. She smoked perpet-ually, unable to abandon the habit. Mrs Wiltshire was small. Shyness caused her to coil herself up in the presence of other people so that she often resembled a ball. Tonight she was in pink, a faded shade. Mrs Mace-Hamilton was carelessly plump, a large woman attired in a carelessly chosen dress that had begonias on it. She rather frightened Mrs Wiltshire. Mrs Arrowsmith found her trying.

'Oh, heavenly little drink!' Mrs Arrowsmith said, briefly drooping her blue-tinged eyelids as she sipped her gin and tonic.

'It *is* good to see you,' Mrs Mace-Hamilton gushed, beaming at everyone and vaguely raising her glass. 'And how they've all grown!' Mrs Mace-Hamilton had not had children herself.

'Their boobs have grown, by God,' the older Arrowsmith boy murmured to his brother, a reference to the Wiltshire twins. Neither of the two Arrowsmith boys went to their father's school: one was at a preparatory school in Oxford, the other at Charterhouse. Being of an age to do so, they both drank sherry and intended to drink as much of it as they possibly could. They found these family occasions tedious. Their sister, about to go to university, had determined neither to speak nor to smile for the entire evening. The Wiltshire twins were quite looking forward to the food.

Arrowsmith sat beside Mrs Wiltshire. He didn't say anything but after a moment he stretched a hand over her two knees and squeezed them in what he intended to be a brotherly way. He said without conviction that it was great to see her. He didn't look at her while he spoke. He didn't much care for hanging about with the women and children.

In turn Mrs Wiltshire didn't much care for his hand on her knees and was relieved when he drew it away. 'Hi, hi, hi,' he suddenly called out, causing her to jump. Wiltshire and Mace-Hamilton had appeared.

The physical similarity that had been so pronounced when the three men were boys and had been only faintly noticeable between Wiltshire and Mace-Hamilton in the Vine was clearly there again, as if the addition of Arrowsmith had supplied missing reflections. The men had thickened in the same way; the pinkness of Arrowsmith's countenance was a pinkness that tinged the other faces too. Only Arrowsmith's grey thatch of hair seemed out of place, all wrong beside the baldness of the other two: in their presence it might have been a wig, an impression it did not otherwise give. His grey flannel suit, beside their pinstripes, looked like something put on by mistake. 'Hi, hi, hi,' he shouted, thumping their shoulders.

Further rounds of drinks were bought and consumed. The Arrowsmith boys declared to each other that they were drunk and made further *sotto voce* observations about the forming bodies of the Wiltshire twins. Mrs Wiltshire felt the occasion becoming easier as Cinzano Bianco coursed through her bloodstream. Mrs Arrowsmith was aware of a certain familiar edginess within her body, a desire to be elsewhere, alone with a man she did not know. Mrs Mace-Hamilton spoke loudly of her garden.

In time the party moved from the bar to the dining-room. 'Bring us another round at the table,' Arrowsmith commanded the lipsticked barmaid. 'Quick as you can, dear.'

In the large dim dining-room waiters settled them around a table with little vases of carnations on it, a long table beneath the chandelier in the centre of the room. Celery soup arrived at the table, and smoked salmon and pâté, and the extra round of drinks Arrowsmith had ordered, and bottles of Nuits St Georges, and bottles of Vouvray and Anjou Rosé, and sirloin of beef, chicken à la king and veal escalope. The Arrowsmith boys laughed shrilly, openly staring at the tops of the Wiltshire twins' bodies. Potatoes, peas, spinach and carrots were served. Mrs Arrowsmith waved the vegetables away and smoked between courses. It was after this dinner six years ago that she had made her suggestion to Wiltshire, both of them being the worse for wear and it seeming not to matter because of that. 'Oh *isn't* this jolly?' the voice of Mrs Mace-Hamilton boomed above the general hubbub.

Over Chantilly trifle and Orange Surprise the name of Torridge was heard. The name was always mentioned just about now, though sometimes sooner. 'Poor old bean,' Wiltshire said, and everybody laughed because it was the one subject they all shared. No one really wanted to hear about the Mace-Hamiltons' garden; the comments of the Arrowsmith boys were only for each other; Mrs Arrowsmith's needs could naturally not be voiced; the shyness of Mrs Wiltshire was private too. But Torridge was different. Torridge in a way was like an old friend now, existing in everyone's mind, a family subject. The Wiltshire twins were quite amused to hear of some freshly remembered evidence of Torridge's naïveté; for the Arrowsmith girl it was better at least than being questioned by Mrs Mace-Hamilton; for her brothers it was an excuse to bellow with simulated mirth. Mrs Mace-Hamilton considered that the boy sounded frightful. Mrs Arrowsmith couldn't have cared less. Only Mrs Wiltshire had doubts: she thought the three men were hard on the memory of the boy, but of course had not ever said so. Tonight, after Wiltshire had recalled the time when Torridge had been convinced by Arrowsmith that Buller Yeats had dropped dead in his bath, the younger Arrowsmith boy told of a boy at his own school who'd been convinced that his sister's dog had died.

'Listen,' Arrowsmith suddenly shouted out. 'He's going to join us. Old Torridge.'

There was laughter, no one believing that Torridge was going to arrive, Mrs Arrowsmith saying to herself that her husband was pitiful when he became as drunk as this.

'I thought it would be a gesture,' Arrowsmith said. 'Honestly. He's looking in for coffee.'

'You bloody devil, Arrows,' Wiltshire said, smacking the table with the palm of his hand.

'He's in the button business,' Arrowsmith shouted. 'Torridge's, you know.'

As far as Wiltshire and Mace-Hamilton could remember,

Torridge had never featured in an Old Boys' magazine. No news of his career had been printed, and certainly no obituary. It was typical, somehow, of Arrowsmith to have winkled him out. It was part and parcel of him to want to add another dimension to the joke, to recharge its batteries. For the sight of Torridge in middle age would surely make funnier the reported anecdotes. 'After all, what's wrong,' demanded Arrowsmith noisily, 'with old school pals all meeting up? The more the merrier.'

He was a bully, Mrs Wiltshire thought: all three of them were bullies.

Torridge arrived at half-past nine. The hair that had been like a mouse's fur was still like that. It hadn't greyed any more; the scalp hadn't balded. He hadn't run to fat; in middle age he'd thinned down a bit. There was even a lankiness about him now, which was reflected in his movements. At school he had moved slowly, as though with caution. Jauntily attired in a pale linen suit, he crossed the dining-room of the Woodlands Hotel with a step as nimble as a tap dancer's.

No one recognised him. To the three men who'd been at school with him the man who approached their dinner table was a different person, quite unlike the figure that existed in the minds of the wives and children.

'My dear Arrows,' he said, smiling at Arrowsmith. The smile was different too, a brittle snap of a smile that came and went in a matter-of-fact way. The eyes that had been small didn't seem so in his thinner face. They flashed with a gleam of some kind, matching the snap of his smile.

'Good God, it's never old Porridge!' Arrowsmith's voice was slurred. His face had acquired the beginnings of an alcoholic crimson, sweat glistened on his forehead.

'Yes, it's old Porridge,' Torridge said quietly. He held his hand out towards Arrowsmith and then shook hands with Wiltshire and Mace-Hamilton. He was introduced to their wives, with whom he shook hands also. He was introduced to the children, which involved further hand-shaking. His hand was cool and rather bony: they felt it should have been damp.

'You're nicely in time for coffee, Mr Torridge,' Mrs Mace-Hamilton said.

'Brandy more like,' Arrowsmith suggested. 'Brandy, old chap?'

'Well, that's awfully kind of you, Arrows. Chartreuse I'd prefer, really.'

A waiter drew up a chair. Room was made for Torridge between Mrs Mace-Hamilton and the Arrowsmith boys. It was a frightful mistake, Wiltshire was thinking. It was mad of Arrowsmith.

Mace-Hamilton examined Torridge across the dinner table. The old Torridge would have said he'd rather not have anything alcoholic, that a cup of tea and a biscuit were more his line in the evenings. It was impossible to imagine this man saying his dad had a button business. There was a suavity about him that made Mace-Hamilton uneasy. Because of what had been related to his wife and the other wives and their children he felt he'd been caught out in a lie, yet in fact that wasn't the case.

The children stole glances at Torridge, trying to see him as the boy who'd been described to them, and failing to. Mrs Arrowsmith said to herself that all this stuff they'd been told over the years had clearly been rubbish. Mrs Mace-Hamilton was bewildered. Mrs Wiltshire was pleased.

'No one ever guessed,' Torridge said, 'what became of R.A.J. Fisher.' He raised the subject suddenly, without introduction.

'Oh God, Fisher,' Mace-Hamilton said.

'Who's Fisher?' the younger of the Arrowsmith boys enquired.

Torridge turned to flash his quick smile at the boy. 'He left,' he said. 'In unfortunate circumstances.'

'You've changed a lot, you know,' Arrowsmith said. 'Don't you think he's changed?' he asked Wiltshire and Mace-Hamilton.

'Out of recognition,' Wiltshire said.

Torridge laughed easily. 'I've become adventurous. I'm a late developer I suppose.'

'What kind of unfortunate circumstances?' the younger Arrowsmith boy asked. 'Was Fisher expelled?'

'Oh no, not at all,' Mace-Hamilton said hurriedly.

'Actually,' Torridge said, 'Fisher's trouble all began with the writing of a note. Don't you remember? He put it in my pyjamas. But it wasn't for me at all.'

He smiled again. He turned to Mrs Wiltshire in a way that seemed polite, drawing her into the conversation. 'I was an innocent at school. But innocence eventually slips away. I found my way about eventually.'

'Yes, of course,' she murmured. She didn't like him, even though she was glad he wasn't as he might have been. There was malevolence in him, a ruthlessness that seemed like a work of art. He seemed like a work of art himself, as though in losing the innocence he spoke of he had recreated himself.

'I often wonder about Fisher,' he remarked.

The Wiltshire twins giggled. 'What's so great about this bloody Fisher?' the older Arrowsmith boy murmured, nudging his brother with an elbow.

'What're you doing these days?' Wiltshire asked, interrupting Mace-Hamilton, who had also begun to say something.

'I make buttons,' Torridge replied. 'You may recall my father made buttons.'

'Ah, here're the drinks,' Arrowsmith rowdily observed.

'I don't much keep up with the school,' Torridge said as the waiter placed a glass of Chartreuse in front of him. 'I don't so much as think about it except for wondering about poor old Fisher. Our headmaster was a cretin,' he informed Mrs Wiltshire.

Again the Wiltshire twins giggled. The Arrowsmith girl yawned and her brothers giggled also, amused that the name of Fisher had come up again.

'You will have coffee, Mr Torridge?' Mrs Mace-Hamilton offered, for the waiter had brought a fresh pot to the table. She held it poised above a cup. Torridge smiled at her and nodded. She said: 'Pearl buttons d'you make?'

'No, not pearl.'

'Remember those awful packet peas we used to have?' Arrowsmith enquired. Wiltshire said:

'Use plastics at all? In your buttons, Porridge?'

'No, we don't use plastics. Leathers, various leathers. And horn. We specialise.'

'How very interesting!' Mrs Mace-Hamilton exclaimed.

'No, no. It's rather ordinary really.' He paused, and then added, 'Someone once told me that Fisher went into a timber business. But of course that was far from true.'

'A chap was expelled a year ago,' the younger Arrowsmith boy said, contributing this in order to cover up a fresh outburst of sniggering. 'For stealing a transistor.'

Torridge nodded, appearing to be interested. He asked the Arrowsmith boys where they were at school. The older one said Charterhouse and his brother gave the name of his preparatory school. Torridge nodded again and asked their sister and she said she was waiting to go to university. He had quite a chat with the Wiltshire twins about their school. They considered it pleasant the way he bothered, seemingly genuinely to want to know. The giggling died away.

'I imagined Fisher wanted me for his *bijou*,' he said when all that was over, still addressing the children. 'Our place was riddled with fancy larks like that. Remember?' he added, turning to Mace-Hamilton.

'*Bijou*?' one of the twins asked before Mace-Hamilton could reply.

'A male tart,' Torridge explained.

The Arrowsmith boys gaped at him, the older one with his

mouth actually open. The Wiltshire twins began to giggle again. The Arrowsmith girl frowned, unable to hide her interest.

'The Honourable Anthony Swain,' Torridge said, 'was no better than a whore.'

Mrs Arrowsmith, who for some minutes had been engaged with her own thoughts, was suddenly aware that the man who was in the button business was talking about sex. She gazed diagonally across the table at him, astonished that he should be talking in this way.

'Look here, Torridge,' Wiltshire said, frowning at him and shaking his head. With an almost imperceptible motion he gestured towards the wives and children.

'Andrews and Butler. Dillon and Pratt. Tothill and Goldfish Stewart. Your dad,' Torridge said to the Arrowsmith girl, 'was always very keen. Sainsbury Major in particular.'

'Now look here,' Arrowsmith shouted, beginning to get to his feet and then changing his mind.

'My gosh, how they broke chaps' hearts, those three!'

'Please don't talk like this.' It was Mrs Wiltshire who protested, to everyone's surprise, most of all her own. 'The children are quite young, Mr Torridge.'

Her voice had become a whisper. She could feel herself reddening with embarrassment, and a little twirl of sickness occurred in her stomach. Deferentially, as though appreciating the effort she had made, Torridge apologised.

'I think you'd better go,' Arrowsmith said.

'You were right about God Harvey, Arrows. Gay as a grig he was, beneath that cassock. So was Old Frosty, as a matter of fact.'

'Really!' Mrs Mace-Hamilton cried, her bewilderment turning into outrage. She glared at her husband, demanding with her eyes that instantly something should be done. But her husband and his two friends were briefly stunned by what Torridge had claimed for God Harvey. Their schooldays leapt back at them, possessing them for a vivid moment: the dormitory, the dining-hall, the glances and the invitations, the meetings behind Chapel. It was somehow in keeping with the school's hypocrisy that God Harvey had had inclinations himself, that a rumour begun as an outrageous joke should have contained the truth.

'As a matter of fact,' Torridge went on, 'I wouldn't be what I am if it hadn't been for God Harvey. I'm what they call queer,' he explained to the children. 'I perform sexual acts with men.'

'For God's sake, Torridge,' Arrowsmith shouted, on his feet, his face the colour of ripe strawberry, his watery eyes quivering with rage.

'It was nice of you to invite me tonight, Arrows. Our *alma mater* can't be too proud of chaps like me.'

People spoke at once, Mrs Mace-Hamilton and Mrs Wiltshire, all three men. Mrs Arrowsmith sat still. What she was thinking was that she had become quietly drunk while her husband had more boisterously reached the same condition. She was thinking, as well, that by the sound of things he'd possessed as a boy a sexual urge that was a lot livelier than the one he'd once exposed her to and now hardly ever did. With boys who had grown to be men he had had a whale of a time. Old Frosty had been a kind of Mr Chips, she'd been told. She'd never ever heard of Sainsbury Major or God Harvey.

'It's quite disgusting,' Mrs Mace-Hamilton's voice cried out above the other voices. She said the police should be called. It was scandalous to have to listen to unpleasant conversation like this. She began to say the children should leave the dining-room, but changed her mind because it appeared that Torridge himself was about to go. 'You're a most horrible man,' she cried.

Confusion gathered, like a fog around the table. Mrs Wiltshire, who knew that her husband had committed adultery with Mrs Arrowsmith, felt another bout of nerves in her stomach. 'Because she was starved, that's why,' her husband had almost violently confessed when she'd discovered. 'I was putting her out of her misery.' She had wept then and he had comforted her as best he could. She had not told him that he had never succeeded in arousing in her the desire to make love: she had always assumed that to be a failing in herself, but now for some reason she was not so sure. Nothing had been directly said that might have caused this doubt, but an instinct informed Mrs Wiltshire, that the doubt should be there. The man beside her smiled his brittle, malevolent smile at her, as if in sympathy.

With his head bent over the table and his hands half hiding his face, the younger Arrowsmith boy examined his father by glancing through his fingers. There were men whom his parents warned him against, men who would sit beside you in buses or try to give you a lift in a car. This man who had come tonight, who had been such a joke up till now, was apparently one of these, not a joke at all. And the confusion was greater: at one time, it seemed, his father had been like that too.

The Arrowsmith girl considered her father also. Once she had walked into a room in Lagos to find her mother in the arms of an African clerk. Ever since she had felt sorry for her father. There'd been an unpleasant scene at the time, she'd screamed at her mother and later in a fury had told her father what she'd seen. He'd nodded, wearily seeming not to be surprised, while her mother had miserably wept. She'd put her arms around her father, comforting him; she'd felt no mercy for her mother, no sympathy or understanding. The scene formed vividly in her mind as she sat at the dinner table: it appeared to be relevant in the confusion and yet not clearly so. Her parents' marriage was messy, messier than it had looked. Across the table her mother grimly smoked, focusing her eyes with difficulty. She smiled at her daughter, a soft, inebriated smile.

The older Arrowsmith boy was also aware of the confusion. Being at a school where the practice which had been spoken of was common enough, he could easily believe the facts that had been thrown about. Against his will, he was forced to imagine what he had never imagined before: his father and his friends as schoolboys, engaged in passion with other boys. He might have been cynical about this image but he could not. Instead it made him want to gasp. It knocked away the smile that had been on his face all evening.

The Wiltshire twins unhappily stared at the white tablecloth, here and there stained with wine or gravy. They, too, found they'd lost the urge to smile and instead shakily blinked back tears.

'Yes, perhaps I'd better go,' Torridge said.

With impatience Mrs Mace-Hamilton looked at her husband, as if expecting him to hurry Torridge off or at least to say something. But Mace-Hamilton remained silent. Mrs Mace-Hamilton licked her lips, preparing to speak herself. She changed her mind.

'Fisher didn't go into a timber business,' Torridge said, 'because poor old Fisher was dead as a doornail. Which is why our cretin of a headmaster, Mrs Mace-Hamilton, had that Assembly.'

'Assembly?' she said. Her voice was weak, although she'd meant it to sound matter-of-fact and angry.

'There was an Assembly that no one understood. Poor old Fisher had strung himself up in a barn on his father's farm. I discovered that,' Torridge said, turning to Arrowsmith, 'years later: from God Harvey actually. The poor chap left a note but the parents didn't care to pass it on. I mean it was for you, Arrows.'

Arrowsmith was still standing, hanging over the table. 'Note?' he said. 'For me?'

'Another note. Why d'you think he did himself in, Arrows?'

Torridge smiled, at Arrowsmith and then around the table.

'None of that's true,' Wiltshire said.

'As a matter of fact it is.'

He went, and nobody spoke at the dinner table. A body of a schoolboy hung from a beam in a barn, a note on the straw below his dangling feet. It hung in the confusion that had been caused, increasing the confusion. Two waiters hovered by a sideboard, one passing the time by arranging sauce bottles, the other folding napkins into cone shapes. Slowly Arrowsmith sat down again. The silence continued as the conversation of Torridge continued to haunt the dinner table. He haunted it himself, with his brittle smile and his tap dancer's elegance, still faithful to the past in which he had so signally failed, triumphant in his middle age.

Then Mrs Arrowsmith quite suddenly wept and the Wiltshire twins wept and Mrs Wiltshire comforted them. The Arrowsmith girl got up and walked away, and Mrs Mace-Hamilton turned to the three men and said they should be ashamed of themselves, allowing all this to happen.

GOING BACK

EMMA DONOGHUE

C yn kicked the machine systematically. She glanced down at Lou, who was scrabbling under the radiator for a pound coin. 'Come on, wimp, help me kick,' she told him. 'I'm not letting you deflower me without a packet of Thick-Ribbed Ultras.'

Lou's response was to embed his ears between his knees and gasp. Passersby were lingering at the nearby jobs noticeboard, all studious expressions and pencils in hand.

'So much for chivalry,' Cyn announced loudly. 'No rubber no jolly rogering. That's fifty pee I've wasted on you already.'

She slung her scarred jacket over one shoulder and headed for the stairs. Lou hauled his red face up and stumbled after her. Once through the rainbow-muralled doors of the community centre into the noisy Brixton street, they let rip with laughter.

'Pathetic,' Cyn reproached him. 'Didn't they ever teach you how to keep a straight face in that seminary of yours?'

'If they'd taught me how to keep anything straight, sweetie, I wouldn't have been thrown out on my ear.'

'Poor ear,' murmured Cyn, flipping its pointed tip with one finger as they paused at the pelican crossing.

He writhed away. 'That's sexual harassment of a co-worker, that is. And you who always meant to be a separatist.'

'I'm a respectable woman now; I've been seen trying to buy condoms on a public corridor.'

'Yeah, but which of us would have got to wear them?'

Cyn gave him a mistressful scowl. Then the skin around her eyes crinkled. 'Did you spot May from Accounts at the noticeboard, ears flapping? Our reputations are saved.'

They had met at Pride the previous June. Cyn, on a day off

from her temping job, leaned her elbows on a steel barrier and watched the crowd whoop by. Lou was one of the boys in gleaming white jockey shorts, funking along behind the Sisters of Perpetual Indulgence. What made her notice him was the shamrock in relief on the back of his No. 2 shave; when he dropped out for a rest against the barrier, it was two inches from her face. The most testicular of symbols, she commented afterwards. Lou claimed it represented a triad of Celtic goddesses, but, when pressed, could not remember their names.

Then a few weeks later, on her way back from a James Dean double-bill at the Roxy in Brixton, Cyn happened to spot the Rainbow Centre and remembered something that nice boy-germ had said about working there as a set painter. Lou recognised the woman in the navy suit only when she hoisted herself onto the stage and introduced herself as 'Whatshername from the march'. She hadn't been on the boards, she said, since her days of teaching heel-toe in the parish hall under the knobbly crucifix.

August was nearly over when the two of them came face to sweaty face in Oscars. She reached over a line of men and bought them two lime and sodas. In return Lou remembered to tell her that they needed a dance person at the Rainbow to add a chorus of local ten-year-olds to *Fee Foe Fie Fum*.

It was one of Cyn's unspoken superstitions that if you met someone accidentally three times in as many months, the friendship had to happen.

She turned up Monday morning, surprising them both. Over polystyrene cups of tea, her voice relaxed and dipped. Lou's ears recognised it as Irish, and he was suddenly awkward. He wiped his hands on a crusty blue rag. 'You didn't tell me you were one of us.'

'Who's us?' she asked.

'Ah, you know, Gay-lickers. Little green fairies.'

'I've never felt like one of an us.'

209

Lou let it drop. He led Cyn round the back of the set and pointed out details on a painted dragon to make her laugh.

As the first knot of kids trickled in, she stepped carefully over some chickenwire, introduced herself to them, and began inventing a Digestion Dance for Act II. Smacking her hip for the rhythm, Cyn stopped herself after one '*haon dó trí*', realising that these kids would have no idea what it meant. Somehow 'one two three' sounded much flatter.

Two months slid by, three and a half, and Cyn was still working at the Rainbow. Or, as they variously called it on idle mornings round the drinks machine, the Rambo, the Brainrow, or the Puddle.

Lou she addressed as her toy-boy, her babe, her gentleman friend, her Martin Luther Queen. He borrowed her big leather jacket; she stole the last mouthful of his tea. The other workers didn't know what to make of them. Cyn and Lou didn't know what to make of themselves, nor did they worry about it.

One Friday in December Lou noticed her mouth sagging at the corners, so he dragged her to Oscars. 'Would you go halves on a packet of crisps?'

She straddled a stool. 'No point, English crisps are horrible. I stay faithful to Tayto Cheese 'n Onion.'

'So you binge on them when you go back?'

Cyn spun a beermat on a fingertip. 'Haven't been back.'

'In how long?'

'At all.'

Lou curled his feet round the bar of the stool. He tried to take it in. 'What, since whenever?'

'1980. John Paul II was blessing ze young people of Iyerland as my plane took off. I could see the crowd shrinking behind the wing.'

Lou bit the corner off his peanut packet. 'Not even for Christmas?' He heard his voice, like a disappointed child's.

Cyn grinned over her upturned collar. 'I suppose you'll be zooming home to the Mammy on the 23rd of December?'

'And stay till after the New Year's hangover. This year she wants me till Epiphany but I've told her we've a show on.'

'Liar.'

Lou bent his head. 'Let's get the full confession over: I forget all my vegetarian principles when I smell the turkey stuffing.'

'And do you delight the family with your *Queer as Fuck* T-shirt?'

'Ah, get away with you.' Lou's voice sank.

'Let me guess: you're not exactly out to them.'

'Not in so many words, and certainly not in those particular words.' Lou pulled at his ear lobe. 'You've forgotten what it's like back there.'

'I remember too well.' Cyn took a deliberate sip. 'So why fold yourself back into the closet once a year?'

He made a face. 'Because being a bit discreet is better than the ructions it would cause if I said anything. Besides, I couldn't miss the Christmas.'

'Missing it's easy after the first time,' Cyn assured him. 'I get an old friend to send me a box of Tayto each year.'

'But you must feel a bit . . . cut off.'

'Ah get lost laddy.' She looked at him with amusement that had a warning behind it. 'Can you see me ever fitting in?'

Lou frayed the edge of his beermat with one nail. 'You wouldn't have to . . .'

'Listen, I felt more of an exile for twenty years in Ireland than I ever have in the twelve I've been out of it.'

He contemplated the mark his glass had made on the polished wood.

Three hours later their speech was slower, more circuitous. The conversation had meandered through SM, the best temperature to drink Guinness, god, nephews and nieces, and was circling back to Ireland and its many embarrassments.

Lou knew some activists over there working for decriminalisation. Cyn tried three times to pronounce the word, and snigg-
ered into her beer. She shut one eye and fixed him with the other.
'What's the Irish age of consent then?' she asked.

His forehead hurt. 'There isn't one. I was telling you, it's a
Victorian statute – '

'No,' she interrupted him, 'I mean what's the age of consent
for being Irish?'

Lou was massaging his temples, too hard.

'I mean, I don't seem to remember ever being consulted.
Correct me if I'm wrong.' She pointed a stubby finger. 'Were you
ever asked if you agreed to be Irish?'

He shook his head carefully, once.

'All that cultural baggage foisted' – Cyn paused, checking the
word – 'absolutely *foisted* upon us without a by your leave.'

She continued, her finger dipping on every important work
like a conductor's baton. 'And what happens if you try and refuse
it or leave it behind? Everybody freaks out as if you've dumped a
baby in a carrier bag at the airport.'

Lou opened his mouth, but could think of no remark that was
not sad or silly.

Suddenly very much the personal secretary, she smoothened
out a bus ticket and began a list of Reasons for Not Living in Our
Dear Native Isle. It began to expand beyond the limits of the ticket,
into rural depopulation and the violent habits of Celtic heroes, so
Lou proposed they turn it over and restrict the list to new factors
since 1980. On the plus side – Lou insisted there be a plus side,
so Cyn drew a narrow margin down the edge of the ticket – all
they could think of was crisps.

By the time he came back from the loo, Cyn had sagged over
the counter. He could see a tear shining on the wood, and her
shoulders were heaving. Putting one arm around her, he tried to
shield her from the blank stares of the other drinkers.

After a minute, Cyn sat up and wiped her face on her denim sleeve. 'Sorry.'

'No problem,' he said, too heartily.

'Christ,' she roared, pointing one accusatory finger behind the bar.

'What is it now?'

'Page Three calendar. Typical bloody men. Even bloody faggots like a few bloody tits on the wall.'

Lou got her out the door before the barman could take action. They walked in silence to the Tube.

She cleared her throat with a husky roar. 'Sorry. One pint too many.'

'Sure.'

'It wasn't about anything.'

'Mmm.'

Cyn turned a wet repentant face. 'And what I said about faggots – I didn't mean you. I mean men are shits but you're alright, Lou – Lou.'

'I quite agree.' He pushed her through the turnstile. As she drifted towards the escalator he shouted, 'You will receive my severed balls by the next post in a plain brown wrapper.' He made a few jaws drop, but Cyn glanced over her shoulder and seemed comforted.

By the time they met up after Christmas, Cyn had worked her way through her box of Tayto. The next two shows were planned around gospel choirs rather than dance choruses; Cyn gave herself a week of moody unemployment, loitering in galleries and parks, then rooted out an old pair of navy tights and went back to temping.

One evening her Looptheloop came round to her flat for tuna bake. (Not that he was not a vegetarian, but somehow he always thought of tuna as a vegetable, just like anchovies.) He accepted seconds and thirds, to keep her company. Then they sat in front of the television with the sound turned down, and burped, and laughed in disgust at themselves. Each told the other they looked tired.

'Luther?'

He glanced up, startled by the full name.

She passed him the biscuit barrel. 'Why don't you go out and have a wild passionate affair?'

'No particular reason.'

'You're so post-Aids.' Cyn sighed. 'Have you calmed down after a riotous youth, is that it?'

'Not really. All through adolescence I painted trees. Then the seminary, painting Jesuses.' Lou paused to remember, staring at the television screen, where a man and a woman were silently shouting at each other over a car door.

'And then a few wild oats?'

'No, then I hung around Limerick for a few years, wondering whether I'd go back to the seminary if they asked me. But in the back of my mind I knew well that the priests would never have me back without me volunteering for ECT or something. So finally I rolled up my vocation, left it under the bed, and took the boat over to London.'

'And then some wild oats?' Cyn dipped another gingernut in her tea.

'One or two.'

She rolled her eyes. 'How can I be a faghag if my only fag is so damn respectable? I'm going to enrol you in a nude painting class tomorrow. You're in a rut.'

'Am not.'

'Are so. I can hear it in your voice.'

'You're just projecting your rut onto me.'

'Sounds painful!' she murmured.

Cyn didn't want to talk about herself tonight. She wanted to make fun of models in shampoo ads and maybe play Off the Couch if there was nothing on after *The Golden Girls*. With Lou she could almost touch the sixteen-year-old girl she'd never been.

Lou was sticking out his tongue at her lasciviously. 'Don't you go inventing ruts for me. Those who can't live, counsel.'

Cyn stared into the biscuity dregs of her tea.

It was a cold, clammy evening in March. Lou sat on the Tube, counting the stops, reminding himself not to bend his ticket in case the machine would spit it back at him. He had four layers on to keep out the howling draughts; his face felt damp and hot. Cyn had rung to say he had to come over.

'What, now? Cyn-ful, I'd have to take three Tubes.'

'Please, I'm really sorry but please.'

'OK pet, no worries. Give me an hour.'

Lou watched the grey wall of the tunnel hurtle by. Paper corners of old ads flapped in the breeze as the train came alongside a platform. Things had been strange with Cyn recently. Once they went dancing together in a dyke club which let boys in as friends or slaves on Mondays. He and Cyn had worn matching Pervert T-shirts, and danced like lunatics under a full moon, and in the toilet queue Cyn had told a curious woman that yes, Lou was her son, and she was very proud of him. It was a hilarious night, something to write home about, if his letters to his mother had ever told her anything that mattered.

But ever since, Cyn and he had been getting on each other's nerves. Silences and mishearing and prickliness; it seemed a silly way for a friendship to peter out.

On a lunch break last week, he had consulted Jazz, the counsellor at the Rainbow. Jazz advised sitting down together to share feelings and negotiate new terms. Lou nodded and squirmed. The best thing about friendship was not having to have all those heavy analytical conversations lovers had. Friends could just get on with living it.

His stop; he lunged for the door.

Cyn met him at the top of her stairs but didn't hug him. He had never known her to gabble quite like this. She told him how worried she was about the rumour that her landlord was planning to gentrify the block. Also she was thinking of changing to an agency which didn't mess temps around quite as much. The punnet of imported raspberries was a shocking price, but she had felt an urge to anticipate summer. Which laces did he think would go with her new boots?

Lou stayed patient until the third cup of tea. 'Is anything the matter?'

'No, just wanted to see your ugly mug really.'

'Any time.'

Cyn sat on the arm of the sofa, her arms folded round a big patchwork cushion. Her feet tucked under the leg of his jeans, for anchorage. They watched a gorgeous dancer in a pop video.

'What a sulky face on your woman.'

'It's a man in make-up,' he told her.

'No way.'

They argued the matter idly. She talked as if she had been drinking but her breath smelt of nothing but raspberries. Her fingertips were stained with them.

Lou accepted one, delicate-haired and slightly bruised. He kept his eyes on the television, nodding and keeping the occasional yawn inside his jaw. Only when he realised she was talking about the two of them did he look up and grin at her.

Cyn was telling him stuff he already knew but it was nice to hear it. How interesting it had been this year, something she had never done before, getting to know someone who was gay but of the opposite sex, like having so much in common yet being so far apart. It was the perfect situation for friendship, actually, because she was a completely woman-identified woman and he was, well, she supposed the equivalent phrase was a totally man-identified man, though that sounded a bit fascist, but she meant it in a nice way.

Lou assured her that he took it in a nice way. He stole the third last raspberry from the punnet in her lap.

Cyn was in full flow. How brilliant it was that the two of them could sort of share their thoughts without having them sort of curdled by heteropatriarchal patterns. (And to give her credit, she did grin as she dredged this phrase up from her feminist race memory.) A faggot and a dyke could balance each other, Cyn was explaining to him. They fitted. They knew who they were.

Lou nodded. His eyes slid back to the screen where Wogan was interviewing someone interesting for a change.

And then Cyn forgot what she was saying, forgot herself, and kissed him on the ear.

The rest was a blur to him, afterwards. He could never remember many details of that night. Maybe because he was so curious, so busy watching from outside, that he had not been really involved at all. Or maybe it was as if nature had edited out of his memory an experience irreconcilable with the rest of his life, like some women forget the pain of childbirth. But what Lou would always remember was that slow kiss on the ear that made every hair on his body stand up.

When he woke they were lying back to back. It was oddly comforting, the weight of his hip against the small of her back, her soles against his heels. The bed was damp, the wrinkled sheets still warm; he must have only dropped asleep for a few minutes.

Lou lay awake, not moving a muscle in case the two of them would become aware of each other and have to talk. He wanted to hold still and run it back through his head, but already it was blurring. The strange female shapes, the unexpected timing. And then, after all, the human similarity; the results of hands on bodies turned out to be not so different after all.

He had never been to bed with a woman before. Did it count if she was a lesbian? In some ways, Lou thought, stifling a giggle, it was the most logical choice.

Behind him Cyn shifted, her back pulling awake from his; a draught wound in to separate them. He had to move his leg or it would cramp. He twisted to face her, and rested his head on her shoulder, but lightly.

She found she could hear him thinking, like a pulse in the head on her shoulder.

'Hi,' he said at last, rather squawkily, and Cyn was overwhelmed with fondness for him.

'Hello,' she reassured him.

After a gap of half a minute, Lou got his question over with. 'Was that all right?'

'Yeah.' What a bland word, an insult, a mere grunt. What could she tell him about something so recent and brief that her brain had hardly registered it? 'Rather different from how it used to be.' Cyn added in an undertone.

'When?'

'Fifteen years ago.'

'Fifteen years ago I was taking my first holy communion in velvet knickerbockers.'

Cyn cleared her throat. 'I meant with other men.'

'I know.' Lou turned his face up to the cracked ceiling. Silence covered them like a blanket, stifling the words. But if he didn't ask these questions now they would hammer in his head. 'How different, exactly?'

Her face was angled into the pillow. What she said was muffled and he had to ask her to repeat it. 'Not different enough,' Cyn said at last.

'I'm sorry. I mean, that's fine. No sweat.' What was he rabbiting on about? There was sweat everywhere, cooling the sheets against them like a mummy's wrappings.

It wasn't bright enough for Lou to see her eyes, but he could feel their gaze on his skin. 'It's not you, it's me,' she said, as if to a child. 'You're very different from them, you make a totally different . . . shape. But I'm afraid I still can't quite see it.'

He lay still, then scratched his ear. Why was he feeling bleak when it was such a relief? The things he had been dreading, ever since he woke up, were enthusiasm, romance, or a dreadfully earnest renegotiations of the terms.

Lou exhaled a quick prayer to the god he didn't believe in anymore. What he would have liked to say to the woman breathing beside him was a simple thanks that she seemed to have got about as much as he did out of the whole business and no more. But some things couldn't be said, even between friends. 'Tea?' he asked, leaning up on one elbow.

'Please.'

It took two months for them to feel safe enough to curl up on a sofa together. Lou's sofa this time, to avoid memories. It was May, and the sun sifted across the cushions. When he took her hand this time there was a layer of airiness between their bodies; it cushioned them, saved their nerves from jarring. They kept talking. Lou delivered a rant, punctuated with laughter, about the Rainbow's Artistic Director, who was so paranoid about Clause 28 that he had instructed Lou to paint over the giants' moustaches and bandannas in case the Council withdrew funding. By the end of an argument about the Labour Party, Cyn decided that the electricity between them had been earthed and laid to rest. It felt so wonderfully ordinary, her hand lying on his. Laying her head back on one of Lou's granny's cushions, she decided she wouldn't have to unearth that 'Bi Any Other Name' badge after all.

Lou watched her eyelids float in a sea of tiny lines. 'Your accent's coming back these days, you know,' he remarked.

'It is not!'

'Listen to yourself. '"Tis an' all",' he added in a stage-Oirish quaver.

She grinned and slid farther down the sofa arm, putting her boots up on his jeans. 'Must be your evil influence.'

If he didn't push it now he mightn't get another chance. 'They say it's getting better over there, Cyn-ful.'

'Don't they always.'

'Ah but seriously. The Government are finally going to have to make us legal; they've promised to bring in an equal age of consent by July.'

'Speak for yourself, I was never illegal.'

'They'd have to get you for general indecency.'

'They'd have to catch me first.'

Lou rapped on her soles. 'Stop messing. Why don't you come home with me at the end of June for Pride?'

Cyn opened one eye.

'Dublin has its very own Pride March now, isn't that the cutest thing?'

Her eye shut. 'Dublin's not home. I grew up a hundred and fifty miles away. I've been to Manchester more often than Dublin.'

'Well, think of it as a halfway point, then. Halfway between the Rainbow Centre and your parish hall.'

The cushion dropped to the floor. 'I'd rather think about tandoori chicken. Come on, my treat.'

Lou followed her down the stairwell. The sun was pale yellow, snagged on a city spire; fingers of cloud stroked it as they passed.

'I just can't believe in an Irish Pride March,' Cyn commented, as they crossed the street to avoid a knot of skinheads. 'It'd be a contradiction in terms. Pride is sun on the lions in Trafalgar Square and bobbies in helmets and that transvestite dressed up as Margaret Thatcher.'

'What a traditionalist you are, for a deviant.'

The point struck home. Cyn's walk slowed; her fists went deeper into her pockets. 'Where'd we stay, if we did, which we won't?'

'I'll find a nice queer B&B in Dublin. Separate rooms, I assure you.'

'But of course.' She grabbed his hand, gave it a quick and only partly mocking kiss.

'It'll all be so different from how you remember it.'

'How different exactly?'

'Let me guess what you're going to say: "Not different enough"?'

He caught the edge of a sheepish grin, as she turned her face away.

'Cyn, it's a new decade. Condom machines — '

' — much good that does me — '

' — a female president up in the Park. How about if I pay the price of your ticket if you're not entirely satisfied?'

'You couldn't afford to, unless you've been turning tricks in your lunchbreaks.'

'I know,' sighed Lou, 'but didn't it sound impressive?' The campness left his tone. 'Listen, you have to come back with me. If I went with English mates they wouldn't understand. Ireland's growing up, we have to be there.'

'Oh really? Puberty is not a pretty sight. Tantrums and spots,' Cyn reminded him, folding her arms across her jacket.

'Think of it more like a gorgeous teenager, with very soft eye-lashes.'

'Paedophile.'

He pulled a hideous leer.

Cyn yawned as they turned the corner onto the high street. 'I don't know, Lou-Lou, the very idea makes me tired. Wake me up when Ireland starts consenting to us instead of kicking us in the teeth.'

'Any day now,' he promised her, doubtfully.

'I'll believe it when I see it.'

'You'll never see it unless you believe it a bit.'

They wandered down the street past the restaurant, past the pub, coming to no conclusion. Like tails of cloud, their voices winding around and in and out.

RINGSEND

FRANK RONAN

S tanley waded out of the sea, calf-deep, and the water threw patterns of reflection on his bare legs. He had, he considered, rather good knees. Other parts of him were faulted: his hands too narrow and tapering; his nose amorphous; his feet marred by tufts of hair, but his knees were a source of constant satisfaction to him. They were round and flat like the knees of horses he remembered from the time when there were horses. He came out of the water, dripping and cold, and dressed on the high tide mark. Because the morning was already hot, he wondered, not for the first time, why he felt compelled to wear clothes at all these days. He knew he would feel silly walking naked through the empty streets, but there was something more than that: with all the clothes in the world at his disposal it might be wrong of him not to use them. A sin, perhaps, to waste them.

That speculation made him remember that he was running low on socks and he decided to make a detour through Grafton Street on his way home. He liked the excuse to go shopping, but had to discipline himself. In the beginning he had collected so much clutter, and his house had become so full of everything that had taken his fancy, that he was forced to move next-door and use his own house as a sort of Museum of Materialism. These days he went through the shops trying to take only what he could persuade himself he needed.

His bicycle ride from the beach to the city centre took him through the suburbs, and then the streets, of North Dublin: pedalling fast where the roads were clear; swerving and weaving in other places where cars had been abandoned all that time ago. Was it three or was it four years? He had meant to keep a record of the passing time, like Robinson Crusoe, but had soon given it up. Time, now that he was the only guardian of it, was counted, not in months but in phases of depression and anxiety, which were fewer and fewer as time went on, and bouts of giddy happiness, which were constant, and states of complacent normality, such as now. He was a little surprised that loneliness was not an emotion he suffered from. He had read a book about repression once, and that had given him cause for anxiety, until he considered his circumstances and decided that loneliness was best left repressed for the time being, if repressed it was.

He left the bicycle outside Browne Thomas and pushed through the doors. It was lucky, he supposed, that the cataclysm or whatever it was had happened had occurred on a Tuesday morning when all the shops were open, so that they had been left open in perpetuity for him. He would not have felt quite the same about his shopping trips had he to smash windows or crow-bar shutters before every acquisition, perhaps setting off burglar alarms and wrecking the perfect silence of the city. He treasured that silence, broken only by the clicking of his bicycle wheels and the sound of breath leaving his body.

He made his way between dusty counters to the menswear department, where he chose a dozen pairs of socks in thin black silk. He liked the sort of socks that were so fragile and expensive they could be worn only for a day and then thrown out, just as he liked the sort of shoes that were so expensive they lasted forever. Not that a word like expensive had any currency anymore, though it was hard for him to think of another to replace it. He wrapped the socks in tissue paper and put them in a bag. Before he left he wiped the dust from a couple of mirrors and tried on the cashmere jacket which he had been considering for some months. He studied himself with lips pursed for a few minutes before deciding that it did not really suit him. And, anyway, there was plenty of time to change his mind before autumn and the cold weather.

Leaving the shop, swinging his carrier bag between the perfume counters, he thought he heard a noise. A faint rustle perhaps, but certainly a noise of organic origin. He stopped, stiff in his tracks. Such a noise was not possible. He wanted to turn and look, but couldn't. Fear had frozen every muscle in his body. He was too frightened to shake, but could feel a sensation in his jaw as though his teeth were about to chatter.

Then a voice, emphatic with surprise and delight, said, 'Stanley Baldwin.'

It was a girl's voice, from somewhere on his right, behind the stack of moisturising lotions and the scratch'n'sniff display. He closed his eyes, and it crossed his mind that madness had crept upon him, and that the voice had its source in his insanity and not in reality. He was interested to notice that of the possible explanations of the voice, his preference was for madness. But he could hear footsteps, and the voice again.

'I thought it was you. Of all the people.'

Of all the people indeed. He recognised the voice. There could be no mistaking it, and of all the people left living, it would be Miriam Burke. Her voice was scored in his brain since the day he had first met her in the radiotherapy waiting room of the Mater, in the days when the desperation of cancer had led him to believe that he should have one, final, try at making a conquest of a woman. It was partly his experience of Miriam Burke which had sown the seeds of misanthropy in him, and left him one of the few people who might enjoy being, as he had believed he was, the last inhabitant of the planet.

His first practical thought, once he had accepted that the voice behind him was real, and that it was hers, was the realisation that he couldn't be sent to prison for her murder. The comfort of that allowed him to force a smile, open his eyes, and turn towards her.

'Well,' he said.

'Well indeed,' she said. 'You're just in time. You can help me with this for a start. I was just trying it on when I heard you.'

She was wearing a short black dress of cut velvet and she turned her back to show that the zip was undone. She wriggled slightly as he pulled the mechanism upwards, over her bare suntanned back.

'What do you think?' she asked, doing a twirl for him.

'A bit old-fashioned,' he said. 'I haven't seen anyone wear one of those for years.'

She laughed and poked him in the ribs. 'You were always a smart-alec.'

They stood for several minutes with nothing to say. She, not knowing whether to laugh or cry; he, fighting an instinct to leg it and get far away from her until he had time to consider the implications of not having Dublin all to himself; both of them having mislaid what conversational skills they had, in the years of silence.

A folk memory stirred in his brain, and he said, 'D'you feel like a gargle?'

'Davy Byrne's?' she said.

'No,' he said. 'That place was always full of yuppies. I like the Parliament.'

In the pub he put himself behind the bar to pour the drinks, and stayed there while she perched on a stool the other side of the counter. He made her some sort of blue and green cocktail according to her instructions, but refused to search for a paper umbrella to decorate it. He pulled a pint of Guinness for himself.

'The last barrel,' he said. 'I have the place nearly drunk dry. I already ran through what was in the George before I came on to this place.'

She made no response, and he wondered if what he had said had sounded like boasting. Perhaps she was sulking about the paper umbrella. She was making him feel awkward and, at the same time he felt she was gaining power over him and he resented it.

He said, 'It's a bit of a coincidence, isn't it? The two of us being the only ones left and us knowing each other.'

'Not at all,' she said. 'I knew everyone.'

'I suppose,' he said.

'So,' she said, 'where were you when it happened?'

They told each other their stories of the Tuesday morning. He had been in the Mater having his radiation treatment. They had strapped him into the machine as usual, but instead of coming back for him after a few minutes, they left him for what seemed like hours, until he thought he was going to fry, and then he got himself out of it. And then there was no-one. Every living creature in the world had turned to vapour. As for the cancer, there had been no sign of that since. And she had more or less the same story, except that it had happened to her in a London hospital, and she had spent the years between in England, driving from one empty city to another until she finally took the risk and crossed the Irish Sea to find out if there was anybody left at home.

'Lucky I knew how to handle a boat,' she said.

'Yes,' he said, hoping for the sake of politeness that she wouldn't hear the tone of regret in his voice.

'Do you think,' she said, 'it was a war, or what?'

Her question produced symptoms of discomfort in him. He said, 'I used to worry about that. I started to read what I could about the weapons and that. But there didn't seem much point in the end. Whatever it was, it was fairly conclusive.'

'Do you think it was fate?' she said. 'Just the two of us left in the world?'

He squirmed with uneasiness. 'How do you mean?'

She reached a hand across to where his lay on the counter, and he flinched and drew back. 'Like Adam and Eve,' she said. 'It's up to us to get the whole thing going again.'

Her directness gave him the courage to defy her. He looked at her coldly, and said, 'You're taking a lot for granted.'

'What?'

'Paradise ended when Adam and Eve started that sort of hanky panky.'

He said it with such deadly seriousness that she assumed, naturally, that he was joking. She laughed, loudly. 'You're deadly, Stanley Baldwin, so you are. Still the same.'

He let it drop at that, for the moment. Never having spelt it out in his previous life, he was disinclined to allow a creature like Miriam Burke to be the first to hear him say it. He had hoped that by bringing her here, to this pub with its homoerotic posters and long established reputation, she would get the message of her own accord. From the way she was gazing at him and sucking on her swizzle stick it was obvious that a little bluntness might be called for. He pulled another pint for himself, while reviewing in his mind some of the less messy forms of murder. Just in case.

She wanted to see where he lived and, after a lot of persuasion, he agreed to take her out to his house in Ringsend.

'Ringsend?' she said. 'What are you living out there for when you could have any house in Dublin? What's wrong with Merrion Square?'

'I like the sea,' he said. 'Anyway, Merrion Square is all banks.'

'Not anymore, it isn't,' she said.

Her second disappointment was that he travelled by bicycle.

'What do you have that yoke for when you could have any car in Dublin?

He shrugged his shoulders and could think of nothing he wanted to say, but wheeled the bicycle between the two of them, down College Green, while she talked about the Trinity Balls of long ago.

Dublin, that had been such a comfort to him while it was empty, seemed eerie in her presence. The doubling of footfalls and the sound of her voice echoed too loud, drowning out the click of bicycle spokes that was normally his only companion. He thought of leaping onto the saddle and pedalling away up Nassau Street, but what then? He couldn't spend the rest of his life hiding from her. And how could he deny her a bit of company, when she had been craving it for so long? Craving it probably as much as he had been enjoying the silence.

'Offer it up,' his granny would have said. He offered it up, for the moment.

He hated her coming into his house and looking at his things, and he winced every time she touched something. He finally shouted at her when she put her arms about his neck and tried to kiss him.

'No,' he yelled, pushing her away. 'I thought I told you. I don't want any of that.'

'Oh come on,' she said. 'What's the matter?'

'Nothing's the matter. Or nothing was the matter until you came along.'

'I don't understand you,' she said. 'You told me at Sally Dawes' twenty-first that I was the girl of your dreams.'

'And you laughed at me and went off with some rugby-playing ape from Killiney.'

'Oh I see,' she said. 'Playing hard-to-get now, to punish me.'

'No,' he said, and then, with his head averted he mumbled, 'Anyway, I'm gay.'

'What?'

'Gay,' he shouted. 'G-A-Y: queer.'

'Don't be stupid,' she said. 'You can't be gay. There aren't any men left. Anyway, you never were before. You were all over me at Sally Dawes'. And Finnoula Robinson did it with you. I know 'cause she told me.'

'Well I am now,' he screamed, and then, more calmly, said, 'The thing with Finnoula Robinson was a disaster. I was only covering up for what was going on between her brother and me. You've no idea what it was like in those days.'

'Henry?' she said, with some astonishment. 'My Henry? Henry Robinson? But we were practically engaged. Sweet Jesus.'

'Look,' he said. 'It doesn't matter now, does it? What can I say to you? For three years now I've been in love with someone who happens to be a man; who happens to be myself, and I've been perfectly happy. As far as I'm concerned that makes me gay, no matter who or what I shagged in the old days. I don't want to start the human race all over again. I like things the way they are.'

'Ssh,' she said. 'Don't talk. You're upset.' She pulled him down on the sofa beside her and put her arms around him and he, unresisting, allowed himself to be comforted.

'I'm sorry I can't be what you want,' he said. 'If you're staying around anyway, I suppose we could just be friends.'

She wasn't paying attention. She was looking out through the back window. 'What kind of tree is that in the yard?' she said.

He looked up. 'An apple tree, I think.'

'There'll be fruit in the autumn, so.'

She was thinking about the children they would have once he had overcome his present, illogical, way of looking at things. She wondered if history would repeat itself, and whether her first-born son would murder her second.

'No,' he said. 'You're out of luck there. There are no insects left to pollinate the flowers. Fruit is off the menu. Forbidden or otherwise.'

BIOGRAPHICAL NOTES

PATRICK BOYLE
Born Ballymoney, County Antrim, 1905. Worked for forty-five years for the Ulster Bank before turning to writing. He published a novel, *Like Any Other Man,* and four collections of short stories. Died 1982.

ITA DALY
Born Drumshanbo, County Leitrim, 1944. Twice a winner of a Hennessy Literary Award, she has published four novels, two children's books and a collection of short stories.

EMMA DONOGHUE
Born Dublin 1969, she has published a book on British Lesbian culture and a novel, *Stir-Fry.*

MARY DORCEY
Born Dublin 1950, she is a founder member of the first Irish Gay Rights group. She won the 1990 Rooney Award for Irish Literature with her short story collection, *A Noise from the Woodshed.*

DESMOND HOGAN
Born Ballinasloe, County Galway, 1951. Winner of the John Llewellyn Rhys Memorial Prize in 1980, he has written three novels, two collections of short stories, and a play.

JOHN JORDAN
Born Dublin 1930. Literary critic, short story writer, poet, academic and broadcaster, he died in 1988.

RITA KELLY

Born Ballinasloe, County Galway, 1953, she has published one collection of short stories, *The Whispering Arch*.

RAY LYNOTT

Born Manorhamilton, County Leitrim, 1943. Winner of a Hennessy Literary Award both in 1975 and 1976, he has published one collection of short stores, *A Year in the Country*.

COLUM McCANN

Born Dublin, 1967, he won a Hennessy Literary Award in 1990 and has published a collection of short stories, *Fishing the Sloe-Black River* which won the Rooney Prize in 1994.

VAL MULKERNS

Born Dublin, 1925, she won the Allied Irish Banks Prize for Literature in 1984. She has published four novels and three collections of short stories.

EDNA O'BRIEN

Born Tuamgraney, County Clare, 1932, she has published six collections of short stories and eleven novels, and is one of Ireland's most distinguished writers.

JULIA O'FAOLAIN

Born Dublin, 1932, she has published two collections of short stories and four novels.

SEAN O'FAOLAIN

Born Cork, 1900, he was for most of his life Ireland's leading man of letters. Best known for his short stories and editorship of *The Bell*, he also wrote biographies, travel books, literary criticism, novels and an autobiography. He died in 1991.

TERRY PRONE
Born Dublin, 1949, she is a leading communications expert and has written a number of books on the subject. 'Blood Brothers, Soul Sisters' is the title story of her first collection of short stories.

FRANK RONAN
Born County Wexford, 1963. He has published three novels, the first of which, *The Men Who Loved Evelyn Cotton*, won the 1989 *Irish Times*/Aer Lingus Irish Literature Award.

PADRAIG ROONEY
Born County Monaghan, 1965, he has published one novel, *Oasis*.

WILLIAM TREVOR
Born Mitchelstown, County Cork, 1928, his second novel *The Old Boys* won him the Hawthornden Prize. Since then his many distinguished novels and short story collections have won him the Royal Society of Literature Award, the Allied Irish Banks Prize for Literature, the Whitbread Prize for Fiction and an honorary CBE.